PRAISE FOR THE
SUGARLAND BLUE SERIES

Sworn to Protect

"Davis's new Sugarland Blue series, a spinoff of the Fire-fighters of Station Five series, features detectives from the Sugarland, Tennessee, police department. In the strong series launch, Detective Shane Ford can't forget his brief affair with fellow officer Daisy Callahan. Though hurt and betrayed by his rejection, Daisy doesn't hesitate to offer Shane support when his best friend, NFL star Brad Cooper, is found dead from a suspected drug overdose, and Shane becomes the guardian of Brad's sixteen-year-old son, Drew . . . a satisfying, fast-paced read."

—*Publishers Weekly*

"What's not to love about sexy men in blue with fast hands, true hearts, and the courage of their convictions? Davis certainly knows how to draw the perfect balance of vulnerability and strength, giving readers a superhero without a cape and pairing him with his perfect mate. She wraps it all up in an action novel that falls just shy of a police procedural, but with plenty of pure steamy romance and family drama. A great start to the Sugarland Blue series!"   —*RT Book Reviews* (4½ stars)

"*Sworn to Protect* by Jo Davis brings us characters we are familiar with and the long-awaited return to Sugarland, the setting of the Firefighters of Station Five series. This book was well worth the wait and Jo Davis delivers a rich story filled with emotion and intrigue."

—Night Owl Reviews (top pick)

continued . . .

PRAISE FOR THE FIREFIGHTERS OF STATION FIVE SERIES

Ride the Fire

"The perfect blend of romance and suspense. Neither element overshadows the other. Jo Davis creates a great combination of romance, steamy love scenes with mystery and suspense mixed in. I was pulled right into the book, and before I knew it, the last page was turned. I wasn't ready to let go." —Fiction Vixen Book Reviews

"Once again, Jo Davis has rocked it in this series!"
—Night Owl Reviews

"Jo Davis continues her steamy, heat-packed romantic suspense stories with *Ride the Fire*. This book is a great blend of hot romance with suspenseful, well-plotted action." —Fresh Fiction

Line of Fire

"Grab a fan and settle in for one heck of a smoking-hot read.... Fiery-hot love scenes and a look inside the twisted mind of a killer make *Line of Fire* stand out. Add in the behind-the-scenes look at the other characters and I could read this book over and over!"
—Joyfully Reviewed

"Full of romance and steamy love scenes with a splash of mystery and suspense. This combination had me eager to turn the page and left me wanting more. The love scenes were scorching hot!" —Fiction Vixen Book Reviews

Hidden Fire

"Surprisingly sweet and superhot ... one of the best heroes I've read in a long time. If you want a hot firefighter in your room for the night, grab a copy and tuck right in with no regrets. Four hearts." —The Romance Reader

"A fast-paced romantic suspense thriller."
—The Best Reviews

BOOKS BY JO DAVIS

The Sugarland Blue Novels
Sworn to Protect

The Firefighters of Station Five Novels
Ride the Fire
Line of Fire
Hidden Fire
Under Fire
Trial by Fire

HOT PURSUIT

A SUGARLAND BLUE NOVEL

JO DAVIS

A SIGNET ECLIPSE BOOK

SIGNET ECLIPSE
Published by the Penguin Group
Penguin Group (USA) LLC, 375 Hudson Street,
New York, New York 10014

USA | Canada | UK | Ireland | Australia | New Zealand | India | South Africa | China
penguin.com
A Penguin Random House Company

First published by Signet Eclipse, an imprint of New American Library,
a division of Penguin Group (USA) LLC

First Printing, December 2013

ISBN 978-0-451-41501-1

Printed in the United States of America
10 9 8 7 6 5 4 3 2 1

Acknowledgments

As always, special thanks to:

My wonderful family for always being there to support and encourage me. I love you all.

My best friend, Debra Stevens, for saving my sanity with impromptu lunches and refreshing spiked beverages, and always being there when I need a shoulder to cry on.

My friend Mary Anne Rocha for making sure I take a "gamble" on life and unleash my inner wild child from time to time.

My agent, Roberta Brown, for always being my cheerleader and my guide.

My editor, Tracy Bernstein, for endless support, patience, and words of wisdom.

All of the crew at NAL, including the managing editors and copy editors, art department, marketing team, and publicists. You guys are awesome!

And the readers. Your support for our boys in blue means the world to me. You rock!

1

God help me, I'm only twenty-eight. Too young to die.

Taylor Kayne bolted upright in bed, bathed in sweat, heart beating a sharp, painful rhythm against his sternum. The ghost sensation of cold steel pressing into the back of his head slowly evaporated, bringing him to wakefulness. The nightmare was usually the same each time. Once, the real-life incident that spurred the terror had been nicely suppressed and compartmentalized in a tight little box in his brain, but lately the dream descended with alarming frequency.

Delayed PTSD. Wouldn't that tidbit give the Sugarland PD's shrink an orgasm?

Shane Ford, Taylor's partner in Homicide, would be shocked, too. Shane knew the story of what had happened four years ago, but had no idea the past was riding Taylor hard. Driving him to lose sleep, affecting his appetite, costing him focus at work. And nobody could find out, especially Shane. Why the hell was this happening *now*, when his life was mostly together?

Pushing from bed, he stood and shook it off one more time. One more day. He could do this.

Glancing at the clock, he grimaced. Just shy of five thirty in the morning. Jesus, that sucked. But since he'd skipped his run for the past few days, he might as well take advantage of the extra hour before he had to get ready for work. He knew he'd feel better once he got his blood pumping, but lately it had been damned hard to get motivated.

"Get your ass moving, slacker," he muttered to himself.

In less than two minutes, he was dressed in jogging pants, a T-shirt, and tennis shoes. Sucking in a deep breath he headed downstairs and out the front door, locking it behind him and then hanging the spare key on a cord around his neck. After tucking it under his shirt, he started off.

Settling into a brisk pace, he regulated his breathing, enjoying the feeling of stretching neglected muscles, his soles hitting the pavement. He loved to run. He wasn't a fitness nut, not even close, but the fresh air was good for him. Helped him clear his head. Especially in the early summer, like now, before the weather turned too hot.

As always, he admired the older homes in his neighborhood, with their tidy yards and beds full of flowers. He had a healthy competition going with the neighbors on his street as they tried to outdo one another for who could cultivate the best yard. They even held a yearly contest at their block party. Shane liked giving him shit about that. *Sue me—I like plants and flowers, and I'm social.*

Whatever. Focusing on his home gave him something

to do to take his mind off his single, lonely status for a while. Besides, ladies loved that sort of shit, right? When he found The One, she'd admire his botanical handiwork and realize she'd found the *perfect man*. The idea made him smirk at his own idiocy.

He was so into his thoughts, the steady pounding of his feet on the asphalt, that he didn't register the whine of an approaching engine. Acceleration.

Not until it was almost too late.

Out of habit, he glanced over his shoulder—and his eyes widened. A black pickup truck was barreling down on him and swerved in his direction. Twisting his body, he dove for a row of hedges just as the bumper of the truck clipped his left side. The shock of the impact barely had a second to register and then he was flying over the bushes. He hit the ground hard, skidding, one knee and an arm taking the brunt. Coming to a stop, he rolled to sit up, half-expecting the truck to burst right through the hedges and mow him down.

At the sound of the vehicle squealing around the corner, he let out a sigh of relief and sat there, pushing a shaking hand through his hair.

"Shit!"

Sharp pain began to make itself known, and he inspected the damage. His right forearm was scraped, bloody, and dirty, but once it was cleaned it wouldn't be too bad. The laceration across his kneecap might be more problematic. Probing it, he hissed a breath. The cut was nasty, and he was bleeding like a stuck pig. It was a tricky spot for stitches, though, so he'd just have to tend it as best he could.

Getting to his feet was more difficult than he expected. He was already hurting all over, getting stiff. Of course, there was nobody around on this quiet street to help him, and he hadn't brought his cell phone. He'd jogged about four miles and his watch showed it was after six, and he was looking at a painful walk home. He was going to be late to the station.

He started off, wincing with every slow step. His body was throbbing everywhere, so to occupy his mind, he tried to focus on what he recalled about the truck.

The vehicle was black. Completely. Tinted windows that were beyond legal. Thinking harder, he realized it was a Ford. Newer model, from the grille and logo. He hadn't been able to get a glimpse of the driver or the plates. As for who might hold a big enough grudge to try to run him down? Fuck, he'd been a cop since he was twenty-one. That list would take all day to compile.

That was all he had, and it wasn't much.

The walk home took almost an hour. By the time he limped up the porch steps, he wanted nothing more than to crawl back into bed and give the finger to this whole day. Instead, he took a hot shower, paying special attention to getting the dirt out of his scrapes and the cut on his knee. It hurt like shit, and he knew he'd feel worse tomorrow. *Joy.*

Once out of the shower, he toweled off and gathered some first-aid supplies, then sat on the toilet lid. The arm could wait. His knee was still bleeding like a bitch, and he doused it with antiseptic. Several gauze pads later, the bleeding had slowed, and he closed the laceration as best as he could using some wound glue he'd bought at the drugstore a while back. It worked okay, and he bandaged and taped it for good measure. He'd have to watch that wound for infection.

The scraped-up arm he couldn't do much for. He hit it with antiseptic as well, downed a couple of ibuprofen, then hobbled into the bedroom and spotted the time. Just after seven. Before getting dressed, he had to make a call. Picking up his cell, he sat on the bed, brought up his contacts, and punched the number.

Shane answered on the second ring. "Hey. What's up?"

"I'm going to be a little late, half hour or so. I, um, had an incident."

"What kind of incident? What happened?" He could hear the concern in his partner's voice.

"Truck tried to turn me into roadkill while I was out running this morning."

"On purpose?"

"Yeah."

"Fuck," Shane breathed. "You okay?"

"I'm fine, just moving slow. Scraped my arm and cut my knee after he hit me—"

"The bastard actually *hit* you?" his friend barked. "Why the hell aren't you in the ER, getting checked out?"

"Calm down, partner. Like I said, it's not that bad. I got clipped by the bumper is all." He cut Shane off before the man could get started again. "After I get there, I'm going to file a report so the guys on patrol can watch for the truck. Black Ford."

"The one with the fucking *dent* in the front."

He had to smile. "That'll be the one."

"I'm already at the station. I'll give them a heads-up so they can go ahead and start looking," he said, an angry edge to his words.

"Thanks, man."

"You need a ride? I can send a squad."

"No, I'm good." The last thing he wanted was to call even more attention to his situation.

"All right. Take your time and I'll see you soon."

Ending the call, Taylor went to the closet and chose an acceptable pair of jeans that were comfortable. Then he lingered over the shirts. A short-sleeved one would be better because it wouldn't rub on the scrapes, but then he'd have to field questions all day from people who hadn't heard about this morning. Debating, he settled on a dark, long-sleeved cotton shirt that would hide the wounds and any dots of blood that might seep through.

Once he was dressed, putting on his shoes was an effort. Amazing how fast the body became bruised and sore. Good thing he was going into the station—the longer he sat around here, he might never move again.

Downstairs in the kitchen, he settled on coffee and half a toasted bagel. He needed something in his stomach, and he couldn't live without his daily jolt of caffeine. Especially today. He carried both with him, and eyed his new Challenger before climbing in.

He loved muscle cars, and this was a really cool one. But he missed his old Chevelle, which had been fucked up a few weeks ago when he and Shane had taken a dip—car and all—in the Cumberland River while in pursuit of a suspect. The car was currently sitting alone and forlorn in

Christian Ford's big garage out in back of his house. Chris was Shane's cousin and fairly new as a detective at the department, having transferred in from Texas. The three of them tinkered on fixing the Chevelle when they had time and Taylor had the extra cash, which wasn't often.

God, he missed that car.

The Challenger started with a throaty roar, which he had to admit was pretty butch. Too bad he couldn't enjoy driving it today, with his knee screaming every time he switched from the gas to the brake. Maybe he should've accepted the ride. Too late now.

He made it to the station and was thankfully able to give his report with little fanfare. Apparently, Shane had told only those who needed to know, including Captain Austin Rainey and a couple of uniforms, and he was grateful. He had no doubt that the entire department would know within the hour, but at least he was able to have some breathing room. A few minutes later, he limped into his partner's office and closed the door.

Shane looked up from some papers, giving him a half smile. "Hey. He must've winged you good."

"For sure. No point in sitting around at home, though."

"You might reconsider tomorrow, when it's worse."

"We'll see." He wouldn't call in sick unless he was on his deathbed, and they both knew it. Shane just shook his head.

"Tell me exactly what happened."

He spent the next few minutes giving his partner the rundown, though there wasn't much to tell. They went back through some of their most recent cases to try to form a list of who might still carry enough of a grudge to commit attempted murder, but although there were several candidates, none were that strong.

"I might have to go back a few years." Taylor tried to get comfortable in his chair, wincing as he squirmed. "Most of these are in prison or dead. As far as the ones that are out, I can come up with a list as long as my arm of who would run me over if they had the *chance*, but . . ." He frowned.

"What?"

"This had a different feel. More deliberate. Nothing I can put my finger on, just intuition."

"Like he was waiting for the opportunity?"

"Exactly. I've got no proof, though."

"You and I both know people kill for two main reasons: passion or money." His partner eyed him. "Which one do you fit?"

Taylor snorted. "Since I'm not loaded, I'm guessing passion. And there's all kinds of passion-motived killings. Specifically hate, when it comes to cops."

Unbidden, his nightmare intruded. Viciously, he shoved it into its box.

"Okay. Someone you or we arrested, then."

"Maybe." Rubbing his eyes, he let out a tired breath. "Can we talk about this later? It might not even happen again."

"Sure."

Somehow, he didn't really believe that. A chill slithered down his spine, telling him this was only the start. Could be his overwrought, stressed mind, but it didn't seem likely that's all there was to it.

A knock interrupted his thoughts, and Captain Rainey stepped into Shane's office. "We've got a body in the

Sugarland Motel. Anonymous caller reported the sound of a gunshot, and Jenkins found the guy plugged between the eyes."

"Anonymous," Taylor repeated. "A possible lead right off the bat."

"That would be too easy." Shane stood, groaning. "And let me guess: it's our turn."

"Yep, you're on." The captain looked at Taylor. "You up for this?"

"I'm here, aren't I? If I was going to laze around, I'd stay home."

Rainey grinned. "That's the spirit. Now go get fucking busy." Turning, the captain strolled out, whistling.

"He's all heart," Shane said, making a face.

"At least he's in a good mood today. Wonder what's up with that."

Their captain was having serious marital problems— as in going down the tubes permanently. He'd been tired and haggard the past few months, and they had all been worried about his health. Today, however, he had a spring in his step.

"No clue, but let's not rock the boat."

Taylor rose with some difficulty and stiffly followed his partner out the door. Turning down his partner's offer to drive, he slid behind the wheel and they were off.

On the way, he thought he saw a black truck in traffic, three cars behind. Then it turned and was gone.

As though nearly being run over wasn't enough, the corpse with the neat little hole in the center of its forehead turned out to be a harbinger.

A sign of a shit storm heading his way.

Taylor stood next to Shane as both of them studied the dead man sprawled faceup on the floor. His salt-and-pepper hair was surrounded by a sticky pool of blood congealing on the industrial-grade carpet, and his expression was vaguely surprised.

"Who the hell was the poor bastard?" Taylor muttered. "And why did he get popped here, of all places?"

Shane snorted. "He could've had the decency to get his ass killed in Nashville, out of our jurisdiction."

Taylor rolled his eyes at his partner's crappy joke. "You know what I meant."

"Yeah."

Both of them glanced around the small motel room, but there wasn't much to see. At least on the surface. Carefully stepping around the body, Taylor noted a few clothes hanging in the closet next to the bathroom.

"A change of suits, a couple of pairs of jeans, and three polo shirts." He peered into the bathroom. "A shaving kit in there. That's all."

"Got a small leather carryall on the table, containing underwear and socks. A plane ticket, too, round-trip from LAX to Nashville International and back. Looks like he arrived yesterday, was supposed to fly back in three days. Car keys and his wallet beside the bag." Shane left the leather trifold sitting on the dresser and flipped it open with the edge of one latex-covered finger. "Max Griffin, born December twelfth, 1946. San Diego address."

California. Taylor's heart gave a lurch. He stared at Shane, his friend unaware of his sudden chill. *It means nothing. San Diego is not Los Angeles. They're two differ-ent cities 121 miles apart, almost a two-hour drive.*

"Interesting," he managed. "So, the car outside is his rental. He was here for a specific reason, but there's no evidence of what that might've been."

"Not yet." Turning, Shane yelled out the open door to the officer who'd arrived first after the call of a gunshot had come in. "Jenk!"

Aaron Jenkins, their new hire at the department, stuck his head in the door. "Yes, sir?"

"Take these and open that rental. See if you can find anything inside to give us a clue why our dead guy was in town." Shane tossed him the car keys, and the kid caught them one-handed. "Be careful about touching stuff."

"On it!" His boy-next-door face lit up at the prospect of helping with the investigation.

As he ducked out again, Taylor chuckled. "Damn, were we ever that young and green?"

"Probably, once upon a time." His partner quirked his mouth in a half smile. "Don't you ever wish you could go back to your early twenties?"

"For the wild social life and the hot young bod? Sure. For being the low cop on the totem pole again? Not so much."

"True."

"Though my bod is *still* hot."

"If that's what you want to tell yourself, old man."

"Says he who turns the big three-oh next week," Tay-lor shot back. "I'm only two years older than you."

"Just fucking with you."

"When are you not?"

In truth, Taylor gave as good as he got when it came to his partner. He and Shane had worked in Homicide together for more than four years, since Taylor had moved to Sugarland, Tennessee, from Los Angeles. His mind shied away from the disaster that had prompted his move, and he focused on how content he was here, among people he liked and respected.

He and Shane might trade barbs, but it was all in good fun. His partner had become one of his best friends, and he'd do just about anything for the man. He had no doubt the feeling was mutual.

"Nothing much in the car, sir," Jenk said, stepping into the room. "Just some fast-food wrappers and a map. Isn't that odd?"

"What's that?" Shane asked.

"Well, who uses a paper road map anymore, right? Most people use their smartphone or a GPS, especially if they're traveling alone. Hard to read an old-fashioned map when you're driving."

That gave his partner pause. "You're right, though sometimes people prefer the old way of doing things. Reading a smartphone while driving alone would be just as tough." He sighed. "Come to think of it, we didn't find a phone at all. Good work."

The kid beamed at the praise. Taylor suppressed a grin and was about to play Razz the Rookie when Medical Examiner Laura Eden arrived, along with the police department's forensics unit. The cops jokingly referred to them as Eden and the FU, like a rock group, because they tended to arrive en masse, the head honcho and her entourage. And *FU* for obvious reasons—not that the forensics guys were all assholes. The term had just stuck.

The room got crowded, so Jenk, Taylor, and Shane moved outside to let them process the scene. There wasn't much to find, and in less than an hour, Eden was giving them the short version.

"No surprises. Well, not counting the man with the bullet in his brain," she said dryly. "Based on the blood splatter, this is indeed the murder scene. Mr. Griffin was shot in the forehead at point-blank range with a smaller-caliber handgun. Nothing much to bag except a couple of hairs and some other fibers."

"They finding any prints?" Taylor asked.

The striking brunette arched a brow. "In a motel room? Seriously, Detective?"

His face heated. "Right." How stupid of him. Not to mention it sucked to sound like an idiot in front of a gorgeous woman who'd turned him down flat for a dinner date. Twice.

"Anyhow, I'd say he's been dead for about an hour and a half. That's all I know, but I'll send you what I've got when I know more."

Taylor cleared his throat. "We about done here, then?"

Shane nodded, running a hand through his longish brown hair. "Yep. Thanks, Laura."

"No problem. See you guys."

It kind of smarted how she just went inside again without a backward glance, all cool professionalism. His partner must've noticed something in his expression as they walked to Taylor's car, because he couldn't resist making a comment.

"It's not you, buddy. *You're* the one who told me she had a thing for the captain."

"Yeah, I know," he grumped as he slid behind the wheel. "Why do women always want the guy who's not available?"

"They're twisted like that, my friend. Well, not all of them." Shane buckled his seat belt. "Just find a different horse to bet on than Laura."

"Easy for you to say. You snagged a fine woman, and you've got a great kid."

A dopey smile split his friend's face. "I did, didn't I? I'm a lucky SOB."

I will not be jealous. I'm happy for him.

He was, truly. Shane and his new wife, Daisy, had been through hell and so had Shane's seventeen-year-old godson, Drew Cooper. Being colleagues at the police department had been a minor obstacle for the couple compared to their other troubles, especially helping Drew deal with the trauma of his father's death. Then there were the awful secrets Drew had been keeping and the danger those secrets had brought into their lives.

But it was over now, and the three of them were forging a new life together.

"Hey, you're a great guy," Shane said, sensing the dip in his mood. "You're going to find a fantastic lady who loves everything about you. You're funny, easygoing, and you're a good friend to everyone who knows you."

"Is this the part where we hug?"

"Shut up, asswipe."

But he laughed, and Taylor couldn't help but be a little cheered as he pulled out of the parking lot.

Maybe this day would take a turn for the better after all.

Max is dead! Oh, God.

Cara Evans pulled the baseball cap low on her head and watched the activity from her hiding place in the park across the street from the Sugarland Motel. Angrily, she swiped away the tears that refused to quit falling. Just as she'd done for the past four goddamned years.

Max had come to town, looking for Cara. Then he'd phoned, urging her in a hushed voice to meet him at the motel. Why had he come to her? Especially now, after all this time? Who killed him and why? His visit could be related to her sister's murder. Or their father's estate. Any number of things. But the answers to those questions had died with Max in that awful room.

One thing was for sure: the murdering asshole would pay for snuffing out the life of a good man. The only person she had still counted as a friend in the entire, sorry world. Leaning her head against the rough bark of the tree, she gave up and let the tears flow. For several long moments she allowed herself to grieve, barely aware of the sounds of activity across the street. Gradually, however, she gained a measure of control. Her fingers tightened around a solid object she'd forgotten about.

Max's iPhone.

She'd be in a fuckton of trouble if and when the cops thought to track its whereabouts. It would be hard to explain her presence in Max's room and why she'd used the device to make the anonymous call to the police about a gunshot, then lifted it before fleeing the scene. Harder still to convince them she hadn't killed him, that he was dead when she arrived. But she planned to get rid of the phone. As soon as she took a peek to try to determine why he had wanted to see her so badly. Why he had possibly died for it.

Voices across the motel's parking lot snared her attention. Peering around the tree, she saw two men in plainclothes emerge from the room. Detectives, from the glint of the shields hooked to their belts at the waist. She'd been too stricken with panic and raw grief to pay attention when they had arrived, so she studied them now.

Both were tall, but the brown-haired one was taller and leaner than the other. The man who was presumably his partner was maybe an inch or two shorter and more muscular. Golden blond hair just covered his ears, layered in a loose, casual style with some wisps of bangs falling into what looked from here to be quite a handsome face—

Recognition hit her like a baseball bat to the head, and though she'd half-expected him to show up, she felt sick. If not for the tree, she would have tumbled to the ground.

Taylor Kayne. Untouchable. Man's man. Lauded hero.

"Fucking lying murderer," she whispered, rage welling in her chest. Despair, rotten and black, clogged her throat.

Once again, Kayne was smack in the middle of the

hell that was her life. That suited her fine, though. Because the bastard probably didn't know Cara had come to Sugarland or even have a clue who she was in the first place. He sure as hell didn't know he was the reason she was here. Or that she knew where he worked, lived, ate, shopped, jogged.

But he would find out soon. She was biding her time, waiting for the perfect moment. Then she'd spring her trap. Force him to spill every last filthy secret that should have corroded his guts by now.

Detective Taylor Kayne was going to confess to murdering her sister.

And then Cara would exact her long-awaited revenge.

2

His phone call was late. And Snyder knew he hated to be kept waiting.

Rolling his shoulders against the knots of tension, Dmitri Constantine picked up his glass of Scotch and swirled it over the ice. Then he took a generous swallow and walked to the window to stare out at the traffic crawling like ants far below his high-rise condo.

And as always, he thought of *her*.

His fingers tightened on the glass as he battled back the helpless rage. His life had ended four years ago, three times over, and he was the one who ended up paying the price. That, however, was a situation that would finally be rectified.

A vibration in his pocket cut into his stark musings and he pulled his smartphone from his pants. "Give me good news," he said curtly.

"The first target is shaken, not stirred." A chuckle followed Snyder's attempt at humor.

Dmitri didn't laugh. "Alive?"

The man sobered. "Of course. I know my job."

His gut tightened in anticipation. Making Kayne suffer was going to be a glorious thing. "Good. And the second target?"

"On ice, as requested. He didn't have time to pass along what he knew," Snyder said. "I made certain of that."

Now Dmitri sensed a hesitation in his man's voice. "But?"

"I lost the woman after she left the scene."

"Not what I wanted to hear," he said with barely restrained anger. "You'll find her again."

"She's as wily as a fucking fox, but she can't evade me forever. I'll find her."

"Call me when you have more news. And don't make me wait too long."

The news intrigued Dmitri. Jennifer's sister was no doubt spooked by Griffin's murder. But before that, she couldn't possibly have known anyone with ties to her past was closing in. Which meant she had her own agenda in Tennessee—an agenda Griffin had been paid well to inflame.

If he'd done a better job of that, he'd still be breathing.

"Yes, sir. I—"

Hanging up on Snyder, he crossed the room and lowered himself to his leather sofa. Then he placed his highball glass on the coffee table and continued to stare out the window. Anyone observing him now would be fooled by his outward calm. His cool collectedness.

They wouldn't guess that he'd learned his patience in prison. Some lessons in that hellhole had been worth the price.

And the reward would be more than worth the wait.

*   *   *

Cara's brain was rudely snatched from sleep as she registered Steven Tyler screeching about a dude looking like a lady. Rolling over, she blinked at the cheap digital alarm clock near her head. Then she reached out and slapped it multiple times until the annoying thing fell silent.

"Jeez."

Waking up gracefully, not to mention at the butt crack of dawn, was not her strong suit. By far. Her double gig as a bartender and lead singer in her rock band at the Waterin' Hole kept her busy most nights, until closing at two a.m. more often than not. Her band played there only twice a week—a popular local country band ruled the roost the rest of the time—so she filled the remainder of her nights by slinging drinks. She didn't really need the money, but she loved both jobs, even if the place was a little rough around the edges.

Max, however, had been extremely unhappy about her move from Los Angeles *and* her new place of employment. He continually tried to persuade her to come "home," saying L.A. was where she needed to be if she wanted to make it big as a rocker. He didn't understand that just didn't matter anymore. As much as she loved music, she no longer lived for it.

Making Jenny's killer pay had taken top billing.

Groaning at the shaft of pain at the memory of losing Jenny, and now Max, she pushed out of bed. She didn't have time for more tears. Her agenda was packed for the day, and she had to get moving if she wanted to make rehearsal on time.

Reluctantly, she dragged her ass into the shower and let the hot water stream over her protesting body, loosening her muscles and lifting the fog. By the time she'd finished and stepped out to dry off, she was feeling much more human again. Something she was grateful for when her cell phone buzzed and she glanced at the caller ID.

"Just great." She was tempted to ignore the call, but avoidance would only backfire, resulting in a barrage of messages and texts, each one more unhinged than the last. Steeling herself, she picked up.

"What do you want, Mel?" she asked, proud of keeping her tone cool. Unaffected, when she was anything but.

Melinda Evans was like a hungry shark—any scent of blood in the water and she'd attack.

"*Mom*, not Mel," she said tightly. She'd lost that distinction long ago, but continued to mistakenly insist that biology made it so. "And what makes you think I want anything? Can't I call my baby just to talk, see how you're doing?"

Her grip tightened on the phone. "You could, but you don't. Ever."

"I only asked a simple question. You don't have to sound so hostile."

Cara barely stifled a bitter laugh. "I'm surprised you're sober enough to notice."

"Honey—"

"I'm not sending you any money, so you can save us both the pretense." *Stay calm. Deep breath.* "You have a roof over your head, and I have groceries delivered every two weeks. That's all you're getting." *And more than you deserve.*

Most children wanted to believe the best of their parents. Her late father had loved Melinda once, proving that love is truly blind. Especially when it came to his wife's addictions. She had plenty of them, and he had the money to support a better class of loser. But when their father had died, she and Jenny learned that while love was blind, Dad wasn't stupid.

Whatever relationship they'd managed to maintain with the selfish bitch vanished with the reading of Dad's will—when Melinda had been left a minimal allowance to pay for modest niceties, and the bulk of the estate had been left to Jenny and Cara. Of course, Melinda didn't use the money as Dad intended and frequently found herself broke. Any extra cash Jenny had granted Melinda went straight up the woman's nose.

Then Jenny had been murdered. Cara realized that her so-called mother never had any intention of getting clean, and she'd put a stop to doling out the extra cash. Had tossed her in rehab for the first of four visits to date.

Cara wasn't completely heartless—a cruel twist of fate had made this woman her mother, and she wouldn't put her on the street.

Melinda's soft laugh cut through her musings. "You're wrong this time. I really am calling to check on you."

"I'll mark the date on the calendar."

"So cynical." The woman sighed. "Anyway, I also wanted to let you know that Max came by the house and was really upset. Said something about flying out there to see you."

Cara lowered herself to sit on the bed, pulse pounding in her throat. "When was this?"

"I don't know. Yesterday morning or the day before? I can't really remember."

"Think," she ordered, staring at her bare toes digging into the carpet. "What was Max upset about? What did he say?"

"He yelled at me," Melinda said in a small voice. "I don't know why."

Yelling at her now wouldn't do any good, either. The woman's brain was fried from too many years of using. Max had known that, too, which meant his visit to her mother, however futile, was important.

"You must have some idea. Did you try to contact your dealer? Maybe Max found out about it."

"What? No! I haven't in ages!"

That was up for debate. "Did you try to withdraw extra money again?"

"No." Frustration colored her voice. "Nothing like that. Not *really*. I . . ."

"What do you mean, not really?"

"Nothing. I just wanted you to know Max came by, and he was madder than I've ever seen him."

"Okay, listen to me carefully." Cara paused, hoping she had Melinda's attention. "Max *did* come here to see me, but he never told me why. He's dead."

"Dead?"

"Somebody shot him in the head before he could talk to me," she said hoarsely.

"Oh, my God!"

The other woman's shock brought it all rushing back. Tears filled her eyes and her lungs hurt. "I need for you to remember what he said when he came to see you."

"I—I just don't, but I'll keep trying."

"All right. And stick around the house for a while, okay?"

"How come?" she asked, clearly puzzled.

Cara shook her head. Her mother no longer possessed any ability to pursue the thoughts that flitted through her brain. "Max went to see you and he was upset. He came here intending to see me and somebody killed him. Don't leave the fucking house, Mel."

"You don't have to curse at me."

Jesus Christ. "Are you listening? What did I just say?"

"Don't leave the house, and I won't. I'm not a child."

That was irony for you—the child became the parent. "Right. I've got to run, but I'll call you later."

"Okay. Love you, baby."

Thankfully, she hung up before Cara was forced to answer. And for that, she felt miserably guilty. She sat for a moment, collecting herself. The call was even more disturbing than usual where her mother was concerned. Why had Max gone to see her before flying to Tennessee? What the hell was going on? She wanted to head to the police station and demand to know what they were doing to find his killer. But that would mean questions about how she knew of the murder, and the possibility of revealing she'd been in his motel room.

It was clear she wasn't going to get any more answers from Melinda than she'd gotten from Max's phone the night before. The device hadn't been password protected and revealed nothing but a few names she already knew and a few numbers she didn't recognize.

"Shit."

The phone. Pushing from the bed, she hurried into the living room and retrieved the device from the coffee table. She'd completely forgotten about it! Quickly, she disabled the tracking app and then shut the phone off. She didn't know a ton about technology, but with any luck, that would keep anyone from knowing she had it in her possession.

Something told her the police were the least of her worries. She should go to them, tell them what she knew. Which wasn't much. But fear held her back because she'd already screwed up, and, much more than that, she didn't trust cops. Not one iota. Nobody could blame her for that.

After stashing the phone in her closet, she pulled on a pair of old, soft jeans and a T-shirt. Once her hair was dry and tamed, she applied just enough makeup to avoid looking too pale. No sense in wearing the heavy stuff before showtime.

Next she gathered her guitar, amp, and the backpack containing her cords and other equipment, and hauled them out the back door to her truck. Lowering the tailgate, she muscled everything into the back, then retrieved her purse and locked up the house.

As she stepped outside again, the sun's reflection on the front of the truck caught her eye. Or, rather, it was the dent in the right front side that snared her attention. "What the hell?"

Incredulous, she jogged over and squatted, letting her purse drop to the driveway beside her. On close inspection, she could see the damage was slight. If the sun hadn't been hitting the vehicle just right, she might not have noticed for days. As it was, she racked her brain trying to think when this could've happened.

Earlier in the week, she'd gone to the self-service car wash down the road and washed the truck. Was that Wednesday? She thought so. Distinctly, she recalled crouching, drying off the bumper with a towel, and it hadn't been damaged then. She was certain. And she hadn't done it herself.

Peering at the dent, she noted that the area wasn't large, perhaps the size of a football and mostly on the surface. The chrome had taken a hit, as had some of the black paint. There was a slight scratch on the chrome, but that was all, thank goodness. She could probably pop out the dent herself. It wasn't enough damage to alert her insurance company and risk the rate going up because some jerk had obviously backed into her truck sometime since Wednesday and hadn't left a note.

With an irritated huff, she grabbed her purse, palmed the keys, and went around the driver's side to climb in. People sucked. Even moving across the country hadn't changed that fact.

Minutes later, she pulled into the parking lot behind the Waterin' Hole. Shutting off the ignition, she glanced toward the back door and spotted a slight figure huddled against the wall, sitting on the asphalt. *Blake Roberts.* Her heart clenched in sympathy as she got out of the truck, trying not to stare at the young man's ragged appearance.

"Hey, Blake," she called. "Wanna give me a hand?"

As expected, he jumped up from his spot and shuffled over, eager to help. Or most likely hungry and desperately needing the twenty she always slipped him when he was around. He insisted on earning his money, though. No handouts for him.

As she turned to reach for the amp, he nudged her aside. "That's too heavy. Let me get it."

This despite the fact that she outweighed the nineteen-year-old by at least twenty pounds. But she let him, marveling, as usual, that he was stronger than he looked. The boy was too thin, his waiflike frame and adorable face making him appear younger than his age. Tangled brown hair fell to his shoulders, matching doe eyes that set off his delicate features.

And he was as sweet as he was pretty, which caused her to worry about his survival. How the fuck had a nice kid like Blake ended up homeless? She hadn't known him long enough to get the story, but earning his trust was important to her for some reason. She didn't want this boy's life to go to waste if she could help it.

Grabbing her guitar case and backpack, she followed Blake inside. As she maneuvered past the bar and approached the small stage, the young man was already at work. Setting down her case and pack, she studied him thoughtfully as he buzzed like a bee, placing her amp exactly where she wanted it and then dragging out the extension cords. For the first time, she realized the guy paid attention to their setup and *knew* what he was doing. An idea began to form, and as her other band members arrived and started to lug in their equipment, Cara eased toward the bar and leaned against it, watching.

"Wish I could hire that kid."

Cara turned to see Jess, the bar's manager and her

boss, studying Blake as the boy moved around efficiently. "Why can't you? He obviously needs work, and he's a good guy from what I can tell."

"Couple of reasons." Jess crossed his arms over his broad chest. "First off, pretty boy like him would get eaten alive in this place."

"Only if he's out front. What about cooking or washing dishes?"

"That'd work if I had an opening in the back, but I don't." The big man sighed. "The one position I did have, you filled it. I needed a bartender, and Blake didn't have the cash to take the classes and get his license, even if I decided to give him a shot."

"Damn, that's a shame."

"Yeah." He gestured to Blake. "Thing is, I don't know if he'd take the job if I had one to offer. The kid's gonna have to swallow his pride and accept some real help if he plans to get off the street, and me slippin' him a sandwich every day doesn't count."

She frowned. "Back up. Why do you doubt he'd take a job from you?"

"Blake struggles hard with seeing every kind gesture as a handout. He's skittish, too. Keeps his head down and tries not to attract attention, even though he's hungry for a chance and a connection with people around him. There's this cop who's taken a liking to him, struck up a friendship of sorts, and so far Blake hasn't even let *him* help."

Suspicion hit her hard in the gut and she found herself bristling. "Who's this cop?"

Jess laughed. "Down, girl. He's not interested like *that*,

and he means well. He's a detective—name's Tate or something. Nice guy, on the up-and-up."

"A cop with a heart of gold? As if."

"I swear it."

She gave an unladylike snort. "Right. I'll put that on my list of surprises for the week."

Just then, Blake came walking up. "Hey, Cara? I finished."

She gave him a smile. "So you did, and it looks great. You're getting pretty good at the setup."

Blushing, he ducked the compliment and said shyly, "They're ready for sound check. I can make the adjustments so you guys don't have to stop what you're doing."

"That's fantastic—thanks." She nodded at the stage. "If I didn't know better, I'd say you've done this before we met."

He shrugged his slim shoulders. "Some. I was in a band in high school."

"Awesome," Jess put in. "What do you play?"

"Bass. It was fun, but nothing lasts forever, you know." Almost reluctantly, he glanced at the small stage.

Nobody had to tell Cara the reason his dreams had crashed and burned. Even if she didn't know the whole story, it was clear the young man's support system was nonexistent. Someone, maybe more than one person, had dealt this boy a terrible blow.

But luck could turn on a dime.

"Well, I have a bass player right now," she began. Blake's face fell and she hurried on. "But what I don't have is a good sound man. Before you started assisting me, it was taking forever to get things set up so we could move on to rehearsal and be ready for the show. I need someone I can count on to make sure we're ready to go and that the show runs smoothly from beginning to end."

The young man blinked at her, processing. "I— What are you saying?"

"I'm saying I want to hire you for the job." Blake's mouth fell open and his eyes widened, and she couldn't help but smile. "You've been helping with the setup, but this would entail you staying for the whole evening, manning the sound board, and breaking down the equipment afterward as well. It's more responsibility, but, frankly, I think you're ready."

"Why me?" he managed. "I mean, it's not because you feel sorry for me? I don't take handouts—if I can help it." He shot an embarrassed look at Jess, probably thinking of the food the manager sometimes gave him.

Cara shook her head and said firmly, "This is not a handout, Blake. Do I empathize with your situation? Yes, and I won't lie about that. But working for a band is just that—hard *work*. What's more, it's a job I believe you're well qualified to do, when so few are. What do you say? Will you be my sound man?"

The boy opened and closed his mouth, making an effort to keep his composure. "What nights would I work?"

She had him and they both knew it. "We play here two nights a week right now, Wednesday and Friday. We don't normally set up this early, but we're doing an extra rehearsal today. So count on being here around four on those days. We'll do a run-through of the show, then be back onstage at eight. We play several sets with breaks in between, all the way until closing at two a.m."

"That's a long night."

"Will the hours be a problem?"

"No, just thinking out loud."

A light dawned. "You'll need transportation."

He studied his battered shoes. "I'll be here on time, no matter what."

"For the time being, I'll pick you up wherever you're staying and drop you off. And you *will* have a real place to stay before tonight is over," she insisted, cutting off any protest he was about to make. "Nobody who works for me is going to be without a roof over their head, because that'll make me look like a world-class cheapskate and an asshole to boot. You got it?"

A small grin curved Blake's lips. "Yes, ma'am."

"Aren't you going to ask about your pay?"

"I don't . . ." Taking a deep breath, he squared his shoulders and raised his chin. "What's the offer?"

"Confidence—that's good," she observed in approval. "You'll need that, working with my band. They're good guys, but they'll ride you at first to see what you're made of. Give it back to them as good as you get and they'll respect you. To start, I'm thinking seventy-five dollars a night."

The boy hesitated and glanced at Jess, who arched a dark brow. "She's lowballing you, kid. Four in the afternoon to two in the morning is a long-assed day, even with breaks. Don't let her get away with that shit."

Cara could've kissed Jess for latching onto what she was doing and for playing along. Blake's face scrunched as he thought about the offer.

"If you count eight hours of actual work, that's barely more than nine dollars an hour," the young man stated.

"That's more than you're making now."

He met her gaze without backing down. "You pointed out that this job is one not many people are qualified to do. I think I'm worth more."

She wanted to cheer but forced herself to nod seriously. "You're right. How much, then? Ninety?"

"One h-hundred cash." His voice was quiet, but he didn't flinch. "Per nïght."

"That's a good chunk." She pretended to consider for a long moment, then stuck out her hand. "Deal. Do I have a new sound man?"

A wide smile spread across Blake's beautiful face as he took her hand. "Yes, you do. And thank you for giving me a chance."

"I'm happy to have you aboard. Now, why don't you come meet the band officially? They're going to love you."

As she led Blake over to her guys, she was glad to see they greeted him warmly, even if some of their colorful comments caused the boy to blush. She still had to work out where he would stay, but she'd think of something.

By the time they launched into a cover of Heart's "Barracuda," Cara was in her zone. Letting the music wash over her and carry her far from her problems was her crack, and it worked.

At least for the moment.

Taylor climbed out of the passenger's side of Shane's new crossover SUV and slammed the door. "Nice ride, man. Comfortable."

Shane joined him as they walked toward the entrance to the Waterin' Hole. "I can hear a *but* in there."

He shrugged and suppressed a grin. "No *but*. It's a nice vehicle if you're into that sort of thing."

"What sort of thing?"

"You know, the *family* thing."

"You say that like it's a deadly disease."

"If the colonoscopy fits."

"A colonoscopy is a *procedure*, not a disease." Shane snorted. "You're an asshole—you know that?"

"Whatever."

"Now you sound like Drew," his friend grouched. "Damn, I need a beer."

"I think they can handle that request."

As Taylor pulled open the door, the din of partying and rock music hit him, a solid wall of sound that he always found exciting. Something about music, being around other people out to have a good time, pumped his blood. Always had, ever since he'd reached legal age long ago. Lately, though, despite his ribbing Shane about his new status as a family man with a dorky-looking SUV . . .

Yeah, he was jealous. And lonely. After enjoying a few beers and laughs with the guys, Shane had a gorgeous woman waiting at home. *And I have a cold, empty bed.*

It didn't have to be that way. He could troll the room, pick up a sweet honey for the night. Take her to a motel room and act out their own version of that "ride a cowboy" song. But the problem was always how awkward he felt leaving in the wee hours. Empty, too.

No, tonight he'd sit out that scene. He'd enjoy a few rounds with his buddies and call it a night. He was just about to take a seat next to Shane at their group's table when he spotted a familiar figure to the right of the stage.

Nudging his partner, he indicated the young man fiddling with a panel of switches.

"Hey, isn't that Blake?"

Shane squinted. "Yeah, looks like. What's he doing?"

"I'm gonna go find out. Order me a Guinness, will you?"

Without waiting for an answer, he pushed through the crowd toward the Sugarland PD's former police informant. The young man was intent on his task and didn't see Taylor approach.

"Hey, kid!" he called over the canned music blaring over the club's sound system.

Blake's chin jerked up and a broad smile spread across his face. "Detective Kayne. How's it hangin'?" He stood and offered his hand.

Taylor shook it briefly. "Just Taylor, man," he said, then gestured to the board loaded with various knobs. "Did you score a job with the band?"

"I sure did," the kid declared proudly. "Can you believe it? Not playing in the band—though that would be awesome—but setting up, doing the sound check. Making sure the sets go all right, and breaking down afterward. Cool, huh?"

The boy's enthusiasm was catching. Taylor clapped him on the shoulder. "It sure is! Congratulations. I knew something was bound to shake loose for you sooner or later." He was beyond relieved that the boy now had a way to get off the streets. Before he left tonight, he'd make sure Blake had a place to go, whether he wanted to accept help or not.

"Thanks." He glanced behind Taylor. "You here with your cop friends?"

"For a while. Thought we'd have a couple of beers, take in some music."

"Dude, you're gonna *love* this band," Blake said, jerking a thumb behind him in the general direction of the backstage area. "The lead singer is so *hot* and way talented."

Taylor smiled. The young man was out and gay—the reason he'd been kicked out of his house several years ago. "What does he look like?"

"She," Blake corrected. "Her name is Cara."

"Oh? Switching teams already?"

"No! But I'm not blind, man. Cara's the *bomb*."

Chuckling, he shook his head. The woman must be something to have earned Blake's trust and loyalty—not an easy thing to accomplish. "Well, if she's so incredible, maybe you'll introduce me."

Blake eyed him, considering. "Maybe, if you're lucky."

It took him a moment to realize the kid wasn't teasing. "She really must be something."

"She is." The house lights dimmed briefly, and Blake straightened. "Showtime in ten. Gotta get back to work."

"All right. I want to talk to you before I go, though."

The wariness crept back into Blake's brown gaze, but he nodded. "Sure thing."

He probably knew that Taylor wanted to make sure he had a place to stay. Taylor had pushed him about the matter every single time they spoke, to the point he worried the young man would up and disappear for good. But he wouldn't stop until he knew for sure Blake was on the path to putting his life together. And the kid couldn't do that while sleeping behind a Dumpster or in an abandoned building.

Taylor rejoined his group, grabbed his Guinness, and took a long draw. "Thanks for the beer. I've got the next round."

Shane waved him off. "No problem. So, what's up with the kid?"

"Our young friend got himself a job with the band, doing the sound stuff and whatnot."

"Hey, that's great. Maybe you'll stop worrying so much about him now."

Shane didn't fool him—his partner was just as concerned about Blake, especially since he now had a teenage son of his own to raise. Kinda brought home how important family was, and how much Blake must be hurting inside.

"Maybe. I'm still going to make sure he has a roof over his head before I leave tonight. Even if he has to come home with me."

Shane frowned. "Listen, your heart's in the right place, but do you think that's smart? We like Blake, but, truthfully, we don't really know him that well."

"He's a good kid," Taylor said in his defense. "He's assisted the police plenty, stuck his neck out when the risk was greater than the reward, and he deserves better than what he's been dealt."

"And you're going to fix that."

"That's right."

Shane sighed, then lifted his beer and saluted. "Good. I'll help any way I can. Don't hesitate to ask."

"Thanks, partner."

Just then, the lights dimmed and remained that way, signaling showtime. The crowd cheered as Blake stepped up to the microphone to get the party truly started.

"How's everyone doing tonight?" A raucous yell went up at his greeting. Playing them, he called out again.

"Are you ready to *rock*?"

A louder roar met his challenge, beers and shot glasses raised high.

"That's awesome, because we've got a hell of a show for ya'll tonight!" Taking a deep breath, he shouted, "Please help me give a big welcome to a smokin'-hot band we're damned lucky to have stolen from Los Angeles—Cara Evans and the Ten Inch Boys!"

Around Blake, several cops snickered at her backup band's name, and the crowd roared in approval. The words *Los Angeles* bounced around in Taylor's head as the drummer, a bassist, lead guitarist, and keyboardist— all twentysomething guys—jogged onto the stage and took their places. Seemed he couldn't get away from references to that city no matter how far he fled.

The other side of the world wouldn't be far enough.

Then the drummer clicked off the song and they launched into the rousing, fast-paced intro of a current song Taylor heard on the radio all the time but couldn't place. Something with an attitude. He was still trying to name it in his head when the lead singer sprinted out, took the microphone, and belted out the first notes with a husky, whiskey-laced Ann Wilson voice.

Taylor felt like he'd been smacked upside the head with a brick.

As Cara Evans injected a healthy dose of raw sarcasm, singing of a woman missing the man who'd shit on her time and again, Taylor was transfixed.

Oh yes, Blake owed him an introduction.

And he wasn't leaving here without it.

3

Cara's tight little body should be registered as a lethal weapon.

Taylor's eyes were glued to the slim hips swiveling to the beat, low-rise skinny jeans clinging valiantly to slight curves. A cropped tank top rode well above her exposed navel, showing off creamy skin and a flat, toned tummy. Definitely no muffin top there.

She was a short, petite thing, probably no more than five-foot-nothing and one hundred ten pounds soaking wet. And, boy, would he love to get her wet, all right.

Her face was delicate, her nose slim. She had large kohl-lined eyes, though he couldn't tell their color from where he sat. Jet-black hair framed her face and fell just to her shoulders and was streaked with purple. If she had been wearing all black instead of jeans and a tank top, she'd appear to be on the Goth side. Despite her porcelain features, she looked wild, a bit dangerous. Nothing like the women he usually pursued, women like Laura Eden—sleek, professional, and coolly untouchable.

Suddenly, wild and dangerous was exactly his type.

Around him, his buddies alternated between watching the show, talking about work, laughing, and drinking. For his part, everyone faded into the background. Everyone except the sexy little rocker strutting around, owning the stage. Song after song, he devoured her every move. Not only how damned hot she was, but her talent. She was a natural performer, her voice like liquid gold.

A hard thump on his back nearly sent a swig of his beer down his windpipe.

"Hey, earth to Kayne!" Cunningham, one of the night-shift officers, bellowed in his ear. "Whatcha starin' at, huh? Think you're getting some of that? Think again, hound dog!"

"No way would that sweet thing let your ugly ass get too close!" another one called.

A few of the others laughed, and he received a couple of good-natured nudges at being caught completely enamored of the singer. He laughed along with them, but inside he cringed. He knew they were just kidding, but their words stung, given his pitiful lack of success lately.

He went back to ignoring them, nursing his beer and then another. *Working up some liquid courage, old boy?* Maybe. The girl was young. Not jailbait, if he was any judge, but early twenties as opposed to his thirty-two. Just a big enough gap to make him *really* start feeling his age. He didn't even want to *think* about how old she was when he graduated from high school.

Jesus.

Somehow he made it through the set without taking too much more crap from his friends. It seemed they sensed a change in his mood and left him alone. Which left him free to plan what he might say when he met the cutie. Too bad he couldn't come up with anything that didn't sound stupid.

The second the band's first set was done, Taylor jumped to his feet and began to make his way toward the stage. The band members were milling around, mopping their faces and necks with hand towels and drinking a variety of stuff, from bottled water to whiskey shots. As he neared, he was relieved to see that the singer was drinking water, though why he should care was a mystery. Other than the obvious—his being a cop, that is. He hated to imagine her driving home after this, tipsy, and having a wreck.

Being arrested.

God, give it a rest! Be a normal guy, for Christ's sake!

As he stepped up, Blake gave him a knowing smirk. "I'm guessing you're here for that introduction."

"You guessed right."

"You've got a lot of competition, man. Just sayin'."

Indeed he did. Another glance in Cara's direction proved just how much. The woman was holding court over a crowd of fans, the vast majority of whom were men. Particularly irritating was the way her lead guitarist hovered real close, practically draped over her like a damned blanket. He was contemplating how to get through the throng to speak to her when Blake shouted in her direction.

"Cara!" Turning, she smiled, a question in her eyes. "Come over here! There's someone I want you to meet."

Waving at Blake, she returned her attention to the folks pressing in and, after a few moments, managed to break away tactfully. Like liquid sex, she moved, slim legs eating the distance, toward where he stood with Blake. Riveted, he admired her loose-limbed walk, the confidence edged with a bit of attitude. He wondered what it might be like to have all of that intense focus on *him*. Then her gaze slowly slid from the younger man to Taylor.

And the welcoming smile slid from her face and fell to the floor like a stone. For a second, he could have sworn he saw a flash of something dark and poisonous in her eyes, but then it vanished just as fast. Surely he was mistaken. Either way, it was not exactly the type of intensity he was going for.

His stomach immediately plummeted to his toes and he stared at her in confusion. What on earth could he have done already to warrant a negative reaction? They hadn't even met yet! Suddenly he wished he'd stayed at his table with the guys.

"Cara," Blake said, waving at him. "This is my friend, Taylor Kayne. Taylor, this is my new boss, Cara Evans."

"Pleased to meet you." Taylor stuck out his hand, feeling foolish even as he did so. But she took it, giving it a firm shake, lips turning up.

"Same here."

Not precisely a warm welcome, but he'd take it. "You and your band sounded fantastic. There aren't too many females doing rock justice these days, but I have to say I'm a fan. I don't understand why you aren't signed with a big label."

Another troublesome flash in those eyes—he could see now that they were blue—and she gave him a wry smile. "Thanks. There was a time when that dream wasn't so far out of reach. But life has a way of taking a sharp left when you'd planned to go right."

"Doesn't it?"

"Been there, have you?" She gave him the oddest look. Almost calculating.

"Once or twice."

"What do you do for a living, Taylor?"

He hesitated. Some people weren't comfortable around cops, especially those who worked in or hung around clubs. He'd never lied about his job when he wasn't undercover, though, and he wouldn't start now. "I'm a police officer with the Sugarland PD. Detective, actually."

"Hmm." Reaching out, she trailed a black polished fingernail down his neck, into the V of his shirt. Playfully, she ran the tip of her tongue over her lips. "And are you very, very good at . . . detecting?"

With that, Blake made a rude snorting noise and made himself scarce, heading in the direction of the restrooms.

"I like to think so." He leveled her with his best, most charming lopsided grin. Inside, though, he was a quivering mess. His brain screamed at him that he'd finally gotten hold of more woman than he was prepared to handle.

His little head, however, was totally on board with the idea.

Warmth pooled in his groin, gradually spreading to envelop his stiffening cock. He liked her fingernail scratching lightly over his skin, making every nerve ending sing with pleasure. Her warmth and spicy scent teased his nose even through the less pleasant club odors of smoke and beer, and he wanted to get closer. Pull her into his body and find out whether that lush mouth was as good at kissing as it appeared.

"I don't think you are."

He blinked, trying to recall what they'd been talking about. Oh yeah—his detecting skills. "What makes you say that?"

"If you were that good, you'd have figured out that I'm not interested." With that, she placed both palms on his chest and pushed. As he took a couple of steps backward, she turned to walk away.

"Wait!"

Pausing, she turned and looked over her shoulder. "Why should I?"

"Don't I get a chance to change your mind? Let me buy you a cup of coffee after you're done."

"I hate coffee."

Damn. "Hot chocolate? A Coke?"

Eyes glittering, expression unreadable, she studied him for a long moment. He resisted the urge to squirm like a bug under a magnifying glass. Finally, she gave a barely perceptible nod.

"A drink here at the bar," she said. "We play until closing at two, and it'll take Blake and the band about half an hour to break down. You have until they're finished to impress me and not one second more."

A challenge. Why in the hell that haughty declaration, along with the cool fire in her gaze, should make him harder than a frigging rock, he didn't have a clue. Except that he'd always found self-confidence damned attractive and this lady had that in spades.

"You got it." He met her eyes, not allowing his own doubts to show even a bit. That would be the kiss of death with this woman, he sensed. "But maybe you have half an hour to impress *me*, not the other way around." He punctuated the statement with a wink.

She huffed a laugh and shook her head. Then she sauntered away, tight little ass swaying in those sinful jeans. He was just about to head back to his table when he noticed that Cara had stopped to speak with the lead guitarist, who had those pesky boundary issues. Of more importance at the moment, however, was the question Taylor overheard her ask the man.

"Have you seen Blake?"

"Saw him head toward the restroom," the man replied, nodding in the general direction. "He's got two minutes."

Come to think of it, hitting the men's room wasn't such a bad idea. He could take care of business and let the kid know his break was almost up. Making his way down the dim corridor away from the main room, he was knocked aside by a big, burly asshole with enough grizzle on his face to use as sandpaper. On his heels was a slightly shorter man, dressed similarly in biker boots and motorcycle leathers.

The Waterin' Hole was somewhat rough around the edges, but it wasn't a biker bar. This place typically catered to a blue-collar crowd, but they didn't get many bikers here. They were making tracks, too. A ball of dread settled in his gut.

Hurrying, Taylor pushed through the restroom doors. "Blake?"

A groan was his answer and he followed the sound to the last stall, where he found Blake crumpled in a heap on the dirty tile. "Shit," he hissed. "Are you all right?"

Another pain-filled moan was his answer as the young man struggled to sit up. Crouching at his side, Taylor saw the boy's bloodied face and a slow burn of anger flared in his chest.

"Who did this?" He already guessed, but wanted to see if the boy would tell the truth.

"Two big motherfuckers," Blake wheezed. "Looked like Hells Angels."

"Ever see them here before?"

A pause. "No."

"Don't lie to me, kid," he said in a low voice, tearing off a wad of toilet tissue. He helped Blake press it to his nose. "What did they want?"

"To remind me what happens to police informants. Guess they didn't quite believe I'm retired."

"So it wasn't a bashing?"

"Not really," he said quietly. "They weren't here to beat me up for being gay. That was just a bonus."

Taylor wanted to crack both of their skulls. Over the past few months he'd become protective of Blake and worried about him plenty. Maybe it was because he'd never had kids of his own, but this one got to him. Blake reminded Taylor of himself at that age. Alone and vulnerable. Smaller than the average kid and a perfect target. He had nobody around who cared.

Until one day someone did. And made all the difference.

"Come on. Let's get you washed off," he said gruffly,

hauling the boy to his feet. Blake was holding his side. "They hurt your ribs?"

"I took a shot or two. But I'm tougher than I look."

Taylor almost smiled at the younger man's fierce scowl, but refrained. As he helped Blake to the sink, the boy shook him off and insisted he could handle washing his own face. Taylor stood by, lost in thought, and jumped when someone pounded on the bathroom door.

"Blake? Honey, are you in there?"

"Cara," Blake said, groaning. "I've already fucked up on my first night. She'll probably fire me."

"No, she won't." Crossing to the door, Taylor opened it and took in her surprised face. "Blake had a mishap. He'll be right out."

If he thought that was going to put her off, he was mistaken.

"Get out of my way," she growled and marched right past him. "What happ— Oh, my God! Who did this?"

The boy turned and gave her a wan smile as he used wet paper towels to wipe the last of the blood from his swelling nose. "My face ran into some dude's fist. I'm good."

"You are not *good*. Not even a little bit." She rounded on Taylor. "Did you do this? Because if you did—"

"Whoa there, boss lady," Blake said, intervening. "Taylor's cool. He came in after those big assholes left. The cop here always helps me, even when I don't want him to."

As she glared at Taylor, he could see her working that out in her head. He also detected a faint look of disbelief, quickly masked, before she spoke.

"You're Tate!"

"Say what?"

"Jess told me some detective had taken an interest in Blake's well-being, but he thought his name was Tate or something. But he meant *Taylor*," she said almost to herself. She was staring at him in shock. "That's you."

"Um, yeah . . ." He exchanged a puzzled look with Blake, who shrugged as if to say he had no idea, either, why she was so hung up on that fact. Almost amazed. "Am I missing something here?"

She recovered quickly. "No. I'm just surprised to meet the guy Blake speaks so highly of—that's all."

The young man blushed. Not meeting Taylor's gaze, he tossed his paper towels in the trash. "We need to get going or you're gonna be late for your set."

"The band can wait. I think you should get to the hospital, get checked out," she said, frowning in concern. "And you need to file a police report."

"No way. I'm totally fine." Blake's lips pressed into a grim line, his expression determined. "And no police. Taylor knows what happened and that's enough."

Understanding the boy couldn't afford a hospital visit, Taylor felt bad for him. Since he didn't seem to be that badly hurt, he wasn't about to push the issue. He didn't blame the boy for not wanting an official police report, either. He knew male pride, not to mention suspicion of authority figures, all too well. Especially being young, with nothing and no one to turn to.

Taylor interjected. "That's fine—no hospital or police. But if you see those guys anywhere around again, you *will* tell me so Shane and I can deal with them."

The boy nodded, looking shaken. "Promise."

Cara sighed, giving in. "Okay. But if you get a bad headache or blurred vision or can't breathe—"

"Yes, Mom," Blake interrupted. "I'll go if I think I'm gonna keel over. Okay?"

"You're damned right you will."

Cara headed out of the restroom behind the boy, hovering over him like a mother hen. Taylor thought that was funny. Sweet, too, and directly opposite the prickly attitude she'd shown Taylor. Fascinating.

Is it all men who're interested that she doesn't like, or is it just me?

"Taylor?" Blake paused, letting him catch up. "Thanks for being there."

"Always, kid."

Cara gave him an inscrutable look and said, "See you at closing time."

Then she was gone, ushering her charge though the crowd. Humming to himself, Taylor went back to his table, where Shane immediately pounced on him.

"Where the hell have you been?"

"Making a hot date for later," he said, trying not to sound smug.

"Really? Damn, you work fast." His partner took a swig of his beer. "Who is she?"

Just then, the band kicked off their new set, and the floors vibrated as Cara's smoky voice crooned the first lines of "Barracuda." Grinning, Taylor pointed toward her.

Shane followed his finger, then looked back at Taylor, mouth open. "Her? No fucking way."

"Way."

"You dog! How'd you score that?" Cunningham bellowed above the music.

"It's a talent," Taylor shouted back. Ignoring his friends' whistles and jokes, he sat back and enjoyed himself.

And if his love interest wasn't quite as enamored as he believed? Well, they didn't have to know that.

But he was going to change her mind if it was the last thing he did.

Watch me.

Cara watched the handsome blond all through her sets. Couldn't take her eyes off him no matter how hard she tried.

Taylor fucking Kayne. He wasn't supposed to be so together. So damned *nice*. On top of that, he obviously cared a great deal about Blake, and the feeling was mutual. Nothing weird about their relationship that she could tell—just a man who'd befriended a homeless teen and wanted to see him succeed. To be almost an older brother figure.

On their set breaks, the detective didn't seek her out the rest of the night. Why had that become increasingly more irritating as the night wore on? Her attraction to him was nuts. She didn't just dislike the man.

She hated his *fucking guts.*

Or thought she did. Until she met the man and he wasn't anything like the monster she'd imagined. Now she was baffled. Curious completely against her will. She wanted—no, *needed*—to find out who the real man was behind the cute, lopsided smile and gorgeous green eyes. Looked like she'd get her chance, too.

Maybe a golden opportunity had been dropped into her lap. Instead of watching and waiting for an opportunity to destroy him from afar, she'd do it from within his inner circle. Sort of like the Trojan horse—come as a friend, then vanquish the enemy in his own yard.

When the last song was finished and she took her bow with the band, she searched the area where Taylor and his friends had been sitting. He was still there, but the others were apparently getting ready to leave, which suited her fine. She needed to get into his confidence, but that didn't mean she wanted to get too close to his friends. Too many cops in her face was *so* not a good thing in her book.

After putting her own guitar in its case, she made her way to the bar and took a seat. "Scotch on the rocks," she told Chandler, one of the bartenders she sometimes worked with.

"You got it, Cara. Great show, by the way."

"Thanks." She eyed her coworker as he fixed her drink, and wondered why he didn't rev her motor.

The guy was good-looking, for sure. He was former military. Beefy arms and torso, gorgeous face. But his brown hair was buzz cut—not her preference. He was a little too muscular for her taste, too much like a serious weightlifter. She preferred sexy blonds. Ones with plenty of gorgeous locks for a girl to dig her fingers into.

Like Taylor.

"Shit."

"Hey, you're getting a head start on me," a deep voice said.

She turned slightly to see Taylor take the stool beside her. His smile made her breath hitch, and those green eyes held her captive. He was just the right height, somewhere around six feet, and perfectly muscled. God, the man could model for a calendar or something.

What's more, his eyes and his demeanor were kind. She'd seen that before when he was talking to Blake and hadn't wanted to admit it. But it was hard to deny what she could see plain as day. Maybe his kindness was only because he'd learned some hard lessons from his mistakes. Maybe these days he was trying to make up for the lives he'd taken years ago.

As if he ever could. That steeled her resolve once more. She'd set her hook and then reel in her big fish.

"Not too big a head start," she said with a slight smile. "You can catch up."

Chandler set her drink down. "What'll it be?"

"Just water for me," he told the bartender. "I've had enough."

Her coworker filled a glass with ice and water, then set it in front of Taylor. He took a healthy drink.

"A man who knows when to stop," she observed. "Sort of the exception around here."

"Well, it *is* a bar. But you're right—I make a point not to overdo the alcohol."

"A regular Boy Scout, huh?" She couldn't keep the slight edge from her tone. With his next words, she wished she had.

"Hardly." He gave a low chuckle. "I had a dad, loosely termed, with a drinking problem, a nasty temper, and a hard fist. He left a lasting impression."

Her glass froze halfway to her lips, and she set it down. "He beat you?"

Taylor made a face. "What a downer. I didn't mean to get into that."

"I'm so sorry." She meant it. Because now the kindness in those eyes was tinged with sadness, and it was her mocking that had brought back a horrible memory and put it there. *Shouldn't I be glad?*

"Don't be. It's ancient history."

Not so ancient that it no longer hurt, but she didn't say it aloud. "Is that why you became a cop? To help people who went through what you did?"

"Partly. I meet people like Blake all the time and it never ceases to sicken me how one human being can treat another."

"You really love your job."

"Most of the time, yes. I like being a detective, putting puzzle pieces together to solve a crime. Or stopping criminals before they hurt someone again."

Right there. Right that moment, she almost blurted out the whole reason she was in Sugarland—because of the one time he'd failed. Not only failed, but fucked up spectacularly and gotten her sister killed. Something made her hold her tongue, though, and simply let the conversation take its natural course.

"And how often does that actually happen? That you get to put away the evil ones and all is well for the good citizens of Metropolis?"

"Not as often as I'd like," he admitted. "But the ones we win are rewarding."

"What about the ones you lose?" The edge was back. *Dammit.*

He paused. "We have to do our best and move on," he said quietly. "We lose some and it hurts, but that's all we can do."

With that, a vivid image of Jenny lying dead on her living room floor, brains splattered all over her priceless Persian rug, slammed into Cara hard. She drained the rest of her Scotch and signaled Chandler for another.

The silence that followed while the bartender refreshed her drink was surprisingly comfortable. In spite of the tension Taylor wasn't even aware of, he was easy to talk to. He waited until Chandler moved away again before speaking.

"Are you just curious about my job, or is there some reason you're asking these questions?"

Okay, perhaps not so unaware.

"I'm curious. Is that a crime?" she quipped.

"It's not the questions, it's the way you're asking them." Taking another sip of his water, he shook his head. "Never mind. It's been a long week and I'm beat."

"I should let you go, then."

He grinned. "Not *that* beat. Besides, my ride is gone."

"How convenient." She slanted him a look. Oh, she knew what he wanted. The question was, would she play his game? "Your time is up."

"What?" Blinking, he looked around. "It hasn't been thirty minutes."

"My band is ready to go, and Blake needs a place to stay, whether he wants to accept help or not."

"I was thinking the same thing. Thought I'd offer to let him crash with me for a while."

"Or me. Why don't we let him decide?"

"Works for me," he said. "Am I to assume I failed to impress you?"

She mostly finished her second drink, then slid off the stool. Taylor stood next to her and she felt his nearness, his heat. Like before, when she'd teased him on her break, he smelled so good, of sandalwood and spice. She conjured what he'd feel like, pushing her into the mattress, sliding his cock deep, fucking her hard and fast. All those muscles, his sexy maleness, his skin.

"You know what they say about assuming." She let her mouth hitch into a small smile, which he returned.

"Indeed I do. Let's go find Blake."

He was waiting out back and gestured to her truck as they approached. "I loaded your guitar and amp in the back for you."

"Thanks, hon. You earned your money tonight. I'll pay you when we get home."

It took the boy a couple of seconds to process. "What do you mean, *home*?"

"My home. Where you're going to be staying until you're on your feet," she clarified.

"Cara, I can't accept—"

"Yes, you can," she said firmly. "I told you we were going to discuss this, and I meant it."

"There isn't much discussion if you're telling me what to do," he shot back.

Taylor added his two cents. "She's right, kid. I've told you before that there's no shame in accepting a hand up. I had to do that myself when I was around your age."

The boy's eyes widened, his face barely visible in the dim lighting. "You? I . . . You seem like a guy who's had it easy. I mean, you're successful."

"Only because I swallowed my pride and let the people who cared about me lend a hand. You do the same, and I promise you I'll tell you the whole story one day soon."

"Blake, you'll never reach safety if you don't grab the life preserver," she said. "What's it going to be?"

"You can stay with me as another option," Taylor put in. "I'd be glad to have you."

Blake thought about that for several long moments. This was so difficult for him, but in the end there really wasn't a choice. "I'll stay with you." He jerked his chin at Cara. "I'm working for you now, so it's just easier until I can get my own wheels."

She beamed at him. "Great deal. You won't be sorry, kid."

"Almost twenty here, not a kid." He rolled his eyes.

"Come on," she said, laughing. "Let's go."

As they approached her truck, Taylor's steps slowed. She noted how he stopped and stared, seeming to pay particular attention to her front bumper. Weird.

"What are you looking at?"

"Nothing. Are you fine to drive?"

Okay. "I'm good."

"Let me drive anyway? You just had two drinks, and

I quit a while ago." He held out a hand. "Occupational hazard. Sorry."

Shrugging, she fished the truck's keys from her pocket and handed them over. They got in and Taylor fired up the ignition, with Cara seating herself in the middle, and again his wonderful scent assailed her. Trying to ignore it, she turned to Blake on her other side.

"Taylor's going to drop you off at my place first. Then I'll take Taylor home. I won't be long."

Blake's knowing grin was visible in the dark. "Uh-huh. I'll bet you won't."

"Shut up, twerp." Taylor reached across her to give him a playful shove, and the two of them scuffled a bit.

"Hey! I'm in the middle here!"

The two guys finally settled down, but all three of them were smiling by the time they did.

All the way home, she had to remind herself that the cop was the enemy.

But already, that was becoming almost impossible to remember.

4

Taylor chose to wait outside while Cara got Blake situated in her house. If it were anyone besides that boy, Taylor would never have trusted him alone with her *or* her belongings. But this was Blake, and he knew the young man was a good soul.

Besides, Taylor wanted to take a look at her truck. A black newer-model Ford, just like the one that had hit him earlier in the week. His hip was still bruised, but at least he could walk now without pain.

Casting an eye toward the house, he got out of the truck and walked around to the front bumper. The light being emitted from the lamppost above illuminated the area just enough to see what he was looking for. And then he wished he hadn't.

On the right side, above the front bumper, was a dent. It wasn't that big, but it was large enough to have resulted from smacking into a person. His heart sank as he positioned his body the way it had been just before he'd been struck, and he lined up perfectly.

"Fuck." How could this possibly be a coincidence?

And yet how could she be after him? He and Cara had only just met. He'd approached her at the bar, not the other way around. Hell, she wasn't going to give him the time of day, but somehow he'd managed to finagle a second glance. This didn't scream setup to him.

But his instincts had been wrong before.

"Well, Blake is settled in the guest room," her voice said, startling him. He turned to see her coming down the walk. "He's beat and is getting ready for bed."

"That's good."

"You were looking at my new dent, huh?" She pointed, a frown marring her pretty face. "That totally sucks. Somebody must've backed into me earlier this week, and they didn't even leave a note."

He hesitated. If she already knew how the damage happened, that meant *she* was the one who'd struck Taylor, on purpose. That she'd known his identity before they met—and she would've realized he'd figure that out immediately. The ruse would be exposed. Yet she looked and sounded sincerely mystified by how the damage had happened. What were the odds it *wasn't* Cara behind the wheel? Or that this wasn't even the same truck?

"You don't remember hitting anything?" he asked carefully. *Or any*one.

"Of course not. I'd remember that," she said, looking at him as though he was an idiot. If she was acting, she was good.

"Right." He'd have to look into this more closely, but he'd do it discreetly. For now, he changed the subject. "You sure Blake will be okay here by himself?" She seemed to understand that he meant emotionally.

"Yeah. He's uncomfortable accepting help, but, like we told him, he'll have to get over that to get on his feet. And I'm fine with leaving him alone, because he's not truly alone, if you know what I mean."

"He's not on the street, worried about survival."

"Exactly." She gestured toward the truck. "Ready for me to take you home?"

"Sure."

He gave her back the keys to the truck and told her the address. "I'm just three streets over, so we're practically neighbors."

She smiled a little. "Who would've thought?"

Again with the secretive edge to her tone. What was with that? When they arrived on the street in front of his house, she let the truck idle.

"Nice street."

"Thanks. I love it here. We have block parties once in a while with food, music, raffle drawings, and such. We even have a competition with a prize for the best yard."

"Sounds like fun," she said thoughtfully. "Have you ever won?"

"Couple of times." He was kind of proud of that, stupid as it sounded. "Don't know if you got the flier, but we're having another one in a month or so, if you'd like to come."

"I don't remember seeing it, but I might just do that."

He shifted awkwardly, unable to remember when he'd ever felt so out of his depth with a woman, even with his sorry track record. The silence stretched taut between them, the night and its blanket of stars closing in. His cock, half-hard the whole evening since they'd met, swelled in his jeans. He wanted to touch, taste, get lost in her softness. Maybe he'd been too long without a woman, but the strange pull in his gut told him it was something more than lust. Though there was plenty of that.

Man up, old boy. What's the worst she can do?

Reject him, sure. It would sting, but he'd live. *Nothing ventured, as they say.*

Cara was studying him, making no move to leave. Taking that as an encouraging sign, he moved forward, so close their bodies were almost touching. Tentatively, he reached out and brushed her cheek with his knuckles. When she didn't move away or protest, he cupped her face and brought their bodies together.

Fire. She scorched him from chest to groin, setting him ablaze. The firmness of her breasts pushed into him as she tilted her head up and met his gaze. He hoped the hunger he read there matched his own, because he was done waiting to find out.

Lowering his head, he captured her lips with his. He could swear he felt the shock of pleasure rush from his brain to his toes. So good. Electric. Wrapping her arms around his back, she urged him closer, opened for him. Happy to oblige, he slipped his tongue into the moist heat of her mouth, exploring. She met his searching eagerly, her response so passionate it made him dizzy.

Breaking the kiss, he slid a hand down to the curve of her ass. "I want you, Cara. I know it's way soon, but—"

"I want you, too," she breathed. A hand slipped under his shirt, rubbed his abdomen. "But I have to go."

"Stay? Just for a little while?"

"Taylor . . ."

"Don't make me beg. It's not pretty."

"Don't give me that damned lopsided smile," she said in a low, husky voice. "It won't work."

"I think it already has."

"It's almost three in the morning. I should go."

Should wasn't *have to*. He smothered her weakening protests with another kiss, this one as hot as the first. Her lips were velvet, devouring him in return, and she writhed against him. He wanted more of the same, only with no annoying clothes to get in the way.

"Stay," he pleaded, nipping at her lips.

Crickets chirped around them. Somewhere a cat screeched. It seemed an eternity before she nodded, and his blood sang.

"For a while, I'll stay."

For a while, I'll stay.

The instant the words were out of her mouth, Cara cursed herself for being a moron.

Not that she didn't want his gorgeous body—oh no, that definitely wasn't the problem. With that shaggy blond hair falling into those beautiful, earnest green eyes, hard muscles tensed and ready to pounce . . . the man was her fantasy in the flesh.

He was the enemy. And right now the woman in her didn't care.

"Let's go inside," he said, voice husky.

Taking her hand, he led her to the porch steps. Fished out a key and let them in. After he'd locked the door behind him and flipped on a lamp, he pushed her against the door and ate her mouth again. A whimper escaped her throat and she was too aroused to be ashamed of her response. She needed him like she needed air. It had been far too long.

"My bedroom?"

"Yes."

Quickly, he led her up the stairs and down a hallway to his bedroom, switching on a lamp on the nightstand. It was a nice room with a big, attractive four-poster bed, but, frankly, her attention was on other things besides the decor. Her mouth watered as he yanked off his T-shirt to reveal a sculpted chest that was lightly hairy. Manly and just right. He had a nice six-pack going, and a treasure trail of dusky hair that ran from his belly button, disappearing into the waistband of his jeans.

"Take off the rest," she said. "I want to watch."

One corner of his mouth quirked up. "I've got myself a voyeur? Sweet."

"Only when it comes to crazy-hot men undressing just for me."

His expression sobered some. "I don't do this often. Haven't in ages, so I don't want you to think I'm some man-slut who trolls the Waterin' Hole on a weekly basis."

"Good to know. But what if I'm a girl-slut?"

"Well, honey, I don't judge." His grin told her that he was teasing.

She smiled back, and it felt foreign on her face. What was it about this man that had her relaxing her guard when she damned well shouldn't? Now wasn't the time to analyze, though. She pointed to his lower half. "The rest, cop."

"Ooh, I love when you say *cop* like that. Sounds dirty."

"Have a fetish about that, do we?"

"Among other things." He unfastened the jeans, then worked down the zipper.

"Do tell."

"Even better, I'll show you sometime."

They'd see about that. For now, she feasted her eyes on him as he pushed his jeans and boxer briefs down his legs, then stepped out of them. His thighs were hard, just as toned as his torso, and he had well-shaped calves. His cock was thick and long, a good eight or nine inches, and was curved upward, purplish red and weeping precum. She caught herself about to lick her lips in anticipation of tasting him.

"Your turn."

His gaze was hot as she pulled off her tank top and discarded it. Next came her lacy bra with the front clasp, something she knew men liked. Flicking it open, she watched his expression darken as she parted the cups and let herself spill free.

"God, you're beautiful."

She was glad the room was a bit dim and hopefully hid her blush. "I'm not very big."

"You're just right," he said reverently. "Perfect."

"Thank you." The compliment was unexpected and very nice. She wasn't used to lovers saying sweet things. Even when she and Jinx, her lead guitarist, had been an item and burning up the sheets, he'd never wasted time with gentleness or sweet nothings.

After kicking off her shoes, she peeled off the trendy designer jeans that hugged her like a second skin. He took in her every move, especially attentive when she saved the purple thong underwear for last.

"It matches the streaks in your hair," he observed.

"You haven't seen nothin' yet." Slowly, she pushed down her panties and his mouth fell open. His eyes widened as he stared at her trimmed black landing strip streaked with purple. She grinned. "I like for the carpet to match the drapes."

"Holy shit," he breathed. "Somebody in heaven really does love me."

"You like?"

"Come here and let me show you how much."

Taking her hand, he pulled her to the bed and urged her onto her back. As he climbed over her, she spread her legs to accommodate him. He kissed her senseless, his erection trapped between them, pulsing and hot, burrowing into her stomach. This was the part she'd always loved best—a strong man covering her body with his, showering her with attention.

And that was an area in which Taylor clearly excelled. He was very skilled in using his teeth, tongue, and hands. Bending his head, he nibbled along her jaw to her neck, and the tiny bites raised goose bumps on her skin. She liked the sensation and squirmed underneath him, which in turn made him growl and rub his cock against her even more.

Reaching between them, he rolled one nipple between his thumb and forefinger, using just enough pressure to send a delicious sting of pain singing to her nerve endings. Heat flared between her legs and she knew she was already wet for him. She liked some edge to her play, and he didn't disappoint.

After twirling one nipple and then the other with his fingers, he moved lower to pleasure them with his mouth. He licked the tip of the first, which was now standing at a tight peak. She savored how his tongue rasped against the nub and then how he sucked it, making sure to graze it with his teeth. Once he'd repeated the process on the other nipple, she was moaning her approval.

Without a word, he began to kiss his way lower. Finally—thank God—he was lying between her thighs, face practically buried in her mound.

"I'm gonna feast on you, baby," he murmured.

"Please." She spread wider.

Maybe she loved *this* part best. Being completely exposed, spread for her lover. Offering herself to his lips and tongue, fingers and cock. She loved how powerful this made her feel. How wanted. Needed.

"So pretty. I love when a woman is bare here," he said, laving the slick lips of her folds.

Most men did, in her experience. They liked a trimmed bush above, but the labia waxed bare was a sensual playground during sex. Taylor sure seemed to agree.

The man licked her like a cat lapping cream, and she arched into him, burying her fingers in his silky hair. His tongue worked between her folds, too, and he fucked her like that, stroking the appendage in and out of her slick channel. Waves of heat pooled in her core and rippled outward to her limbs. He began to eat her in earnest, driving her out of her mind.

"I don't want to come yet," she panted, yanking on his hair. "Need you in me."

Nodding, he wiped his face on the sheets and rose. She almost protested until she saw that he was just moving to the nightstand to fish for protection. Removing a foil square from the drawer, he ripped it open and deftly sheathed his rod. Then he returned to his spot between her thighs and remained on his knees, positioning himself at her entrance. Cupping her bottom with his hands, he lifted her slightly.

Then he worked his thick cock into her, careful not to cause any pain. Not that he could have. She was so overheated she was ready to combust. "Fuck me," she begged.

"Hard and fast, honey?" A thin bead of sweat rolled from his temple, down his jaw. She wanted to lick it.

"Yes!"

She didn't have to ask twice. He plunged in to the hilt, held steady for a moment, letting her adjust. Then slid out, slammed in again. As he increased the strength and tempo of his thrusts, his eyes never left hers. The intensity of his gaze, his raw sexuality and comfort level in his own skin, was damned arousing. She'd never felt anything like the shudder than ran to her soul as he looked into her eyes. Watching her reaction. Seeing his male satisfaction at pleasing her.

Soon he was pounding deep, the sounds of rhythmic fucking like music. He was a skilled lover, his cock angled to rub her clit, bringing her to the edge of orgasm. She staved it off as long as she could, but not nearly long enough. Once release was imminent, she shattered with a cry, her walls clenching around his length, hands clutching his back.

In seconds he followed her over, plunging one last time, his cock jerking and twitching until at last he was spent. Body still draped over hers, he lowered his face into the curve of her neck and shoulder, breathing hard. Sated, she let her palms roam over his spine and downward to squeeze his tight ass. *Very nice.*

After a couple of minutes, he moved to the side, his spent cock slipping out. She had to squelch a bout of disappointment at his loss, and wondered at that. She'd never really felt that way before. Sadly, she was usually glad for the guy to be done and get the heck off her. With Taylor, it was different.

That wasn't good. At all.

When the bed dipped, she realized she'd been so caught up in her thoughts she'd missed him going to the bathroom. He'd discarded the condom and cleaned up some. He held out a damp cloth.

"A clean one for you."

"Thanks," she said, taking the cloth. No one had ever taken care of her afterward, she was certain. It was a sweet gesture that confounded everything she'd believed about Taylor.

For some reason, wiping off with the cloth under his watchful eye was somewhat embarrassing where the actual sex hadn't been. Probably due to coming down from the rush of hormones or something. After she was done, he took the cloth, tossed it into the bathroom, and crawled back into bed.

Snuggling in, he pulled her close so that her head was on his chest. "Is this okay?"

"This is just fine." She smiled to herself, determined to think of the complications of getting involved with this man tomorrow. Or later today. "Do you have to work today?"

"No, I'm off." He laughed softly. "This old man can't handle partying all night, then showing up for work at eight in the morning anymore. Did that plenty in my twenties, but now it would probably kill me."

"You are *not* old." She trailed a finger through his chest hair.

"I've got a few years on that guitarist of yours. The one who was stuck to you like plastic wrap on your set breaks."

She snickered. Men were so transparent. "That was Jay, or Jinx, as we call him, because he's got the worst karma of anybody we've ever met."

"He seemed into you."

"Nah, not so much anymore. He's a friend and watches over me."

"Yeah, I could see that." He didn't sound thrilled about it.

"We had a thing for a while. It blew over and we're cool, end of story."

That's honestly all there was to it, but men were as bad as women about the jealousy thing. Maybe worse. "Why does it matter to you, anyhow? This is a hookup, right?"

Underneath her, he tensed. "Is it?"

"I think that's best. Don't you?"

He was silent for a long moment. She could almost feel him struggling with his reply.

"I think I'm too old for hookups."

"I don't know if I have more to give, or if it's smart to get involved."

"Does anyone really know?" he pointed out. "Isn't it worth the risk to find someone special?"

"Maybe. But taking risks isn't something I've been good at these past few years."

"You might learn."

"I might." It was as far as she was willing to concede, and even that confused her. She hated this man, with good reason. "I need to get home."

"It's late. Or early." He yawned. "Stay. Sleep for a while. I'll make you breakfast later."

Breakfast. How . . . domestic.

With the cop who'd killed her sister.

She rose to dress, turned away from the flash of disappointment that shadowed his green eyes. "Some other time."

"Sure." He paused. "Do you have a cell phone?"

"Yes." Sliding it from her jeans pocket, she held up the device.

"Put me in your contacts?"

"Okay." That could be useful. *Keep your friends close, your enemies closer.* Instantly, she hated the surge of guilt in her chest at the thought. He rattled off the number and she saved it. Then he grabbed his jeans and pulled them on, fishing his phone from his pockets as well.

"Call me, and I'll have yours, too."

She did, and Taylor saved her contact info before walking her out the door and to her truck. He helped her inside and stood there, studying her for a moment.

"I'm sorry if I pushed too hard," he said with a slight frown. "I don't want to scare you away."

"You didn't." *Liar.* "How about we take things slow, see where this goes?"

His smile lit the night. "I'd like that."

He leaned in for a last kiss, and she accepted it wholeheartedly. This was a dangerous game she played, but it was like she had almost zero willpower around Taylor. He seemed like the real deal. Kind, genuine.

And if he was, then she'd have to give some serious thought to Jenny's murder. Specifically, if what she'd been told and had always believed about that day was the truth—or a pack of lies.

Dmitri was nursing his morning coffee when the phone interrupted his solitude. He picked up on the second ring. "Yes?"

"There's been an interesting development," Snyder informed him with a sneer in his tone. "She and the cop have become . . . acquainted."

His hands tightened around his mug. "How so?"

"My guess? In the biblical sense, seeing that they hooked up in the bar last night and ended up at his house just long enough to scratch a mutual itch."

"She's been watching the cop much longer than we have. Now she's playing him," Dmitri guessed.

"Maybe so. But since she hasn't killed him by now, my guess is she's not going to. We have to stick to the original plan—get them both out of the way. Now more than ever, before they compare notes."

"Yes." He sighed. "Forget trying to make it look like she took out the cop. Just get rid of them."

"Yes, sir."

Ending the call, Dmitri went back to his coffee and his newspaper. But the brew was cold and the words blurred.

All he could see was Jenny's beautiful face. The destruction of his plans.

Kayne would pay dearly for the loss of both.

Saturdays were usually Cara's lazy days. No bartending, no band practice. Just a whole day to herself with nothing to do but sleep in, maybe go for a walk. Read a good book. Anything to take her mind off Jenny and dreams of revenge.

Today she had a different sort of distraction: Blake. The young man was asleep in the guest room, and she had no idea what to do, seeing as she rarely had visitors, much less overnight guests. Should she cook breakfast? Let him sleep?

Suddenly anxious, she rummaged through the refrigerator and pantry, searching for something impressive to cook. If not impressive, she'd settle for edible. Somehow she didn't think wilted salad and a few slices of mushy, half-dead cantaloupe would be very appetizing. On the heels of that thought, she wondered why his comfort and well-being were so important to her. It wasn't like he was a lover or anything.

But he could've been, had he not been gay. With a

start, she realized that Blake was much closer to her age than Taylor. What a strange thought. She cared for Blake. In fact, she was beginning to think of Blake as a brother, but the detective was the one who got her motor running.

Dammit! She didn't want to like Taylor, much less be attracted, but her body had gone and parted ways with her common sense. Last night had been a huge mistake. What had she been thinking, playing a game of sexual cat and mouse with the man?

"I can't do this," she muttered, leaning against the kitchen counter. "I can't get involved with him." No sooner had the thought left her lips than a buzzing noise came from the counter. A text had come in on her phone, and, peering at the display, she groaned.

It was from Taylor. *Just want to say have a great day.*

A pause, then another one. *Hope to see you again soon. ;)*

Damn. Her heart beat a little faster and she felt a warmth in her chest that had been absent for a very long time. The thaw was almost painful and not entirely welcome. To reply or not? She was somewhat pissed at herself for even considering it. She picked up her phone, stared at it. Put it down. Finally, she decided to let it wait, for now. If he was truly interested, that wouldn't change in just a few hours.

Cursing herself again, she was about to dig through the pantry once more when she heard a noise behind her. Turning, she saw Blake standing in the doorway to the kitchen, dressed in the same clothes he'd had on the night before. He'd showered, though, and she could smell the fresh aroma of soap wafting from the young man. His hair was damp but combed. Giving her an uncertain smile, he edged inside.

"Hey. You shouldn't have let me sleep so long. I'll get out of your hair."

"What?" She scowled at him. "You're not *in my hair*. Don't you trust me to tell you if you were?"

His face flushed red. "Um, I guess. Sure," he said with more conviction. "You're a pretty direct person."

"That's right. If I wanted you to leave, I'd just say so." She crossed her arms over her chest. "Have you already forgotten our conversation from last night?"

"No. But I don't want to be a burden—"

"Nope, you're not. You're my sound man, and you need a temporary place to stay while we find you a second job to supplement your income. You'll be independent before you know it, and I don't want to hear that crap again. Understand?"

One corner of his mouth kicked up and relief shone in his weary brown eyes. "Yeah, got it."

"Good." She waved a hand toward the kitchen. "I was going to cook, but unless you like rotted produce, we're going to the diner for some breakfast."

His stomach rumbled and though he looked embarrassed, he laughed. "I'd say that sounds pretty damned good."

"Great! Let me grab my keys and purse and we'll go."

Soon they were in her truck and on their way to the old part of Sugarland. One of the first things she'd loved about the place was the old-fashioned town square with a gorgeous old courthouse that sat smack in the center.

Retail shops lined the square on all four sides, including the diner. The restaurant served home-cooked meals in a friendly atmosphere that had become such a rarity across the country.

Pulling into a parking spot in front, she shut off the engine and they walked inside. Immediately she was enveloped in the wonderful smell of bacon, eggs, and something sweeter. Maybe waffles or pancakes.

An older waitress led them to a booth, where they took seats opposite each other and studied the laminated menus. The diner fare was simple, but she knew from experience how good the food was.

"The cowboy omelet for me," she said, closing the menu. "You?"

His voice was quiet. "Maybe the short stack of pancakes?"

"Is that all? What about some bacon?"

"No, thanks." But his stomach rumbled and his eyes remained downcast, belying his words.

"Blake, look at me." When he did, she smiled encouragingly. "I'll say this again, and this time get it through your head. We've become friends over the past few weeks, and now you're a member of the band's crew as well. Our group is essentially family, and we help each other out when we're needed."

"Yes, but—"

"No *but*s," she said firmly. "If you fight me at every turn, not only will that be counterproductive, but you'll piss me off. Is that what you want?"

His lips curved up some. "Well, no. I've seen you in ninja mode and it's not pretty."

"Exactly. Besides, if the situation were reversed, would you help me?"

"Of course! I'd do anything in my power to give you a hand. You know that." His expression was earnest.

God, the guy was cute. "Then just cut us both a break and go with the flow, okay? The best thanks you can give me is to take this chance and run with it."

After staring at her for a few moments, he nodded. "All right. I'll stop being such a pain about it."

"Promise?"

"Yes, I promise."

The waitress came and took their order, and Blake shyly asked for the tall stack of pancakes with a side of bacon. Cara felt like she'd made major headway with him, and it was only a six-dollar breakfast, for God's sake. She couldn't wait to see if he'd forget his vow and balk when she took him shopping for clothes.

They chatted a bit, and after their food arrived, Cara carefully probed into his past when the opportunity presented itself. She found out Blake was from Clarksville, and that his parents still lived there. He had an older brother who no longer lived at home and had a decent job and an apartment in Nashville.

"Well, last I heard," he added sadly.

Cara frowned. "I thought you were an only child."

"No." He gave a bitter laugh. "As far as my parents are concerned, *Jonathon's* the only child."

"I'm sorry." She paused, wondering how much more he'd allow her to push. "Are you sure your brother feels the same? Maybe if you gave him a call—"

"Don't you think I tried that already?" he asked

sharply. "I haven't been living on the street for no reason. Jon told me I disgusted him and then hung up on me."

Her heart broke for him. "He wouldn't even hear you out?"

"No. And I never really got the chance to come out to him, either. My loving folks must've beat me to the punch."

"Must have? Don't you know?"

"What do you mean?"

She leaned forward, elbows on the table. "When your brother said he was disgusted with you, did he say *why*? Are you sure it was finding out you're gay?"

"No . . ." His eyes widened. "But I thought that's what he meant."

"What was Jon like before your falling-out? What kind of person was he?"

Blake's brows drew together. "He was cool. A nice guy to everyone, even kids like me who are . . . different. He never struck me as the judgmental type *before*. I know I've heard him make comments about how people should be able to love who they want."

She thought about that for a few seconds. "Considering what you just told me, is there any chance your parents lied to Jon about you? Drove a wedge between you by telling him you had done something he *would* have a problem handling?"

For the first time since she'd gotten to know Blake, the young man's face lit in an expression of real hope. "My brother hates liars, people who steal and cheat. You think they told him something like that?"

Reaching across the table, she grabbed his hand. "There's only one way to find out."

He bit his lip. "Would you go with me? When I'm ready, I mean."

"I'd be glad to, sweetie. Just let me know when you want to go."

"Let me think about it." He paused. "I'd like to have my shit together before I face him, you know? I want to have a job, be ready to stand on my own two feet. I don't want him to see me as his poor little worthless brother, looking for a handout."

"Well, you have a job with me. But I know what you mean." Something told her Jon would be glad to hear from Blake once he knew the truth. *Please let me be right.*

He looked her in the eye. "I'm grateful you gave me a chance, and I'll give you one hundred percent. It's just that I need a second job if I want to rent an apartment and pay for utilities and groceries."

She nodded. "You're thinking ahead. That's good."

The rest of breakfast passed pleasantly enough, despite the previous heavy subject, thanks in part to Blake's excitement over not only his job with the band, but finding a second one he was suited for.

"Did you know they opened a Guitar Center over by the mall a few months ago?" His eyes were bright for a change. Excited. "I'd be perfect for that job."

"You know the employees have to audition to work there, right?"

He snorted. "Obviously you've never heard me play."

She smiled at that. "I'd like to sometime."

"Really?" His happiness dimmed some. "I don't have my equipment anymore. Had to leave it at home, and my parents have probably hocked all of it by now for the cash."

The idea made her furious, but she kept her feelings hidden. "The band can hook you up with a guitar and amp to practice with. And if—*when*—you get that job, you'll be able to buy your own."

He brightened again. "Yeah."

After they finished eating, Cara paid the bill and they climbed back into her truck. "Let's do some shopping. Then we'll go around and let you pick up some applications to different places, including Guitar Center."

"Most of the applications are online now, aren't they?"

"Most, but not all. And it's always good to speak to a manager in person anyway. Makes a better impression."

"Okay."

The rest of the day couldn't have gone better. Blake was surprisingly easygoing about her buying him new jeans, shirts, and shoes, though he fussed a little over prices and vowed to pay her back every penny the moment he was able. Ignoring him, she bought designer stuff that looked damned good on him and was pleased with the cool-looking guy that emerged from the cute but scruffy waif. Especially after she took him by the barber and had his hair trimmed.

He made a bit more noise over having his pretty, shoulder-length tresses clipped, but they compromised on a cut that still covered his ears and was layered in a trendy style that gave him a sexy, just-out-of bed look he could brush into place with his fingers. All told, he was happy with the look when they were done.

"Jesus, is that me?" he murmured, staring at his reflection in the stylist's mirror.

"I knew there was a handsome man hiding under all that hair and yards of material!" She enjoyed seeing him blush. "Now, on to visit with some managers."

Confidence bolstered, dressed to impress, and hair styled, Blake made the rounds. He had a new spring in his step that was nice to see, and bounded to the truck after each stop, beaming. He collected a few paper applications, made some connections, and even bragged that he'd gotten his flirt on with a couple of sexy prospective coworkers who were more than receptive to the attention. She worried privately about that last part, only because she didn't want him to get hurt.

But Blake couldn't live in a glass bubble, and his friends wouldn't always be around to protect him. At some point, he had to fly on his own.

They were halfway home when he glanced at her, a smirk on his lips. "So, have you texted him back yet?"

"Who?"

"Don't play dumb with me," he said with a laugh. "You've been sneaking peeks at the same message all day when you think I'm not looking."

"I have not!" This earned an arched brow and a droll stare. She sighed. "Fine. So what? It's not like I'm hung up on Taylor."

"Aha! So it *is* our Hottie McCop. Yeah, I totally believe you don't have a thing for him when you kept staring at him last night like you wanted to eat him topped with cherries and whipped cream."

"I did not." Her protest didn't sound very convincing, even to her own ears.

"If you don't want him . . ." Her friend licked his lips and waggled his brows.

Snickering, she smacked his arm. "He's too old for you, and *way* too straight, you little shit."

"Not *so* little. In fact—"

"TMI, my friend!"

Laughing, Blake started to fire back a retort. "Yeah, your Ten Inch Boys might get jealous if— Shit! Watch out!"

From nowhere, a big SUV came barreling around her from the left and cut sharply in front of her. She knew a split second before the jolt that the driver wasn't going to clear the front end. The awful crunch, the squeal of tearing metal, rang in her ears as she fought the wheel.

And lost. With no time to correct her truck, it jerked to the right, flew toward a curb. Jumped the small barrier and shot straight toward a telephone pole. She had no time to scream as the truck plowed into the pole.

The impact stole her breath.

And then the lights went out.

5

Murphy's Law decreed that Taylor should get called in to work on his day off. A lead on a case wouldn't wait, and he wasn't too thrilled about it.

He strode into the station, dragging a bit and wanting nothing more than to head straight for the coffeepot. He'd gotten little sleep last night, thanks to a woman who'd rocked his world, then run like her ass was on fire, and now refused to acknowledge he was alive.

Of course, that was par for the course in his luck with women. He'd texted Cara earlier, just wishing her a good day and saying he hoped to see her again, not really expecting a response. There hadn't been one. Then he spent the morning moping as he worked, interviewing witnesses and doing mounds of paperwork. Now he was edgy and feeling like taking it out on someone, unfair as that might be.

The irritability lasted until he spotted Christian Ford sitting at his desk, head in his hands. The younger detective was slumped in his chair, elbows on the desk top, his defeated posture giving Taylor pause. Chris was one of the most exuberant, positive guys he knew, almost to the point of being an annoying pest, and to see him like this set off alarm bells.

Taylor tried a bit of ribbing to draw him out. "Hey, man. You got the workday flu? I could've told you those extra beers aren't worth the pain."

Chris was typically primed and ready to engage in a round of witty comebacks, but this time he was strangely sluggish in responding. Slowly he raised his head, sat back in his chair, and blinked at Taylor. "I'm sorry. What?"

"You look like crap," he said with a slight frown. The man's face was pale, eyes dazed and a little bloodshot. "What's going on?"

"Nothing. Just didn't get much sleep last night." But the way he stared at the desk top as though it contained the answers to his troubles told a different story.

"Welcome to the club. Anything you want to talk about? We can go for a cup of coffee," he offered.

"I . . . Sure." He blew out a breath. "Sounds good."

"I'll drive."

"Works for me. I've been waiting my turn to ride in that butch new car of yours." He shot Taylor a wan smile. "It's the least you can do since I *am* housing your old Chevelle and helping you work on it."

"You're right. But be prepared to turn green with envy."

Chris fell strangely quiet again on the way to the hip new coffee bar on the mall end of town. Taylor had chosen that place instead of the diner because they'd be too visible at the aging eatery. It was the type of establishment where everyone knew everyone else and noticed when something was up. Which was definitely the case with Shane's cousin.

The coffeehouse smelled good when they walked in, a mix of coffee beans, sugar, caramel, and baked goodies. They ordered lattes, and after picking them up from the other end of the counter, took seats at a table in a corner. Sipping in companionable silence for a few moments, Taylor studied his friend. The man truly didn't look physically well.

"Okay, man. What's eating you?"

Chris stared at the top of his cup. "That's just it—I don't know."

"What do you mean?"

"If I tell you, you have to promise not to say a word to anyone." He looked up, held Taylor's gaze, expression uncharacteristically serious. "Not even to Shane."

Taylor whistled softly. "I don't keep secrets from my partner. Never have."

"You'll keep this one or this conversation is done." Swallowing hard, Chris admitted, "I really don't have anyone else to confide in."

"Why not Shane? He's your family."

"That's just it. He's my *only* family. Might as well be my brother." He took a sip of his latte, and Taylor noted how his hand shook. "I can't worry him until I know what to tell him."

"Christ. If Shane finds out I knew something about you and didn't say anything, he's going to kick my ass."

"Please." That one word, spoken with such bald need, did him in.

"All right," he said with reluctance. "I won't say a word as long as you'll talk to him the second you know something solid."

"I will." Nodding, Chris took a deep breath. "I haven't been feeling well. You probably didn't know 'cause I've been hiding it pretty good."

"Until today."

"Yeah. I haven't been up to par in the past few weeks, but lately I'm so fucking *tired*. Sometimes I get dizzy and I can't see very well."

"This happens a lot?" he asked with concern.

"More and more lately. I've lost a few pounds, too," the other man admitted.

"Are you overly stressed at work? Not sleeping well?"

His friend shrugged. "No more stress than usual, and I've been sleeping fine until recently."

"You need to get to a doctor, Chris. Those symptoms can overlap with a bunch of different conditions, some of them dangerous."

"I will, I just . . ." Trailing off, he looked away. "What if it's something really bad? I don't even want to speculate what."

"All the more reason to call today and make an appointment. Don't wait."

"I don't want to think about it, much less go through a crapload of tests and then have to hear what the doctor will tell me." Chris was really freaked out.

"I know you don't, but you have to do it. You could be wasting valuable time," he said bluntly.

That got Chris's attention. "God. Don't even say that."

"You *needed* me to say it. That's why we're here."

"I suppose so," he admitted quietly. "Thanks, Taylor."

"Don't mention it."

On the tabletop, Taylor's cell phone buzzed and the display lit up. His heart jumped when he saw an incoming call from Cara, and he grabbed it without thinking twice. "Hello?"

But the voice on the other end wasn't the one he expected. "Taylor?"

"Blake? What's up?"

"Someone ran us off the road," the younger man blurted, breathless. "Cara didn't want me to call you, but—"

Taylor shot to his feet, almost knocking over his latte. Chris rose, too, expression concerned. "Where are you?"

"About a mile east of Walmart. We'll be the ones on the side of the road, with Cara's truck smashed into a telephone pole," he said dryly.

"Are either of you hurt?" For a second, he couldn't breathe.

"Just a couple of bruises, nothing serious."

Thank God. "On my way."

Leaving behind his drink, he was barely aware of Chris on his heels. Sliding into the car, he fired it up and was out of the parking lot before the other man could get his seat belt buckled.

"What the hell?" Chris sputtered.

"Couple of friends of mine were run off the road out by Walmart," he said.

"Shit. Are they okay?"

"Blake said they had some bumps and bruises. But

I'm worried because he used Cara's phone, instead of her calling me herself."

"Blake? He's that kid you've been trying to get off the streets?"

"He's twenty now, not exactly a kid, but that's him. You saw him last night. He's started working for Cara and the band."

Chris's eyes widened. "You mean Cara *Evans*, your hookup from last night?"

He winced at the term *hookup*. It implied something less than what their time together meant to him. But for simplicity's sake, he nodded. "The same."

"Just friends, huh? Right."

"Barely, if that. We have great chemistry in bed, but I don't think she likes *me* very much." And didn't that suck?

"And yet Blake thought you rated a phone call, and you're running off to the rescue. Interesting."

"Calling her a friend is a stretch. But Blake *is*, whatever *she* thinks of me and whether she likes it or not."

Chris made a thoughtful humming noise, but thankfully let it rest for the time being. "They catch the other driver?"

"I don't know. But if they did, it damned well better have been an accident and not road rage or something. If that's the case, the bastard's in for a world of pain."

The drive across town had never seemed to take so fucking long. Taylor swerved around slow-moving traffic and construction barricades, ignoring Chris's occasional curse. After an eternity, he spotted a black pickup off to the side of the road, front end crumpled into a telephone pole. A quint and an ambulance were on the scene, and a tow truck was backing into place, getting ready to hook on to the rear bumper of Cara's pickup. Blake was hovering near the back doors to the ambulance, anxiety written in his stance and the flat line of his mouth.

Screeching to a stop, Taylor jumped out of the car and jogged over to the ambulance. He nearly sagged in relief to see Cara sitting in the open double doors, loudly complaining to two of the firefighters/paramedics from Station Five whom Taylor happened to know fairly well. Lieutenant Zack Knight and Clay Montana were patiently trying to explain why she should go to the emergency room, while a uniformed traffic officer stood by *not* so patiently, rolling his eyes and likely waiting to finish his report so he could leave.

"I am not running up a bill for an ambulance ride and an ER visit just for a tiny cut on my forehead," Cara insisted, scowling.

Clay piped up, giving her what Taylor knew was the man's best attempt at a charming grin. "Honey, that's what health insurance is for."

Unfortunately for Clay, his brand of charm wasn't well-received. "I *know* what health insurance is for, and I also know my own body. I don't need a checkup, and my name is *Cara*, not *Honey*."

As Taylor approached, he suppressed the suicidal urge to laugh—both at Cara and at Clay. Clay didn't always know when to quit, and Cara wasn't falling for the firefighter's smooth brand of persuasion.

"Unfortunately, Cara, that's not always true," Zack told her with an understanding smile. "Patients are often the very worst judges of their own conditions, which makes our jobs much more difficult. Remember that country singer who had the bad wreck out on I-49 last year?"

Some of Cara's irritation eased. "No. But I've only been here a few months, and I don't watch a lot of news."

"Well, the point is he refused treatment because he 'felt fine.' Turned out he had a slow bleed in his brain, and by the time his wife realized something was wrong, it was almost too late to save him. He had emergency surgery and underwent months of rehab. He's still not back to a hundred percent."

"I get it," she mumbled. "I'll go and get checked. But I'm not riding in the ambulance."

Zack patted her arm. "Fair enough. I'll just need you to sign a waiver, and for my own peace of mind, I'd like to know who's taking you."

Taylor spoke up. "I am."

Zack turned, then stuck out his hand. "Hey, Kayne! What brings you here? Isn't traffic duty a little off the beaten path for a detective?"

"Zack, good to see you." Shaking the lieutenant's hand, he cut a look at Cara, who quickly masked her surprise at seeing him. "Yeah, I'm a bit out of my realm here, but I spotted a couple of friends in trouble and dropped in to find out what happened."

"That's what I'd like to know," the traffic cop put in grumpily. "You know, sometime *today*."

Chris snorted. "Dropped by, my ass."

Everyone ignored them both—except Cara, who latched onto Chris's words and eyed Taylor with suspicion. "How *did* you know I was here? Did Blake call you after I told him not to?"

Hesitating, he risked a glance at the younger man, thinking he might not want his secret outed. When he merely shrugged, Taylor nodded. "He did, and I'm glad."

"You are? Why?" She appeared truly puzzled.

Was she serious? He couldn't exactly say *because I tend to care about people I sleep with* in mixed company. Though Chris knew the truth, that detail had been shared in confidence. "We have a mutual friend in Blake, and, to be honest, I was worried about you both. I'd like to think you and I are friends, too."

Crap, that sounded lame. Might as well pass her a note in class and ask her to hold hands. He managed not to cringe, just barely. Nearby, Chris was grinning like a jackass, and he shot the man a death glare. Which had no effect at all, except to restore the man's previously missing good humor. At least his friend kept his mouth shut. A minor miracle.

The traffic cop—Schwartz, his tag read—cleared his throat, impatience etched in his posture and expression. "If we're finished with the love fest, I have some questions for Miss Evans and Mr. Roberts."

Blake made a face at the cop, mimicking the words *Mr. Roberts* behind the man's back while he was paying attention to Cara, and Taylor had to stifle a smile. Schwartz, whom Taylor now recalled seeing around the station but didn't know personally, got down to the important stuff and finally earned everyone's cooperation.

"I heard you telling the paramedics you were run off

the road," the officer began. "Can you tell me exactly what happened?"

Cara took a deep breath. "It was so fast. All I know is this car passed me on my side and switched lanes right in front of me. Cut me off."

"What kind of car?"

"It was an SUV," Blake corrected.

The officer turned to look at him. "Did you see what kind?"

"A *big* one."

Schwartz wasn't amused. "Make or model?"

"Didn't catch it."

Cara shook her head. "Neither did I. The other driver cut it too close when he switched lanes, hit my front end, and made me lose control. I was too busy trying not to hit someone else to notice."

The officer took some notes on an electronic pad, making a thoughtful sound. "The driver of the SUV didn't stop at all after hitting you?"

"No," Blake said. "The asshole kept right on going without even slowing down. Cara didn't see because she was knocked out for a minute."

The image of her in the truck, helpless and out cold, made Taylor's blood boil. He'd like to get his hands on the bastard who did this to her and Blake. He listened as Schwartz asked them a few more questions, but there really wasn't much else either of them could relate. Being a detective, Taylor liked details. The lack of them bugged him, but even more so in this case.

Other strange facts teased at the edges of his mind. A few days ago, Taylor had almost been flattened by a truck he could have sworn belonged to Cara. Now that truck was kissing a pole, erasing any evidence that might have supported that claim. Coincidence? He didn't much believe in them. But there was no reason he could fathom why the two incidents should be connected.

"You can take her now," Zack said, breaking in to his thoughts.

Glancing up, he saw Cara and Blake waiting, the two of them regarding him with very different expressions—Blake's open and trusting, Cara's carefully closed. It was almost as if she was trying hard not to show any reaction to his presence, and he couldn't understand why. When she let her guard down they had great chemistry. Then the walls went up again. Maybe she'd been hurt in the past by an old boyfriend or husband. If so, he'd done a real number on her.

"Ready?" he asked them.

"What about my truck?" Cara gestured to the vehicle.

"You'll need to have the towing company take it to a repair shop," he told her. "I recommend Turner Collision, but they charge a bit more than other places. And then there's insurance, and they'll probably want at least two estimates—"

"Screw the insurance company, and I don't care about the money. I just want it fixed."

He couldn't help the short, surprised laugh that escaped. "Really, now? I know a bit about cars, and I'm guessing you're looking at several thousand dollars in repairs. Especially on a nice truck like that one." His detective instincts, which seemed to have dropped into his pants since he'd met her, suddenly kicked back in full force. He narrowed his eyes.

"Come to think of it, where does a bartender and part-time singer get the money to afford a brand-new pickup, a pretty house, and all that band equipment—"

Her gaze turned chilly. "When my finances become your business, Detective, I'll share them with you. Until then, fuck off."

His dick stirred even as anger began a slow burn in his veins. "Rude little thing, aren't you?" Leaning forward, he whispered for her ears only. "Perhaps you need a good spanking. I've got just the right paddle if you want to give it a try."

Heat flashed in her eyes, and for a second he truly thought she'd slap him. But as a slow smile curved her lips, he saw something very different from anger in her gaze. There was amusement and a hint of challenge. And no little arousal, which she barely managed to keep leashed, if the low, husky tone of her voice was anything to go by.

"That's not much incentive for me to behave, cop."

"Oh, my *gawd*," Blake bitched. "Do I have to listen to you guys getting your kink on? I need bleach to scrub that image from my poor brain."

Taylor stepped back from Cara, cursing his lapse in judgment, baiting her with others around. On the job, no less. Looked like stupidity on his part was going to be a regular thing with this woman. "Let's get you to the hospital."

"A complete waste of time," she grumbled.

But she followed, after giving the tow-truck driver instructions to take her vehicle to the place Taylor had recommended. He smiled to himself, pleased that she'd followed his advice.

Blake jogged to the vehicle, reached inside, and retrieved a sheaf of papers. In minutes, they were in Taylor's new Challenger and headed toward the ER. Chris
rode shotgun, and Taylor ignored the detective's smug
glances while Blake *ooh*ed and *aahh*ed over every single
feature of the car.

"This machine rocks," he exclaimed for the third time.

Taylor smiled at the young man in the rearview mirror.
"My *really* cool car is at Chris's place," he said, gesturing
to the man beside him. "You remember my partner,
Shane? He, Chris, and I are working on my old Chevelle,
fixing it up."

"Dude! You have a Chevelle? What year?"

" 'Sixty-nine."

"Shit," the boy breathed in reverence. "If I had a car
like that, I'd drive the hell out of it. I'd wash and wax it
every weekend, and I'd never let it out of my sight."

"Yeah? That's a worthy goal. Now you just have to
save up some money."

"I'm getting a second job," he said with enthusiasm,
holding up the papers he'd fetched from the truck. "Since
I only work for the band two days a week, that leaves me
plenty of hours free to save up for an apartment and a car."

"Is that the reason for the new haircut and the
clothes?"

Blake's voice was excited but laced with a bit of anxiety. "For the most part. I can't show up at an interview
looking like the street rat I was. Do I look okay?"

"Kid, you look fantastic." Taylor winked. "You're
gonna break some boy's heart very soon."

"Boy?" Chris's brows shot up as he got the memo.

"You got a problem with that?" Blake fired back quickly.

"No, not at all," the detective said smoothly, holding up his hands in surrender. "Peace out, man. I say live and let live."

Taylor brought the topic back on track. "Looks like you've got it all figured out." Blake settled down again. The tension had eased as quickly as it had flared.

"Yeah, I hope so. My plans haven't worked out so good until now, but I think I'm due."

"Definitely," Taylor said. "You're gonna make it. Besides, you've got us to support you."

"Me, too," Chris put in. "Whatever I can do."

"Thanks, guys." Blake's voice had a suspicious catch in it, but everyone pretended not to notice.

The hospital loomed ahead, and Taylor parked. They all ignored Cara's grumbling as they trooped into the ER and a receptionist waved her over to begin the paperwork. Taylor looked at Chris as they hovered near a group of chairs.

"Sorry about the side trip. You want me to call someone to take you back to the station?"

"Naw, I'm good."

Blake eyed the other detective. "Man, you don't look so hot. Maybe you should be in there getting checked out instead of Cara."

Chris shook his head. "I'm fine." But his face was pale, and he reached up with a trembling hand to wipe a bead of sweat from his forehead.

Taylor frowned in concern. "He's right. Why don't we—"

"Why don't *we* forget about it?" he snapped, suddenly annoyed. "I'm not doing this right now. You know what? I think I'll call for that ride after all."

"Sorry, dude." Blake stared at Chris, then glanced between the two men, biting his lip. "I didn't mean to stir up any shit."

Just like that, Taylor was pissed, too. Blake had been hurt enough in his young life. He didn't need a simple statement meant as kindness being thrown back in his face. "You didn't," he hurried to assure the younger man. "You did nothing wrong." He turned to take a chunk out of Chris, but the man was already contrite.

"I'm sorry, Blake," Chris said with a sigh. "I haven't been myself lately, and I was an asshole for taking it out on you. Forgive me?"

"Hey, we're cool. Forget I said anything." The apprehension still on his face belied his words.

"No, you and Taylor are right. I'm going to make an appointment with my doctor today."

The younger man began to appear more at ease again. "Good deal."

Chris extracted his cell phone. "Excuse me while I give Shane a call, see if he can come get me."

"See you at the station," Taylor said.

"I don't know," the other man hedged. "I might ask Rainey if he'll let me go home early."

Taylor watched Chris exit through the ER's doors with a sense of dread. "I've known him for about a year and a half, since he moved to town to be near Shane, and I don't think I've ever seen him leave work early."

Blake was frowning. "Any idea what's wrong with him?"

"Could be a lot of things." Taylor clapped Blake on the shoulder. "It's not my place to say."

"I get it."

Just then, Cara walked over from the receptionist's desk to join them. "Frigging paperwork. I could be dead by the time they call me back there."

"Don't even joke like that," Taylor said softly. Placing his hand at the small of her back, he urged her toward the seats. "Come on, let's go sit down."

He half-expected her to retort that she wasn't an invalid, but he was pleasantly surprised. She went without a fuss, and they sat in comfortable silence until Blake piped up.

"So, why did Chris move to town to be near Shane? They have a thing going on? Is Chrissy in denial?" He waggled his brows, and Taylor laughed.

"God, no. For one, Shane's straight and married. Second, he, his twin sister, Shea, and Chris are all cousins."

"Oh." That obviously dashed his hopes of a police bromance going on.

"Chris doesn't have any other family left, so he came to Sugarland, looking for the connection he'd lost when his folks died." He thought a moment. "It must be tough to be alone in the world with no family who loves you."

Blake's gaze sobered. "Trust me, it is."

"Dammit, I'm sorry," Taylor said with a groan. "I wasn't thinking."

The younger man shook his head. "Why don't we stop

apologizing every time something uncomfortable comes up? I'm not that fragile."

"Sounds good." His mouth tilted upward. "And you're not fragile at all. You're strong to survive what you have."

"Well, I'm going to do way better now, thanks to you guys."

For one unguarded moment, Cara smiled at the younger man, and Taylor's world tilted. Stripped of her prickly attitude, the genuine kindness, the warmth, on her face blew him away. These glimpses of what he suspected was the *real* Cara were rare, but they made him long for one of those looks to be turned in his direction.

"Cara Evans? Come on back."

A nurse was waiting patiently in the double doors leading into the ER's examination area. When Taylor and Blake got up and followed, Cara tried to protest, to no avail. There was no way either of them was going to let her get away with downplaying her health if it turned out to be worse than they thought.

They passed several numbered rooms, which were really just cubicles separated by either a solid wall or a curtain. Taylor wasn't sure why some rated a wall as a divider and some didn't, but he was no expert. Perhaps some emergency situations required more privacy.

"Here we go," the nurse said. "If you'll step in here, the doctor will be with you shortly." After casting him and Blake a curious glance, she left.

"I'm surprised they let us come back with her," Blake observed.

"They'll let us come this far, but if they have to take her back for a scan or whatever, we'll have to stay here."

Cara sat with a resigned sigh. "You guys can take a walk or something. There's really no need for us all to be bored, sitting around."

"Not happening," Blake said staunchly. Taylor agreed.

"Besides, Blake was in the same wreck," he pointed out. "Shouldn't he get checked, too? Especially after what happened the other night."

Her gaze snapped to the younger man. "I should've thought of that. Taylor can take you to the registration desk."

"No way. I never even lost consciousness, and I'm not in any pain."

Taylor knew the truth: the boy didn't want to feel as though he was in debt to them for another hospital bill. Blake wanted to pay him back and was about as stubborn as they came.

In the end, he and Cara let the matter drop. Blake settled down, satisfied to have won that round. But they'd both keep a sharp eye on him, Taylor knew.

The doctor came in almost a half hour later and examined Cara, checking all her vitals, the responsiveness of her pupils, and her reflexes.

"You were in an accident?" the doctor inquired, peering into her eyes.

"Yeah. Some jerk cut me off, and I ran into a telephone pole."

"You lose consciousness?"

"Only for a minute or so."

"Hmm." He paused, then rolled his stool back to address her. "I think you have a slight concussion, nothing too serious. But on the side of caution, I'm going to order a CAT scan. If it shows all is clear, which I'm guessing it will, then you'll be free to go as long as there's someone to watch you for the rest of the day and tonight. Do you have any family to stay with you?"

"No," she said quietly, giving Taylor the oddest look. "I had a sister, but she's dead. My mother and I don't get along very well and, besides, she doesn't live close."

"I'll watch her," Blake said, beating Taylor to the punch. "I live with her right now, anyway, so that'll be easy."

The doctor nodded. "Good. I'll go order that scan."

Taylor was disappointed not to be the one taking care of her, though he shouldn't be. He had to work, and even if he didn't, he and Cara had just met. As much as he hated to admit it, Blake was her friend and had more right to see to her than he did.

Well, that was a situation he planned to rectify as soon as possible.

Almost two hours later, they were headed out the door. Cara had received the green light and had stopped grumbling now that she was free. In fact, she lapsed into blessed silence and began to doze in the passenger's seat. Then her breathing evened out.

"Guess the day caught up with her," Blaze said from the back.

"Was bound to happen."

She looked so vulnerable. Young. Seeing her like that did something weird to his heart.

When he pulled up in front of her house, he gently shook her awake. "Hey, sleepyhead." She stirred and blinked at him in confusion. "We're at your house. Let's get you inside."

She didn't protest as he and Blake ushered her into the house and herded her down a hallway and into the bedroom the younger man indicated. Amazingly, she settled on the bed without protest and began to drift off. As her eyes shut, she must've been too tired to protest when he touched her face gently, then kissed her forehead. They left her, pulling the door shut quietly, and went back into the living room, where Taylor stood uncertainly.

"I don't want to leave her, but I've got to get back to work."

"I've got this," Blake assured him. "Come by and check on her later if you want."

Taylor smiled. "She might not like you inviting me here."

The boy shrugged. "She might be confused about what she wants, but it's plain as day to me and anyone else who cares to notice that she's into you. The stubborn little thing just needs a push, that's all."

"More like a hard shove."

"I don't think it'll take much for her to give in."

Taylor regarded his young friend thoughtfully. "Any idea what her problem is with me? She blows hot and cold, and it's driving me crazy."

"Not a clue, but I'm thinking someone took a giant shit on her at some point," he guessed. "You gotta be patient."

"Yes, thank you, oh, wise one," Taylor joked.

"Hey, you asked."

"That I did." Giving the boy a playful shove, he headed for the door. "Tell her I'll be back later."

"Will do. I'm sure she'll be waiting with baited breath."

"Smartass." With a laugh, he left.

His humor didn't last. Thoughts of Blake and Cara being run off the road, and how much worse that story could've ended, tormented him all the way back to the station. By the time he arrived, he had a singular focus.

Search the entire fucking city for a dark SUV that might have been brought into a body shop with damage to the right rear quarter panel or bumper.

Find the bastard and make him pay.

6

Cara awoke slowly, the aroma of something rich filling her senses. Tantalizing her and making her mouth water.

Stretching, she peered at the digital clock by the bed and wondered how she'd lost almost four hours. She'd gone out like a snuffed candle—one second conscious, the next fading fast into nothingness. Her last clear memory was of riding in Taylor's awesome car, the purr rumbling in her head. The scent of his cologne drifting to her nose, making her feel surrounded by his strength.

And then being tucked into her bed, his hand caressing her face. His lips kissing her forehead like a lover would. As though he genuinely cared.

Taylor couldn't care about her. It wasn't possible. Despite his badge and the respect he seemed to command from his coworkers and friends, he was a liar at best, murderer at worst. Wasn't he?

Voices floated to her ears and she sat up in confusion. Two men were talking and laughing from somewhere in the house. One of them was Blake, and the other . . . No way. "Taylor?"

Curious, she slid out of bed and stood, and got a head rush for her trouble. The accident, if it *was* just an accident, had taken more out of her than she'd realized, especially since she and Blake had spent almost a full day together before the incident. The dizziness passed and she left the bedroom, making her way down the hall. The sound of dinner in progress became clearer—the metallic scrape of a lid on a pot, the clang of the oven door, a timer going off. Whatever the smell was, it was damned tempting, and her stomach gave an angry growl.

Entering the kitchen, she was about to call out, ask what was for dinner, but the sight before her stole her voice.

Blake and Taylor were in a standoff across the island, rolled-up kitchen towels in hand. Each one was trying to anticipate the other's move, ready to pursue or be pursued. Then Taylor lunged around the island to the right, popping his towel at the younger man, and Blake took off. Both were laughing like loons as Blake whirled and made a stand, snapping his towel in retaliation and catching his tormentor on the arm.

"Ow!"

"Take that, ya mangy dog!"

"You're gonna pay for that, little shit!"

"Bring it, old man!"

Cara watched them race around like ten-year-old boys and a smile bloomed on her face. They were completely unaware she was observing, and there was such unfettered joy in their game. Such innocence. Her attention was riveted on Taylor, on his smile that lit up the room. The unguarded happiness on his handsome face.

Golden blond hair was disheveled, falling into green eyes that danced with mischief. She damned near forgot how to breathe.

She must've made an involuntary noise, because both men froze, spotting her in the doorway. Taylor spoke first. "Hey! We made you dinner."

"It was my idea," Blake insisted. "I made most of it."

"You boiled the noodles."

"And baked the chicken. All you did was make the sauce." Blake managed to look down his nose at his mentor, even though he was shorter.

"My Alfredo sauce is homemade, if you'll remember. I wouldn't touch that crap from the jar with a ten-foot pole, and it's worth the effort."

Cara giggled. "Enough, you two. I'm sure I'll love the dinner you *both* worked so hard to make for me."

Looking pleased, they stopped their good-natured squabbling and led her into the dining room, where they made a fuss over getting her settled with a glass of iced tea. Impressed, she surveyed the table. They'd gone to some trouble, providing a Caesar salad, bread sticks, and chicken fettuccine Alfredo that looked positively divine.

"Gosh, that smells so good," she said, sitting forward in anticipation. "That's what woke me, and I can hardly wait to dig in."

"Then let's do it." Reaching for her plate, Taylor filled it with a generous portion of salad and fettuccine.

"Thanks."

They ate in silence for a few moments, and Cara studied the detective while trying not to outright stare. It wasn't easy, however. The cop was the finest man to cross her path in a very long time. She couldn't help but wonder what he would think if—no, when—he learned that their meeting would've happened eventually, even if they'd never hooked up at the Waterin' Hole.

She suddenly dreaded that day, when before she'd looked forward to outing him as a fraud and then slamming him with the truth of her identity. But the thing was, nothing about this man, from the moment they'd met, struck her as being the monster she'd been told about.

Twirling some pasta on her fork, she addressed Taylor. "Have they caught the person who made us crash?"

"Unfortunately, no." The detective's expression darkened. "I checked with every local body shop I could find, hoping to get a lead on an SUV that might have been brought in for repair, and so far nothing. Witnesses from the scene didn't have much to add, according to the traffic officer on duty."

Blake spoke up. "I doubt the driver would be dumb enough to take his vehicle somewhere local for body work after committing a hit-and-run. He'd go outside the area." The boy took a bite of his bread stick. "At least that's what I'd do, if I was a piece of shit like him."

"Good point." Taylor sipped his wine. "I'll broaden the search area tomorrow."

Cara had the feeling he would've done that anyway, but was acknowledging that Blake was using good thinking. Despite her reservations, her opinion of him went up a notch.

Okay, I may have been wrong about him. Or, rather, believed the wrong information. So, what am I going to do about it?

"I filled out a couple of those job applications," Blake said, interrupting her thoughts. "I'm gonna turn them in tomorrow."

She smiled. "Good for you. Don't forget to ask to speak to a manager. Makes a more lasting impression."

"Yes, ma'am."

"Don't *ma'am* me," she warned playfully. "I'm not old enough to be your mother."

"You're not?"

She almost choked on her food before she saw the teasing light in his eyes. "Very funny, twerp."

He grinned. "Okay, maybe a much older sister."

She arched a brow. "I can always look for a new sound man."

"I meant *young*," he blurted, laughing. "Young and stunningly *beautiful*. Have I mentioned I love the purple thing you have going on, girlfriend?" He waved a hand at her hair.

The detective snickered. "Looks like I could use some lessons in charm from the kid."

"More like lessons in bullshitting."

Blake stuck his tongue out at her before turning to the other man. "Like you'd need advice from anyone. I'll bet you've got half a dozen ladies eating out of your hand."

Taylor shook his head. "Not so much. I was always kind of a failure with women, even in high school."

"Yeah. Me, too." The boy winked. That prompted more laughter, as the younger man had intended. Once it died down, he regarded Taylor thoughtfully. "Seriously, though, you don't strike me as the kind of guy who fails at anything he does."

The detective's expression softened into something almost . . . sad. "Oh, I've made plenty of mistakes. You can't be a cop as long as I have without fucking up a time or three."

Cara thought Blake would ask for specifics out of curiosity, but he surprised her by staying away from a potentially painful topic. "Have you always worked here in Sugarland?"

"No. I was a beat cop for the Los Angeles PD. Started when I was young." He cleared his throat, looking uncomfortable. "Not much older than you are now, in fact. I made detective not long before I left there four years ago, and then I came here."

"Do you like it here better?"

"Much. There's not nearly as much noise or pollution here, not to mention the added bonus of low gang violence. Don't get me wrong—we still have plenty of crime, or my colleagues and I wouldn't have jobs. But we've got nothing on L.A."

"What's the weirdest situation or call you've ever had?"

Taylor chewed while he considered that one. "Gosh, that's hard to say. There was the time Shane and I were on our way to speak to a witness in a case, and we found a naked eighty-year-old man wandering down Cheatham Dam Road. No relation to our case. Turned out he was off his meds."

Blake wrinkled his nose. "What happened to him?"

"Since he wasn't lucid, we called the paramedics and they took him to the hospital. Don't know what happened to him after that. Depends on whether he had family to take care of him."

"Does it ever bother you, not knowing?"

"Sometimes. It's part of the job, though. We work a case and move on, and we don't always find out what happened to the people we try to help."

Cara absorbed that as they finished eating. It seemed to be more evidence that there was more to this man than she'd believed.

The guys cleaned the kitchen, despite her protests, and insisted she take it easy. Blake disappeared to his room with his new clothes and a netbook of Cara's that she didn't use much. She was letting Blake have it for now, to surf the Internet and job hunt, until he earned enough money to buy his own. She would've just given it to him but he'd insisted. In his eyes, he needed to earn it himself. She could understand and respect that.

"That should distract him for the rest of the night," Taylor commented, settling on the sofa close to her. "He probably hasn't had a computer in years."

"If ever. Things were pretty bad at home, from what I gather, so I'm not sure if that's a luxury he was allowed." She paused. "He told me this morning that he has an older brother."

"Really?" He looked surprised. "I thought he was an only kid."

"I assumed so, too. The brother's name is Jonathan, Jon for short, and the last Blake heard he lives in Nashville."

Taylor frowned. "So, this brother refused to take Blake in after their parents kicked him out?"

"So it appears, but that's the thing. I don't know that Jon knew what was really going on at home. Blake said that after he was forced out of the house, he called Jon. Before he had a chance to say anything, Jon told Blake that he was disgusted by him and hung up."

"And Blake hasn't tried to contact him since?"

"From what I understand, no."

"Then it's possible the parents got to Jon before Blake could and fed him a bunch of bullshit," he speculated. "But why would Jon be so quick to buy it?"

"I don't know. Blake said Jon was a good brother before Jon left home. He made it sound like they were close."

Taylor thought for a moment. "I could do some digging, see what I can find out about his brother. Discreetly, in case he's not the stand-up guy Blake remembers."

"I think that's a good idea," she said. "I could tell by the way Blake talks about his brother that he really misses him. It hurt him when the guy wouldn't give him a chance to tell his side. I can only think the parents purposely drove a wedge between them."

"If so, maybe it can be fixed." He sounded hopeful.

"You really mean that. You want to help."

"Of course I do," he said, cocking his head. "Why would that surprise you? I've known Blake for a few months and I've been working on helping him from day one."

"I guess I'm not used to cops being so nice, that's all." She knew she sounded a little terse and she couldn't keep it out of her tone.

"A lot of people have that perception about us. But, believe me, I didn't get into this profession to ignore those in need or to screw up people's lives."

"But sometimes you do, don't you? Screw up. Just like you told Blake."

"Okay," he drawled, sitting back and giving her a hard look. "Am I missing something here? Because I get the distinct impression that every word out of your mouth is aimed right at my head. Like you're waiting for me to clue in on something I'm the last to know about."

Bull's-eye. That's exactly what I've been doing.

"No, I—"

"Why don't you tell me what the hell your problem is, and then maybe we can move on?"

She stared at him, heart pounding. Five seconds. Ten. It was an eternity. Here was her golden opportunity, laid at her feet. Years of agonizing over her sister's murder, and this man had the answers. He might even give them to her straight.

But that niggle of doubt kept her silent. Letting go of four years of thinking a certain way about the events of that horrible day was so damned hard. She wasn't ready.

"Nothing. I don't like cops much, and it's been an eye-opener for me to realize you're different." There. That much was the truth—it just wasn't the *entire* truth.

"What happened to make you distrust them so much?" he asked quietly. He didn't seem offended. Probably wasn't the first time he'd ever heard someone say that. He seemed genuinely concerned about why she felt the way she did.

"Someone I loved was killed because of a police officer. I don't like to talk about it."

He nodded. Reached over and laid his palm on her

thigh. "I understand. Whenever you're ready to talk, I'm here, all right?"

Mother of all ironies.

"Thanks."

"How's your head?"

"It's good. I didn't mean to sleep for so long, but I think the day and the way it ended caught up with me."

"On top of putting in late nights at the bar. You work too hard."

"Not really." She shrugged. "My day starts later, that's all."

He considered her, as though weighing something. Cara had a pretty good idea what it was: he was still chewing on his earlier question of how she could afford her house, truck, and all the rest on her measly salary. For a nosy detective, it had to be driving him crazy. To his credit, though, he didn't ask again. And she still wasn't ready to indulge him.

Instead, she moved a little closer to him without taking time to examine her actions. Enough to touch, to rest her hand on one hard thigh. His eyes flashed and for a second or two she regretted her impulse. Her touch might not be welcome when she'd blown hot and cold with him since they'd met. Then heat darkened his green gaze and his voice grew husky.

"What kind of game are you playing with me now?"

She licked her lips. "The grown-up kind. Unless you object."

"You won't get much of an argument from me, but be very sure this is what you want."

"I'm sure that you turn me on like nobody I've ever

met. I want you," she said quietly. It felt weird to be unsure of a man's reaction. She needn't have worried.

"I don't think it's a secret that I want you just as much."

Leaning to her, he took her lips in a sensual kiss. Explored her mouth, slipping his tongue inside to twine with hers. He tasted so good, and his male scent, clean and musky, teased her senses. Her body strained for his, seeking to get closer, and she forced herself to pull back.

"Want to take this to my room?"

"I'd love that."

Taking his hand, she led him down the hallway. Inside her room, she shut and locked the door, then pulled him to stand beside her bed. They studied each other for a moment, and then he took her hand.

"You're sure about this?"

It warmed her that he'd ask. In spite of the arousal evident behind his zipper, he still thought of her first. "Very."

She reached for the button on his pants. Her attention never leaving his face, she unfastened them and parted the material. Lowered his pants and briefs until his erection sprang free, and grasped it in her palm as he hissed a sharp breath.

It was hot and silky yet hard underneath the smooth skin. She enjoyed the feel of it sliding through her hand as she started to stroke—and so did Taylor. He widened his stance as much as the restrictive material would allow, tilting his head back and closing his eyes. He made such a decadent picture. So inviting.

Lowering herself to her knees, she flicked the tip of

him with her tongue. Tasted the bittersweet precum ooz-
ing from the slit. She sucked the head and he turned to
putty, holding on to the top of her dresser for support.
She loved rendering him helpless. Incoherent.

"Shit," he breathed. "Stop, or I'm going to come."

Satisfied, she pulled off him with a pop and pushed his
pants and briefs to his ankles. He stepped out of them
and removed his shirt, tossing it to the floor.

"Your turn," he said, lips turning up as he retrieved a
condom from his pants.

Quickly, she shed her clothing and discarded it on the
floor next to his. Whatever illusion she had that she was
in control turned to dust when he walked her backward
to the bed, pushed her onto her back, and covered her
with his body.

"Can't get enough of you," he murmured into her lips.

She loved the feel of him on top of her, surrounding
her with his strength. Their heated skin was pressed together, his steely cock trapped between them. She
wanted him as close as he could get.

"Inside me," she whispered. "Now."

This time there was no foreplay. There was none
needed. Taking the condom, he made fast work of protecting them and positioned himself between her thighs.
As he placed the head of his cock to her opening, he
kissed her neck and buried his fingers in her hair.

"You feel so good, baby. So right." More kisses. He
pushed deeper, his handsome face the portrait of pleasure. And when he looked into her eyes, she swore she
read an emotion greater than lust.

The significance might have scared her had she dwelled

on it, but right then she was carried away on a tide of need as he began to make love to her. His thrusts were languid, every inch of their contact setting her on fire. He treated her as though she was precious, taking her mouth in a slow kiss that curled her toes. Made her feel desired for more than just the sex—for the connection they shared.

His movements sped up and she raised her hips, meeting him eagerly. Higher and higher he took them until her body began to quicken, release building until at last she shattered. Crying out, she clung to him, riding the waves as he stiffened and held her tight. Muscles bunching, he jerked inside her, filling her with heat.

Clinging together, they came down from the euphoria, and he rolled to his back, taking her with him and snuggling her against his chest. Giving in to how good it felt to be so close to him, she laid her head down and listened to his heartbeat. Warm and content, she was drowsing when she felt him begin to shift her to the side.

"Stay," she said, without a second thought. "Please?"

His voice was laced with regret. "I should go. Blake . . ."

"Is almost twenty-one, and an adult. He knows you're here, and he'll be fine with it." She smirked. "Besides, you have to watch me all night to make sure I'm all right after my traumatic head injury."

With a snort, he crawled back into bed and gathered her in his arms once more. "You were right before— you're totally fine. And you're working the system."

"I know you don't have a problem with that."

"You do, do you?" he teased. "Awfully confident there."

"Yep. If you didn't want to be here, you would've left just now."

He laughed softly. "True. I do have to get up for work, though."

"Just get up quietly."

"Damn. The romance is dead already," he said mournfully.

She leaned up on one elbow to see the playful glint in his eyes. "There's cereal. That's the extent of my cooking in the mornings."

"Then you have some culinary skills to learn."

"And you're going to teach me?"

"I'm no expert, but we'll get by." He kissed her lips. "Now get some sleep. I've done enough to finish wearing you out when I shouldn't have."

Content that he was staying, she burrowed into his side and drifted off, feeling safer than ever before.

She would count that as something of a miracle.

Light was streaming from the blinds when Taylor awoke. Cara's form was a small lump under the covers beside him, and he couldn't help but smile.

He'd slept well; not even a hint of a nightmare. That was real progress, and he felt ready to handle the day.

And last night, he'd made progress with Cara. She'd asked him to stay, and she'd meant it. Despite her admitted lack of faith in cops, he hoped that meant she was coming to trust him. The chemistry was still there. Now if only the rest would follow, he'd be a happy man.

Careful not to wake her, he eased from the bed, pulled on his pants, and went in search of the cereal she'd mentioned. He considered making breakfast for them all, but Cara had been sleeping soundly and there was no movement from Blake, either. Perhaps he'd pick up some groceries and make them dinner tonight.

Pleased with that plan, he poured a bowl of corn flakes with milk on them, sat at the kitchen table, and ate while checking his work e-mail and texts. There were a couple of e-mails from Shane saying there was no word yet on the SUV they were looking for. It hadn't appeared at any body shop. There was still no description of the driver, either.

Pushing aside his frustration, he finished his breakfast and decided to check on Cara. She was still asleep, but he was determined that wouldn't last long.

Lowering the covers, he plastered himself to her from behind, nibbling on her neck. She began to stir, waking from the attention, poking her tight butt into his groin. His dick reacted with enthusiasm, hardening to rest between her ass cheeks. Rubbing her and moaning while he kissed, he wanted to do so much more.

"I can't get enough of you," he murmured.

"Mmm."

Reaching around her, he found a breast and pinched one nipple into a tight bead of flesh. It was her turn to moan in pleasure, her body melting for him.

"Wanna fuck you, baby. Can I?"

"Yes," she whispered. "Please."

He liked that, how she was so responsive. So open to letting him have his way. Kissing between her shoulder blades, he peppered kisses all the way down her spine. Then he rolled her more fully onto her stomach, spread her legs.

Eating her was a must. He had to feast on the delicious offering, and from her encouraging whimpers, she was totally on board. Settling between her thighs, he flicked the slick lips of her pussy with his tongue, and was pleased when she opened farther.

He licked her like that for a long time, working her into a frenzy. He tasted her clit, teasing the nub, then lapped at her juices like a starving man. There was something naughty about having her facedown like this, submitting to him. He wanted to take it one step further and hoped she was game.

"Ass in the air."

She got into position, kneeling, shoulders down and her round ass poking up. Begging for more. He was an ass man from the word *go* and was going to get a great deal of pleasure from hers.

"I love your butt," he said, skimming his palm over one round orb. "It's so tight and smooth. So pale. I'm going to spank it a little, just enough to make your skin a pretty pink. Would you like that?"

"Oh! I—I think so . . ."

Immediately, she poked it out even more, and he chuckled. He'd take that as a yes. With his right hand, he gave a light smack. Just enough to make some nice contact, get her used to his palm. She moaned again, a sound that went straight to his cock and stiffened it impossibly hard. He was purple and leaking, he wanted her so badly. But he'd feed this mutual need first.

"You've never had your ass spanked."

"Not like this."

He smacked it again, this time putting some sting behind it. A nice pink hue began to rise on her buttock, and he repeated the process on the other one. She writhed, begging, and he couldn't believe how perfect she was. She was everything he wanted in a sexual partner, a lover. Maybe more, if he was right.

He spanked her with a bit more force, getting her cheeks nice and red. By now she was insensate with desire, and he was fast approaching that level.

"You're so pretty and red. I'm going to slide my cock deep in your pussy and fuck what's mine. Do you understand?"

"Yes! Please fuck me!"

He couldn't hold back anymore. Quickly, he retrieved a condom and took care of protection. Positioning himself behind her, he spread her cheeks and guided the tip of his cock to her wet sex and plunged inside, eliciting a cry of pleasure from both of them.

"Fuck, yes," he hissed. "You're fucking hot, lady. I'm gonna work you with my cock until you scream."

He began to thrust in earnest, flesh slapping flesh, his favorite sound in the world. Except for eating out a woman, there was nothing better than drilling deep into a tight, hot, wet sheath. Relishing the feel of it gripping his dick, squeezing the cum from his balls. Milking him until he spurted.

"I'm close!" he rasped.

His balls drew up and the quickening started low in his groin. Spread like wildfire until there was no stopping the orgasm that tore him apart.

"Yes!" With a shout, he came, filling the rubber, suddenly wishing there was no barrier. The idea of coming inside her, bathing her walls with his seed, made him shudder harder than ever.

She cried out, shivering through her climax with him. Gradually they came down together and he held her for a while, still buried deep.

Make that his number-three favorite thing: keeping his cock inside that hot channel as long as possible.

Her breathing evened out again and he smiled, proud of the fact that he'd worn her out in such a nice way. He could've gone back to sleep, too. Unfortunately, he had to work.

Silently, he debated whether to shower here or head home first. A glance at his watch showed he was pushing it on the time. He hated being late, so he'd grab one here.

His pants could stretch another day. The problem was he hadn't brought an extra shirt, and back in Cara's bedroom, a quick sniff test had him grimacing. *Damn.* He didn't have a spare shirt at work, either.

"In the closet," her sleepy voice mumbled. "There's a couple of men's shirts."

That revelation gave him an unpleasant, greasy feeling in his gut. "From who?"

But she'd already rolled over and gone back to sleep. Annoyed, he padded into the closet and looked around, wondering where in the hell she'd gotten men's shirts. That guitarist, Jinx, with whom she'd had a brief relationship? Fine, but why had she kept them? The question burned in his stomach.

Chill. A lot of people keep things for no reason.

The shirts were hanging at the back of the closet, jammed in such a way it was obvious they'd been long forgotten. That made him feel a bit better. There were only five or six, and most of them looked too small. But one pullover seemed all right and didn't have too wild of a design on it, so he grabbed the hanger and pulled.

Unfortunately, there was some junk piled behind the shirts. The hem of the shirt caught on a box behind it, and when Taylor yanked the shirt from the rod, the box came with it. Tumbling to the closet floor, the box spilled open—and a black iPhone landed at his feet.

Puzzled, he frowned at the device, trying to think why she'd keep a nice phone like that buried in the back of the closet. Then his detective instincts went on full alert.

The phone was hidden. And when people hid things, especially things like expensive smartphones, there was usually a damned good reason.

Picking up the phone, he examined it. Without hesitation, he powered up the device. A few moments later he was faced with a screen he was surprised wasn't password protected. Stupid of the owner not to encode the screensaver, and good for him. That made it easy to go into the phone's profile and access the number, which was preferable to calling his own smartphone with it. A cop never knew how he might have to defend his actions in court.

Working fast, he sent Shane a text with the phone number and the message: *Run this # 4 me—found a phone, need 2 know owner listed.*

Hang on.

Taylor waited what seemed an eternity, but in fact was only a minute. A long one. The answer, when it came, liquefied his guts.

Owner is Max Griffin from San Diego. Our dead guy. Where did u find it?! Call me!

After closing his eyes for a moment, he blew out a deep breath and texted back.

Will do better—bringing in person of interest. C u soon OK

"Oh, fuck." *Have I been sleeping with a murderer?* Taylor was turning, pocketing the evidence, which now had his fucking fingerprints all over it, when Cara appeared in the doorway, wide-eyed and disheveled.

Slowly, he held up the device. "Looking for this?"

Every ounce of blood must've drained from her face, she was so white. "I—I . . . It's not what it looks like. I can explain!"

"You're going to get a chance to do just that," he said coldly. "At the station."

7

Her face was priceless. Had she been any other suspect, he would've very much enjoyed that she looked about two seconds from passing out. He would've egged her on, too, baited her about how much jail time she might get for withholding evidence, at the least.

But he didn't have to say a word. Her terror visibly ramped up without his assistance.

"What's going to happen to me?"

"I don't know," he said honestly. "That depends on several factors. The most important of which is how you came by that phone."

"I—"

"Don't say anything just yet. Save it for questioning."

She flinched, and her fear gave him no pleasure. Typically, when he caught a break in a case, no matter how small, there was the coil of excitement in his gut. Anticipation. Not long ago, he and Shane had discussed this very feeling, and Taylor had told his partner he loved solving puzzles, that piecing together a case was like reading a book backward.

Now he only felt sick with dread. Following a thread back in time to the inciting events always led to someone's pain. He had a suspicion this break was going to lead somewhere he had no desire to go, and he was on the ride whether he wanted to be or not.

The silence was heavy as he waited for her to get dressed, and later grew stifling in his car. She fidgeted with the seat belt, face drawn, but he said nothing to relieve her anxiety. He couldn't, not even after they'd been together.

Especially not after that.

Cara knew he was a detective. She had in her possession a personal item belonging to a dead man, which she'd claimed she could explain. That had to mean she already knew Griffin was deceased and she'd taken the phone for a reason. He just couldn't imagine what the hell that reason might be.

Walking beside him into the station, she came quietly, eyes darting around as though she expected someone to slap handcuffs on her any second. That remained to be seen. Yet despite how bad it looked, he didn't think her capable of killing a man.

Of course, the graveyard was full of victims who'd mistakenly thought the same.

Shane met them in the hallway leading to the interview rooms and Taylor sighed, glad his partner was here for this instead of out on a case somewhere. "I'll put her in this first room. Give me a sec."

"Sure thing." Shane eyed Cara, and gave her a nod to acknowledge her.

Taylor ushered her into the plain room that consisted of a table, three chairs, and a two-way mirror. That's where the captain would stand and watch, if he wasn't busy. A lead in a murder case tended to get bumped to top priority.

"Sit there," he told her, pointing to the single chair on the opposite side of the table. "My partner and I will be with you in a few minutes."

"Okay," she said in a small voice. Then, with more confidence, "I didn't kill Max."

"If not, then you have nothing to worry about." He gave a humorless laugh. "Except for the withholding-evidence thing. We'll be right with you."

He felt her gaze on his back as he left. Now he had to face his partner and the captain. Things were about to get pretty damned awkward.

Closing the door to the interview room, he met Shane and they walked down the hall, out of Cara's earshot. Austin met them and the three of them ducked into an empty room.

"All right, what the hell is going on?" the captain barked.

"This." Removing the phone from his pocket, Taylor held it up for the captain and Shane to see. "I found this in Cara Evans's house. In her, um, bedroom closet."

"In her closet? Why were you ..." Austin paused, made a face. "Aw, shit. You're sleeping with a damned suspect?"

"In my defense, she wasn't a suspect," he said curtly. "As far as I'm concerned, she still isn't. Cara is a person of interest."

"Of *great* interest," Shane said. "She was in possession of a dead man's phone."

Taylor pinched the bridge of his nose. "I know that. I brought her straight here when I realized what it was."

"Was it hidden?" his partner asked.

"Yeah. I was borrowing a fresh shirt and a box fell out on the floor. The phone tumbled out of the box."

"Has she given an explanation for having it?"

"She tried, but I told her to wait until we got here. I didn't want to compromise the investigation more than it already has been."

"Good thinking."

"How serious is it with you and this girl?" Austin probed.

He shook his head. "I don't know. We've been together a couple of times."

"Could get messy."

Damn. "Yeah. Shall we?"

Shane followed Taylor down the hall and into the interview room, but the captain stopped him.

"No way. Chris will handle this with your partner."

With a resigned sigh, he followed Austin into the room next door to watch and listen behind the two-way mirror. Chris walked into the room, and Shane took the lead. Taylor tensed as the scene unfolded.

"Could you state your name and address, please?"

"Cara Ann Evans," she said nervously. Then she rattled off her house number and street.

"Where did you get the phone my partner found in your closet?"

She swallowed hard, her attention divided between the two men. "I took it from Max's hotel room."

The dread that had been sitting in Taylor's gut like a rock grew fangs.

Shane leaned forward. "Which hotel room? Where?"

"The one he rented here in town. I don't remember the name."

"Did Griffin give you the phone? Ask you to hold it for him?" He was giving her an easy out or trying to trip her in a lie.

"No. I—I took it because I thought it might contain a clue as to who killed him."

Shane exchanged a look with Chris. Now they were getting to the nitty-gritty.

"And why would you be concerned about who killed Max Griffin?"

"He was a friend of mine. I've known him for years, and he's been like a father to me." Tears glistened in her eyes.

"Okay. You know he's from San Diego, then."

"Yes," she said, wiping a tear from her face.

"Do you know why he came to Sugarland?"

"No, and I didn't know he was coming until he was already here. He called me when he arrived and wanted me to meet him at his motel, but he wouldn't say why over the phone." She paused. Taylor had an awful feeling he knew what she was about to say next, and he was right. "I went to his room, and the door was cracked open a little. When I pushed it open and stepped in, I saw him d-dead. He had a hole in his forehead."

"Goddammit," Taylor hissed, pushing a hand through his hair. In the small room before him, Cara's expression was one of pure misery.

Shane went on. "What did you do next?"

"Nothing. Except I saw his phone on the nightstand, and I took it on impulse. I shouldn't have." Her expression begged them to understand. "I didn't touch anything else, and I left."

"Where did you go?"

"Home. I looked through the phone, but none of the numbers looked familiar except mine. And, well, my mother's."

There was a new twist.

"Your mother?"

"Yes, Melinda Evans. She lives out in San Diego, at our family estate. Max is a family friend and attorney, not just a friend of mine. He paid my mother a visit before he came out here, but I didn't find out about it until after he was killed. My mother called and said Max came by and yelled at her, but she wasn't sure why."

"She doesn't know *why* he was upset? How could she not know if he was there in person?"

"My mother is an addict." Her tone was bitter. "A well-dressed, attractive, upper-class junkie. I control the money, give her an allowance and such, but that doesn't always stop her from getting drugs. A lot of what she says doesn't make sense anymore, even when she's not using."

There was one of Taylor's questions answered: Cara came from family money. That was how she could afford her lifestyle. It wasn't a stretch, given the picture she painted of home, to see why she'd move across the country to sing and tend bar.

"All right." Shane fell silent, regarding her for a moment. "Anything else you'd like to tell us?"

She bit her lip. There *was* something else, he could tell. After an internal debate, however, she slumped in her chair. "No."

"Then you won't have a problem with us searching your home."

Her head snapped up and her eyes widened as she gaped at his partner, eyes darting between him and Chris. "What? You want to go through my house? I just told you I didn't touch anything else and I didn't kill Max!"

"Then you won't have anything to worry about, Miss Evans." Shane stood. "We'll see about getting a warrant. In the meantime, sit tight."

"I'm not free to go?" She swung her gaze to Chris. "Why can't I leave if I'm not being arrested?"

"You *can* leave, though I suggest you stay here for now," he explained. "It'll be easier for everyone involved."

The look of betrayal pierced Taylor, and it hurt.

"In case you decide to place me under arrest."

Chris didn't deny the charge.

"You all think I had something to do with Max's death," she whispered.

At that point, Taylor couldn't stand to stay away another second. Ignoring Austin's muttered oath, he pushed out of the observation room and into the interview room next door. "Can I have a minute with Cara?"

Glancing at each other and exchanging a meaningful look, Shane nodded. "Now that we're done, sure."

He and Chris left Taylor alone with Cara. Her pale face made his heart clench, and he quickly crossed to her, hoping to reassure her in some way.

"It's obvious you're connected to Griffin's murder in some way. You might even be in danger, since it was you he was coming to see. But, personally, I don't think you did it, and I don't think anyone else does, either."

"Do you think . . . maybe whoever killed him wanted to stop him from talking to me?"

"It's possible." For the first time since he'd found the phone in her closet, he gave her a small hint of encouragement. "I don't want anything to happen to you. So let's do this my way, all right?"

"Sure," she answered with a tremulous smile.

Touching her face briefly, he turned and left. Austin was waiting down the hall, and spoke quietly. "I don't like her for the murder, either. I do agree she's connected, however. If the search of her house turns up nothing, I suggest we keep an eye on her." He shot Taylor a meaningful look. "And not from under her sheets."

Ouch. "If she's cleared as a suspect, then there's no reason I can't see her." He was pushing that issue and he knew it.

"She's a witness, dumb-ass. Do I have to use small words so you can understand the fucked-up nature of this situation?"

He winced, and Shane sent him a look of sympathy. "No, sir."

"Good. Now get going on that warrant so we can figure out why some douche bag offed some lawyer from the land of fruits and nuts in *my* county. Scram."

Taylor stopped by Chris's desk. "Hey, man. Thanks for handling my part of the interview with Cara. I appreciate it."

"No problem." Chris eyed him in concern. "You okay?"

"I will be. Just as soon as we find something useful and clear her, too."

"What else can I do to help?"

"I need you to take a look at Griffin's phone. See what you can find that might give us a lead."

Chris eyed the device. "I'll check out the incoming and outgoing calls. I'll let you know what turns up."

"Thanks again." Some of the tension eased inside him.

"Don't mention it. Just be careful, all right?"

"*Careful* is my middle name." That earned him a snort.

Leaving Chris to his new task, Taylor suddenly stopped, smacking his forehead. "Shit! Blake."

He was at Cara's house, probably still asleep. The kid was going to freak when he showed up with Shane to search her place. God, he hoped this didn't undermine the trust he was building with the younger man. He'd just have to make him understand.

Shane requested the warrant and it didn't take long for the judge to grant one. Cara had been holding a piece of evidence in the murder and had admitted to being on the scene and seeing Max's dead body. That was enough. While Taylor waited, Shane went back to the interview room, showed her a copy of the warrant, and retrieved her house key.

Outside, they climbed in the car, Taylor behind the wheel. He expected Shane to launch into a thousand questions or give him a lecture. He did neither of those. When the silence grew too heavy, Taylor glanced at his partner.

"Whatever is on your mind, spit it out."

"Nothing . . ."

"Bullshit. Come on, you've never held back before. If you start now, you might pop a blood vessel."

"This girl—"

"Cara," he supplied tersely. "She has a name."

Shane paused, gave him a hard stare. "O-kaay. You seem to have it bad for *Cara*. I'm not trying to piss in your Wheaties, but I want you to be careful because something's not adding up with her."

A sharp retort formed on his lips, then died. He'd say the same thing if their situations were reversed. A tired sigh escaped him. "Duly noted."

In less than fifteen minutes, he pulled up in front of Cara's house and they got out. On the front porch, he knocked and waited, in case Blake was still here. He was kind of hoping the boy was out, but no such luck. Time to face the music.

"Hey, dudes," Blake said cheerfully, opening the door for them as they stepped inside. "What's up?"

"I'm afraid this isn't a social visit," Taylor said. Before he could go on, Blake spotted the paper in Shane's hand and his smile faded.

"Oh, shit. You guys here to arrest me? Listen, if I've done something wrong, I sure as hell don't remember what."

Taylor briefly squeezed his shoulder. "No. We've got a warrant to search the house in relation to a case we're working. This shouldn't take long." He might as well have been speaking a foreign language.

"The fuck are you talking about? What case?" He glanced between them. "Is this a joke?"

"I'm afraid not. We need to search the house, and you need to stay out here in the living room while we do."

The younger man's confusion started to give way to apprehension. "Does Cara know about this?"

"Yes, she does."

"What case are you talking about?"

"It's a murder investigation, but—"

"What?" Suspicion crept into his eyes, and his tone sharpened. "Are you shitting me? Did you, like, *plan* this? Is this the reason you've been so chummy with me and her—so you could *investigate* or whatever?"

The accusation hurt. "Nothing could be farther from the truth," he said firmly. "And for the record, though there's a connection, we don't believe Cara had anything to do with the actual murder. We're only here to try to find a thread that will help us with the case. I need for you to believe that."

Giving a snort, he flopped onto the sofa and put his feet up on the coffee table. "Right. Well, you do what you gotta do, Officer, and I'll be right here waiting for you to get done pawing through her stuff."

There was no way to answer that, so he didn't try. Silently, he and Shane started in the living room and kitchen, going through drawers and cabinets. As expected, these rooms yielded nothing more than the usual items one would find. Moving on, they searched the bathrooms. They saved the bedrooms and closets for last.

Searching each bedroom together, they went through every drawer and over every nook and cranny. They even removed the drawers from the nightstands and dressers, looking underneath, and then behind the furniture as well. No stone was left unturned. All that was left was the walk-in master closet, and Taylor had his doubts that they'd find anything.

"I think we're about done."

Shane set a pair of boots back into place and nodded. "Looks like."

"Think Blake will forgive me? He doesn't trust easily, and it must seem like a betrayal to him."

"He will, because you're doing it for the right reasons," his partner pointed out. "You're looking for a clue that might help the case, and finding one doesn't mean that person is guilty of anything. Sometimes it can clear them, or just shed more light on what's going on."

"I know that, but the kid might not be so willing to see it that way."

"Have some faith. He'll come around."

Taylor was about to say more when he spotted a photo album on a shelf above the rod where the clothes hung. "This is an old album," he commented, removing it from its spot. "It's kind of falling apart."

"That's why most people use digital storage now. Saves room in the house, and the photos don't fade."

"Yeah." Turning the book over in his hands, he opened the cover and examined the pictures and the names and dates scrawled in pen. "It starts with childhood photos. Looks like Cara and her sister."

Shane leaned over and smiled. "They were cute kids. And your Cara turned out to be quite the sexy little rocker, didn't she?"

"That she did. But she's not my Cara—yet."

"That's the spirit. Watch out for Austin, though. You'll have to fly under the radar until this case is solved."

"That sucks." Carrying the album, he walked into the bedroom and sat on her bed, turning the pages to examine the contents.

"Looking for something in particular?"

"A photo of Max Griffin, maybe. Could be someone else in here, someone mutual to Cara and Griffin to tie this thing together."

Shane sat beside him and they studied the photos, which were sort of entertaining to him because they represented Cara's young life. But they were innocuous, for the most part. At least until the sisters began to grow up in the pictures.

As Cara and Jenny aged, a strange feeling began to come over him. The strangeness became something darker, more ominous, as he watched Jenny Evans's face slowly morph from little girl to teen to a pretty young woman.

"Oh, my God."

"What is it? Taylor?"

Turning a page toward the back of the album, Taylor froze, staring at the face he still saw in his nightmares. But instead of a happy, smiling face like in the picture, the face in his memories was pale, eyes filled with terror.

"Think you're so smart, asshole? Thought you could come in here and be a big hero?" Connor Wright screamed in his face.

"No, I want to help." Sweat rolled down Taylor's back. *"We can end this peacefully—"*

"Peace? You want peace?" Wildly, he waved his gun at

the three cowering people in the living room. The hostages Taylor had been sent in to help.

One of them was Jennifer Wright—Connor's estranged wife.

"Choose!" Connor bellowed, pressing the gun to the back of Taylor's head.

"Choose what?" Taylor fought to keep calm.

"You want peace? Choose one person to live."

God, no. "Connor, let's talk about—"

"Which one gets to walk out, huh? Choose, goddamn you!"

"Taylor! Partner, where'd you go?"

He blinked at Shane and realized he was breathing hard, the album still clutched in his hands. The nightmare had come full circle and invaded his life. It was back to devastate him all over again, to leave him awash in blood and guilt, on his knees, begging for an end.

Hand shaking, he pointed to the picture. "Cara's sister—she's Jennifer Wright."

"How do you know her?"

"I didn't, not really. She's dead."

"Oh. I'm sorry to hear that, but what—"

"And it was my fault." That statement dropped between them like a stone, Shane waiting for him to explain, expression concerned. "Do you remember the case that caused me to leave Los Angeles?"

That was all it took for the light to break through the clouds.

"Jesus Christ," Shane muttered, hanging his head briefly before looking back at him. "You're saying that *same* woman is Cara's sister? How the hell can that be?"

"That's what I want to know." The reality of Cara moving to Sugarland, meeting Taylor, began to set in. A horrible picture was beginning to form, one that made him sick. "Shane ... I think her truck is the one that hit me the other day."

His friend gaped at him. "You think she actually tried to kill you?"

"No." He pushed a hand through his hair. "I don't know. I spotted a dent in her front bumper that matched the same spot on the dark truck that hit me. At the time I thought it was a pretty strange coincidence and that it might be the same vehicle, but I couldn't think of any reason she'd want to hurt me, so I decided I must've been wrong."

"We could bring in the truck, do some tests."

"We can't. Someone ran her off the road and the front end was totaled. It's being repaired and we'd never get anything off it now." He frowned. "We thought the jerk just cut her off, but what if he was trying to really hurt her? Or worse?"

Shane studied him unhappily. "I think you have to consider that she might've staged the wreck to cover the evidence of trying to run you over."

"It could've happened that way, but I honestly don't think so."

But flashes of how standoffish she'd acted with him when they first met invaded his memory. He thought of how he'd seen something very much like hatred in her eyes when she looked at him. Not lately, though. She was warming to him, and they were getting into each other.

Or so he'd believed.

"She had to have known who I was when she came here."

"Not necessarily," his partner tried. But they both knew the likelihood of that was virtually nil.

"In the hospital," he suddenly recalled. "After her wreck. She told the doctor her sister was dead, and she gave me such a strange look when she said it. I wondered why she'd look at me like that, then I convinced myself it was my imagination. She blames me—and she came here to find me."

"It's possible."

No. Not just possible. He was as sure of that now as he was that he was breathing.

Old pain and new hurt made for terrible bedfellows. He was drowning under the weight of the past and the present crashing together to remind him that a man never truly escapes his mistakes. To push him down into a sea of screams and death.

"Who walks away? Choose!"

One distraught, cuckolded husband pushed over the edge. Three terrified people. One newly minted, inexperienced undercover cop.

Shake well and watch the explosion.

"I caused the deaths of three people that day, including her sister. I've paid every day since then, Shane. Why has this come back to me *now*?"

"I don't know, buddy. But we're going to find out." He paused. "We'll find out what, if anything, Griffin has to do with all of this, too."

"We done here?"

"I believe so. Let's go."

Taylor took the photo album with him, tucked under one arm. On the way out he stopped to reassure Blake as best as he could.

"Everything is going to be fine for Cara, so don't worry. The man who was killed was a friend of her family, and we're going to find out who did it."

"Okay." He seemed uncertain, but relented. "I'll see you after work?"

"Maybe." Dammit, he couldn't look the kid in the eye. Not when he had no idea whether he'd ever darken Cara's door again. "Good luck with turning in your applications today."

"Thanks." That cheered the younger man some, and he smiled a bit as he waved. Then he locked the door behind them.

The drive back to the station was quiet, the mood somber. Shane didn't speak until they were pulling into the parking lot.

"We have no reason to hold her any longer, much less charge her, unless we want to get her on obstruction. But how exactly she was obstructing, we don't know yet."

"I say we cut her loose, but I want to talk to her first."

"All right. I'll be at my desk if you need me."

After acknowledging Shane with a nod, he walked every step toward the interview room feeling like he was going to his execution. It seemed an eternity since he'd left Cara here to wait, but in reality it had only been a couple of hours. When he walked in, he brought forth the photo album and thumped it on the table with more force than necessary. Cara's eyes widened as she saw the album.

"We found nothing to tie you to Griffin's murder, so on that score you can go. But I found something else that might matter in the big picture. Care to tell me what I discovered when I followed your trip down memory lane?"

"Where did you get that?" she asked hoarsely.

"Where do you think I got it? Same place I seem to find all the fascinating items you have hidden—in your closet."

She licked her lips. "I can explain."

"So you keep saying." His voice was low, raw with pain. "Why?"

"Taylor—"

"Tell me! You knew, didn't you? You knew who I was all along."

"Yes." Tears welled in her eyes.

"Why did you come here to Sugarland?" he asked, leaning over the table toward her. "Be honest with me for once."

She flinched, and then spilled the truth he'd been anticipating. Dreading.

"I came here to make you pay."

8

The words were out of her mouth before she could stop them.

But she'd held them in too long. They'd been a part of her soul, the truth that demanded justice. A truth that may have been based on lies and misconceptions.

Now Taylor stood on the other side of the table, expression grim, green eyes haunted. Wounded. "You don't think I've paid? That I don't play out that scene in my head every day, that I get any relief from what happened even after I go to sleep?"

"I didn't know how you felt. I didn't know you!"

"Why did you sleep with me? Why crawl into bed with a man you hated?" he asked, almost physically choking on the words.

"When I met you, you weren't what I expected. I—I wanted to find out about you. If you really were the man I believed."

"That's the only reason?" He gave a bitter laugh. "Wow, I'll try to keep my ego in check."

She rushed on. "That's *not* the only reason. I was fascinated by you, too. I didn't want to be, but I was. I don't have it in me to sleep with a man simply to get information."

"Why should I believe you?"

"Because it's the truth," she said quietly. "I regret now that I wasn't honest with you. I should've just come to see you when I first got to town. I should've asked you directly what I really wanted to know."

"How I could've let your sister die. Meaning it was my fault."

She couldn't deny that, and knew it showed on her face. "I'm only human. I don't understand how you could egg on an enraged man who was threatening everyone with a loaded gun." Her own anger and bitterness were rising again.

"How I could *what*?" His mouth dropped open. "What the fuck do you mean by that?"

"You told him to go ahead and shoot, to ruin his life and go to prison! Didn't you? What was that, some sort of screwed-up reverse psychology? Well, it backfired!"

"Where the hell did you get that garbage? Because that's not what happened!" Agony was etched on his face. Disbelief. "I would *never* risk a victim's life by encouraging the suspect to shoot. I failed in my negotiation, but I was never accused of misconduct like that. Nothing I said to Wright made any difference. Nothing *would* have. Who told you otherwise?"

If he was telling the truth, then she'd been fed a lie. Why?

"No one, at first. The police protected the details like they were the lost Confederate gold, and I wasn't thinking straight for the longest time. All I could feel was grief over losing Jenny. Four years ago, I was younger than Blake and I couldn't process anything but loss. I didn't question."

"What changed that? When did you start to wonder?"

"A year ago, I finally started to emerge from my fog of mourning. I went to the police station, looking for you, but I was told you'd moved away after Internal Affairs finished their investigation and cleared you. Nobody would tell me where you'd gone."

"You started to think there was some sort of cover-up going on," he guessed.

"The seed was planted. Partially because my grief had turned to anger. It didn't seem fair that nobody had really paid for Jenny's death."

"Connor Wright paid," he pointed out gently. "My backup shot him after they busted down the door."

"My brain knew that. My heart was another matter." She paused, trying to form the right words to tell him the rest. "Max found out that I was questioning the details of my sister's death and why Connor went crazy, and he became upset. Then he learned I was trying to find you, and he was livid. He couldn't fathom why I'd invite more emotional pain by locating the cop who got away with murdering my sister."

Taylor stared at her. "So Griffin was the one feeding you this bullshit?"

Unable to meet his gaze any longer, she dropped her attention to her hands, folded and clenched together on the tabletop. "Now I think he twisted the truth, I just don't understand why."

"You *think*?" His voice rang with hurt. "He *lied*, Cara.

And when people lie, it's to further their own agenda. Frankly, given Max's murder and the accidents you and I have both had in the past few days, I'm guessing it's all related and Max isn't the only one with secrets. That's usually the way these things work."

Cold settled in the pit of her stomach, and she met his eyes again. "It's almost as if . . . he pointed me at you like a missile. Like, despite his ranting, he wanted me to find you and make you pay for Jenny's death."

"Yet he had to know what would happen if we compared notes."

"You think he came here the other day to confess what's really going on, and someone wanted to keep him from talking to me?"

"He ended up with a bullet in his forehead. It's not a stretch." Softening his tone, he immediately appeared contrite. "I'm sorry. That was uncalled for."

"No, you're right." Swallowing hard, she said, "It's eye-opening to realize the man I loved like a second father wasn't exactly the man I thought. I want the truth about everything."

"I don't think you do. Not yet—"

"Why would you say that?" she cried. "My sister *died*, and I don't know how Connor could do such a thing, especially to his pregnant wife!"

Her words had the effect of a knife thrust straight into Taylor's stomach. Making a noise that sounded like he'd been stabbed, he stepped back, eyes wide. "Your sister was pregnant?"

"You didn't know?" The silence in the suddenly small room spoke volumes. Finally, he found his voice.

"No. I . . . You're free to go. I'll be in touch."

Spinning on his heel, he turned and strode purposefully for the door, not once looking back before shutting it behind him. Cara stared after him, sick at heart. Taylor had looked like he was about to become ill. If she'd realized he hadn't known, she never would've told him. For several minutes, she sat in the interview room, going back over their conversation in her head.

"You don't think I've paid? That I don't play out that scene in my head every day, that I get any relief from what happened even after I go to sleep?"

And slowly it dawned on her that even if she still wanted to make him pay for her sister's death, there was no need.

Taylor already blamed himself more than anyone else ever could.

He barely made it to the men's room before he hit his knees in front of the toilet and got violently sick.

"Which one gets to walk out, huh? Choose, goddamn you!"

He hadn't been able to do it. And his decision not to choose had cost an innocent baby its life. Oh, God.

He'd never wanted to die more than he did at that very second.

Unfortunately, he kept right on breathing. At least nobody entered the bathroom to witness his shame, for which he was extremely grateful. Still feeling queasy, he rose and splashed water on his face, rinsed his mouth. He wasn't human again, nowhere close, but he could get through the rest of this awful day. Maybe.

Shane was coming down the hallway when he exited the restroom, and frowned. "You all right? I've been looking for you."

"I'm good," he lied. "Must've eaten something that didn't agree with me."

His partner's expression said he didn't necessarily believe that, but he had other pressing concerns at the moment. "If you're going to make it the rest of the day, we got a call from Ace."

A new informant, hopefully taking up the slack from Blake quitting. "He says he's got a tip on Griffin's murder and needs to talk to us, ASAP."

"Did he give any indication what he found out?"

"Nope. But he was nervous, said to hurry."

They were already heading toward the front of the building, then out the door. "Where are we going?"

"Those old apartments off Glenview."

"He live over there?" At Shane's nod, he said, "Christ, a novice. Never, never be seen talking to the cops in your own hood."

"No shit."

The apartments were just shy of an eyesore, an old, worn shoe with a floppy sole among the sleek, modern buildings that surrounded them. Several times the city had proposed tearing them down, only to face fierce opposition from those protecting the lower-income citizens who lived there.

Ace apparently was one of those citizens. He met them near the entrance and led them into an alcove between the buildings. Ace was young, but not as young as Blake. Midtwenties would be Taylor's guess. He was taller than Blake, a handsome boy with chocolate brown skin. His Nikes had seen better days, and though his jeans and T-shirt were worn, they were clean. He struck Taylor as a man stuck in limbo, trying to better himself by taking whatever job would help. But that was only an impression.

Ace turned to them as they found a quiet space near a Dumpster, expression worried. "You got big trouble here, man."

"Who's got big trouble?" Taylor asked. "Me? The city in general?"

"With a dude like this one, there ain't no difference. You got a badass mofo here to do business, is the word goin' around."

"This badass have a name?"

"Snyder is all I know. He's a big fucker. A pro, too. He want you dead, you gonna get that way sooner or later."

Taylor exchanged a look with Shane. His partner was troubled by the news as much as he was. "Any idea who he's after?"

"Man, you slow or what?" Ace eyed Taylor up and down with derision. "Don't know what you did in a past life to end up with a double dose of stupid, but you better figure it out before he kills yo dumb ass."

Despite the tendril of fear that snaked through his gut, Taylor grinned at his partner. "This Snyder is the badass, and I'm the dumb-ass. I don't think that's very fair."

"Hey, you've always got your beauty. That's gotta count, right?"

"Probably not."

Ace was glancing between them as if they were both nuts. Which they probably were. "Whatever, man. I said what I needed to. Cover yo stupid ass, man."

Shane pulled out a fifty-dollar bill and handed it over to the younger man, who quickly pocketed it. With a nod, he vanished between the buildings like a ghost.

"Well, that was informative," Taylor said dryly. "If I'm going to rate a hit man, it had *better* be a badass pro the size of a Sherman tank, or I'd feel cheated."

His partner scowled. "If that's supposed to be funny, I'm not laughing."

He sighed. "I never said it was funny and I'm *not* laughing. I'm trying not to freak out here as I wonder what the fuck this is all about."

"Me, too."

"I guess we see what info we can find on a gun for hire named Snyder. If that's even his real name, which I doubt."

"I'll ask Chris—"

Shane's words were suddenly cut off by a sharp coughing noise, and immediately a spot next to Taylor's head burst in a shower of brick that stung his cheek. Momentarily confused, he instinctively swung his head around to look at the spot, trying to figure out what had caused the shower of shards. Then, with a curse, Shane grabbed his arm and dragged him from where he'd been standing. Just in time.

Another cough, and the brick exploded right where his head had just been.

"Get down!"

Taylor stumbled, yanking his gun from the holster at

his waist, frantically looking for the shooter as they ran in a crouch, ducking around the Dumpster. Bullets pinged off the metal protecting them as they flattened themselves against it.

"Fuck!" Taylor swore, heart pounding. "Where is he?"

"No clue." Shane tried to get a look around the Dumpster, but another shot rang out and he ducked again. "I'm guessing he's down the corridor, past where we were standing."

"Should we make a run for it?"

"It's either that or stay here and wait to become Swiss cheese."

Taylor gestured with his weapon. "I say we break cover, split up. Let's circle behind the building, see if we can cut off his escape."

"Worth a try. On three?"

Taylor nodded, gun at the ready, and waited for his partner to give the count. When Shane said *three*, they bolted from their hiding place and separated. As Taylor expected, he drew the shooter's fire rather than Shane. There was no time for fear, only pure adrenaline as his legs pumped in a ground-eating run. More bullets pocked the wall, and one plucked at the arm of his jacket.

Relief flooded him as he rounded the corner, safe from the onslaught for the time being. But a woman stepped from an apartment, keys in hand, and her eyes widened as she saw him running toward her with a gun in hand.

"Police! Get back inside!"

She wasted no time in complying. He continued on, making for the tree line on the edge of the property, searching in vain for the shooter. It crossed his mind to wonder if Ace had sold him out, bringing him here on pretext. He didn't know the younger man well enough yet to say, but he'd bring him the hell in and find out.

Once he gained the trees, he hustled from one to the next, but caught no movement as he scanned the apartment windows. Then Shane came around the corner of the building, moving fast, shouting, bringing his weapon down to point it toward the parking lot.

"Look out!" Shane yelled.

Fuck. That was his only thought as he realized he'd been looking in the wrong direction, that the hunter had done some maneuvering of his own. As he spun, spotted the bulky figure bracing a rifle with a scope on the hood of a Jeep, Taylor knew he was in big trouble. His arm didn't even make the full swing upward when he saw the weapon jerk, the pop eerily quiet.

Then his head exploded in pain and he felt himself falling.

And he knew nothing more.

"What's wrong?"

Cara slung her purse off her shoulder and walked into the living room, dumping it on the coffee table. She should've known Blake would tune in to the fact that there was something wrong the instant she got home. She'd never been great at hiding her emotions and she figured it wouldn't do any good to start now. In fact, it was time to come clean about several things, before Blake had a chance to speak to Taylor.

"That might take a while."

"Try me." His face reflected genuine concern. "Lean on me for a change, will you? You don't always have to be the strong one."

Feeling numb, she sat on the sofa and waited as Blake took a seat close to her. "You're right. You've been a good friend to me, too, and I do need somebody to talk to." She paused. "My coming to Sugarland wasn't random, like it might seem. I came here because my sister, Jenny, was murdered and I wanted to make the man responsible pay."

His eyes widened in surprise, and he hesitated. "Okay. That's understandable."

"I got to town, set up the gig at the bar. Then most days I watched him, waiting for my chance to make him suffer."

Blake looked worried. "So did you?"

"No. The more I shadowed his every move, the more I began to realize this man might not be the monster I'd been led to believe."

"How's that possible?" he asked in confusion. "I mean, if the bastard murdered your sister, there's no redeeming that."

"There is if I was wrong about the circumstances, which it appears I was." She took a deep breath. "Max, who I thought was my friend, lied about what happened, and his involvement might have gotten him killed."

"Just to clear it up for me, he's not the one you were following?"

"No. Max twisted the story about the other man's involvement, and I believed him, even though he wasn't actually there when my sister died. I don't know why he would lie, and now I've hurt someone who's becoming special to me."

During her pause, Blake put it together. "Taylor?"

"Yes."

"Shit. All that talk about how he's made mistakes, and the weird way you guys were acting around each other . . . That's what he meant, isn't it? Whatever went down with your sister is what caused him to pick up his life and move here?"

"Exactly."

"Do you mind sharing with me what happened?" he asked softly, taking her hand in comfort.

Tears burned her throat, stung her eyes, but she didn't let them fall. "Jenny's husband, Connor, was never a very stable person. He was controlling and insecure in the beginning of their marriage, and only got worse. By the end, he was screaming at her regularly, calling her all sorts of horrible names. Then she got pregnant, and instead of improving their relationship, it made things a thousand times worse."

"Pregnant?" he said in a hushed voice. "Oh no."

"One day my sister had had enough and was packing her bags to leave. She'd told me it was time, and there were some things she wanted to talk to me about. A male friend of hers was there to help her get her stuff out, but Connor came home before they could get away."

"You don't have to finish." He squeezed her hand.

But she had to get it out. "Connor lost it completely. Went right over the edge. He grabbed his gun and took my sister hostage, along with her friend and the housekeeper. But the housekeeper had already phoned nine-one-one, so the police were on the way. The cops arrived and tried to negotiate, but he wasn't having it."

"This is where Taylor comes in?"

Cara nodded. "Connor struck Jenny's friend in the head with the butt of his gun and split open his scalp, knocking him unconscious. After what seemed like an eternity, Connor allowed them to send in a paramedic. The medic was actually Taylor, undercover."

She stared at the carpet for several long minutes before she could continue. Blake just held her hand, lending silent support.

"I don't know what tipped him off that Taylor was a cop, but that was the end. Connor killed . . ." Trailing off, she swallowed hard. "He shot and killed everyone there except Taylor, and the only reason Taylor wasn't killed was because of his bulletproof vest."

"I don't mean to be insensitive, but am I missing something? How is that Taylor's fault?"

"Anger and grief go a long way toward placing blame where there should be none," she admitted. "And for years I lived on that while I just went through the motions of my life. When I started to question what happened, the actual details that led to the shooting, Max told me the undercover cop had screwed up. That he'd tried reverse psychology, egging Connor on, telling him to shoot and he'd lose everything, including his freedom. He said it backfired, and if the cop hadn't made such a terrible mistake, my sister and the others would still be alive."

"But how would Max have known what happened if he wasn't there?"

"I know, right?" Her laugh was bitter. "He claimed he got the information on the sly from an informant inside the LAPD who saw the reports and heard talk from Internal Affairs. I had no reason not to believe him. He was a family friend and the cop a stranger."

"Right," Blake said slowly. "So, the question becomes, what did Max have to gain from pushing this scenario on you and making you believe it?"

"Nothing, except . . . maybe me killing Taylor." She shuddered to think of allowing herself to sink that far. There was a time when, in her grief, she might have attempted it.

"So either he wanted to make Taylor the scapegoat and cover up the real story, or to get you to do someone's dirty work for them."

"How'd you get so smart?"

"School of hard knocks. So, what happened today? I get the feeling there's more."

"Taylor found a photo album here and he took it to the station. He was going through it and saw pictures of me and Jenny and realized she was my sister. It didn't take him long to figure out I had an ulterior motive for being in town."

Blake winced. "I'll bet that went over well."

"Yeah. He was upset and called me on the deception. When I explained to him what I just told you, he denied Max's claims that he antagonized Connor or acted inappropriately. He's got a lot of guilt left over from that day, but not from that."

"You think there's more?"

"Something tells me there is. In any case, he's upset

enough that I don't think he'll want to see me anytime soon."

He smiled. "That may be, but you guys aren't going to solve your problems overnight. What do you say we get out of here awhile? I want to turn in the last couple of job applications, and then maybe we can get some ice cream."

"Sounds good. I could use loads of sugar after a day like this."

They headed out to her rental car and climbed in, and dropped off Blake's applications. Then she pointed the car toward the ice-cream place that was a few minutes from their last stop.

"Jesus, what the hell is going on over there?" Blake pointed.

Stopping at a light, she followed his gesture and gazed out the passenger's window at the sea of blue and red lights at a nearby apartment complex. "I don't know, but it must be something major."

Just then a tap on Cara's driver's window startled her. She lowered the glass to see a uniformed officer looking very serious as he leaned in close. "I'm sorry, ma'am, but I'm going to have to ask you to turn around. We're blocking off the area and I'm not sure when we'll have it reopened."

"Oh, okay. Can you tell me what happened?"

"Shooting," he said curtly, stepping back and waving his arm. "Turn around, please."

Shooting. That word was enough to send her mind tripping down a path she didn't want to revisit. Carefully, she executed a U-turn and was straightening out the car when she gave the scene at the apartments one last glance—and spotted a familiar vehicle in the complex's parking lot.

"That's Taylor's car," she said.

"What?"

"Taylor's car, over there."

He peered across her. "Looks like it."

The sight of the Challenger sitting amid the chaos made her guts twist, as did the fact that she couldn't see Taylor or his partner anywhere. Not that she should be able to—there were so many vehicles and cops—but that didn't alleviate her nerves. At the very next left-hand turn, she swung into a parking lot for the building next door to the activity.

"What are you doing?"

"A little investigating."

"Cara, that cop told us to leave," he said nervously, glancing around as she found a parking space.

"Hey, we turned around like he told us to."

"I'm pretty sure the *and keep going* was implied."

"Relax. We're just going to see if we can spot Taylor and then we'll go."

Shutting off the ignition, she got out and heard her companion mutter a curse. Any other time, she'd laugh at his grumbling, but not now. Something was pulling her toward the scene. A need to be sure he was all right, even if he didn't want to speak to her.

She spotted Shane standing among a throng of cops and firefighters doing duty at this call as paramedics. The detective was pacing anxiously, both hands gripping the sides of his head as he stared at a huddle of paramedics who were crouched over somebody. Without a second thought, she broke into a jog.

"Cara, wait!" Blake called.

Ignoring him, she made a beeline for the group. As she ran up to them, Shane spotted her and immediately intercepted her, grabbing her shoulders.

"You can't go over there," he said hoarsely. His face was drawn, gray eyes wounded.

"Is that Taylor? I need to see him!"

"You can't. Not right now. Let the medics do their jobs and we'll be able to see him at the hospital."

He's alive! Thank God. Her knees almost sagged. "He'll be all right, then?"

"I hope so, but I don't—"

"His head's bleeding!" Blake interrupted, grabbing Cara's arm. "Somebody shot him in the fucking head?"

Blake's loud exclamation got the attention of several officers, who frowned at them. But Cara ignored them, her focus on getting a glimpse of Taylor on the ground. When she did, she was sorry.

He was sprawled on his back, eyes closed. Blood covered the right side of his head, saturating his hair and turning it from blond to a rusty reddish brown. A female firefighter was kneeling at his side and placed a compress on his head, while a studious-looking one in glasses fixed him with an IV.

"Entry wound?" the medic with the glasses asked.

The woman shook her head, glancing at her partner. "Too much blood."

"Let's get him rolling."

Two more paramedics brought a gurney, and as they

were getting Taylor ready for transport, Shane called out
to a firefighter on the fringes who was watching with a
grim expression.

"Howard!"

The man turned, and Cara couldn't help but stare. He
was not like any Howard she'd ever seen, but from the
sheer size of him, his godlike presence, not to mention
the looks to match, he could go by any damned name he
wanted.

Howard walked over, expression serious. "Shane. Hang
tight, man. He's stable, all right?"

"You sure?"

"His vitals are strong. Head wounds always look worse
than they are—you know that."

Cara studied Taylor again and contemplated those
words, though she was still frozen with fear. It wasn't a
definite yes. Beside her, Blake clung to her side like a
piece of Velcro, looking as horrified as she felt.

"Cara . . ." His voice was a whimper. She knew how he
felt.

The big firefighter turned to her. "Are you Taylor's
girlfriend?"

"I— um . . ." She fumbled for the right words. "I'm
Cara Evans, and I'm more like a new friend." The knowing look the man gave her said he had already figured
she was more.

"I'm Howard Paxton," he said, voice friendly. "I'm the
captain at Station Five. I'll see you folks at the hospital
later when I check on Taylor."

"Thanks," Shane answered. "See you."

The captain nodded at Cara and Blake, then went to

join his team. Staring after the man, she couldn't help but feel like his very presence demanded that everything be okay simply because he'd said it.

Shane touched her shoulder. "Come on, they're taking him in. Assuming you two are going?"

"Of course," she said. "There's nowhere else we'd be." Beside her, Blake agreed.

Let them try to keep her away. They'd regret it.

9

The waiting room started out quiet, but soon became crowded with worried cops, pacing and swearing. Even a few firefighters, including the huge Captain Paxton and his team.

Shane was about to lose his mind, from all appearances. But the detective knew a lot of people and was obviously liked by most of them, as was Taylor. There was a constant stream of friends and acquaintances who came in and stopped by to speak with him and a rugged, official-looking man she learned was Austin Rainey, Shane and Taylor's captain.

A short time later, Howard ambled over with the two paramedics she'd seen tending to Taylor. "Cara, I'd like to introduce you to Lieutenant Zack Knight and Eve Marshall. They worked on Taylor in the ambulance and can give you all some information on his condition when he was brought in."

Zack took over, smiling at them reassuringly. He was a handsome man with short black hair, cute in his glasses. "I'm not a doctor, so don't take this as a diagnosis, but an observation. On the way over, I was able to clean the blood to get a closer look at Taylor's head wound, and it appears to be a deep furrow rather than an invasive wound."

There was a general exhale of relief from the group and some mutterings of thanks, Cara's included. Eve, however, had a few words of caution.

"While this is good news, keep in mind that any type of blow to the head will be treated as serious until he gets a full exam. That said, his vitals remained strong all the way here."

"We've got to go, but we'll check back," Zack said. After nodding to the group, he left with Eve.

Howard addressed Shane, his captain, Cara, and Blake. "We're having a party at the park by the river next weekend. We'd love for you all to join us. Taylor too, if he's feeling better."

"Sounds great." Shane shook his hand and Howard pulled him in for a hug and a manly slap on the back.

"Try not to worry. He'll be all right."

"Thanks, big guy."

"Cara, nice to meet you. Hope to see you again soon."

"Same here."

After he walked out the double doors, Cara shook herself. "That's one of the biggest men I've ever seen."

"And hot!" Blake enthused. "Is that a job requirement at the fire department?"

Shane chuckled. "Down, boy. All those guys are straight as can be."

"Still, the view would be awesome."

"Can't argue there," Cara muttered. But with the eye

candy gone, except for Shane, her thoughts quickly returned to the man who was suffering somewhere beyond the doors to the exam rooms. He had to be okay, or she didn't know what she'd do. She needed a chance to make things right between them.

She just hoped she got one.

His head pounded as though someone had driven a rusty spike through his brain.

"Fuck," he whispered. Or thought he did. Couldn't be sure, since he couldn't hear his own voice over the roaring in his ears. The noise made him sick and he sought refuge in the darkness again.

The second time he surfaced, the pounding headache was still clinging to him, but without so much of the dizzying sickness that had rocked him before. Listening, he heard a paper rustle. The sound of someone moving in a chair.

He wanted to speak to whoever was there, but he couldn't think what to say. The words wouldn't form and he was so fucking *confused*.

What day was it? What had landed him here? *Um . . .*

A tendril of fear began to wind its way around his heart and he tried hard to open his eyes. He must've made some sort of movement or sound because instantly a warm, soothing hand landed on his brow and began to stroke.

"Taylor?"

Gradually, he was able to pry open his eyes, but couldn't focus right away. Her features clarified themselves first, and he smiled at her purple-streaked hair. That was kind of cool.

Then it hit him.

"Cara?" he rasped.

"Thank God you're lucid," she breathed. "Well, almost."

"What happened?"

"Shane said you were shot in the head. Don't ever scare me like that again!" Immediately his face and lips were showered in kisses.

The attention was nice, so he took advantage and soaked it up shamelessly. Just Cara being near made him feel better. Gradually, as he relaxed into her touch, the events came back to him.

Meeting with the informant. Learning there was a hit man in town, after Taylor. And then the fucker had shown almost the second their informant had booked out, which made him suspicious. Then the pursuit, he and Shane trying to get behind the suspect to apprehend him.

Yeah, that didn't work out so well.

"How are you feeling?"

"Like I got clubbed with a baseball bat."

"Might as well have been. The bullet grazed your scalp but it still had a pretty nasty impact."

He was goddamned lucky his gray matter was still inside his skull.

"When can I go home?"

"They're keeping you overnight, but the doctor said tomorrow, barring complications."

He made a face. The truth was, though, he wasn't sure he was in any shape to move just yet. "Did they catch the bastard who did this?"

Resuming her seat, she shook her head. "From what I

gathered listening to them, no," she said, looking worried. "Shane thinks this is tied to Max and me somehow, and based on what we'd already discussed, I agree."

"I'm surprised you're still talking to me."

She blinked in surprise. "Me? I was going to say the same thing about you. I've been keeping my identity a secret from you since I came to town. I stalked you so I could make you suffer for what happened to Jenny."

"But you didn't."

"Huh?"

"That's just it," he said with a slight smile. "When it came down to the nitty-gritty, you never did anything about me. Now that I've had time to think about it, I believe the reason you put off confronting me is because you weren't sure about what you'd been told."

"Maybe so," she said thoughtfully.

She was studying him like she had something else on her mind, and he wondered if she could possibly know. . . . But she couldn't, right? She could speculate there was more to the story that had driven him out of L.A., but she couldn't *know*. And he wasn't ready to discuss it yet.

If she didn't hate him before, she might when she learned the whole truth.

Suddenly tired, he melted into the pillows and closed his eyes. He fell into sleep with her touching him, praying the budding relationship between them could survive the coming blow.

Dmitri reined in his temper with a monumental effort. He studied his new man, Web. Allowed him a few moments to stand on the other side of the desk, waiting for his orders. Rage firmly in control, he leaned forward, careful to keep his voice low. Eerily jovial.

"Snyder still hasn't managed to kill one stupid cop." It wasn't a question.

"No, sir."

"Tell me precisely what in the fuck you're going to do about it."

Web hooked his thumbs in his jeans, assuming a casual stance. Unruffled. Smart kid.

"Catch a flight there, make sure he doesn't fuck up again."

Dmitri relaxed a bit. But he looked Web hard in the eye, to make sure there would be no misunderstanding. "Our friend Snyder has outlived his usefulness by screwing up one too many times. Once this job is done, you'll take care of him."

"All right. What about Evans? Still want her dead?"

Dmitri's anger surged anew. "The first clear opportunity that presents itself, kill her. I can't risk the woman putting my future plans in jeopardy. Whether or not her death appears to be an unfortunate accident is up to you."

"What about Kayne? How do you want him done?"

An idea formed in his mind, and the more he considered it, the more he warmed to it. "On second thought, leave him to me. The police will be on guard now, so we'll wait a bit. Then I'll catch a flight with you, and we'll strike."

Web's smile turned nasty. "Do I get to watch you fillet him? After all, you're the only man I know who can make death a form of fine art. Maybe I can learn a new trick."

"If you perform your job well, I might let you partic-
ipate. Now get out. And keep me informed."

"You've got it."

A form of fine art, indeed.

Staring at the small framed photo on his desk, Dmitri's eyes filled, burned with anguish he'd believed long
dead and gone. He traced a finger across the slick glass.

"Kayne will pay," he whispered. "If it's the last thing I
do, I'll get the bastard. I promise."

Taylor had never been so glad to be home.

Wobbling inside, he shrugged off assistance from his
companion and lowered himself to the sofa. "I might
stay right here and not move again."

"Wrong," Cara said with a stubborn light in her eyes.
"You're going up to bed and you're going to stay there
until you're one hundred percent."

"Soon. I just want to sit here for a few minutes." *And
let the room stop spinning.*

The doctor had released him with strict instructions
to come back if he experienced nausea, vomiting, or
blurred vision. So far it was only dizzy spells and a
mother of a headache, so he could cope.

"Are you hungry?" she asked.

"Not just yet. In a little while I will be." He studied
her as she set down her purse and joined him on the sofa.
"Why didn't Blake come with you?"

She smiled. "He's finally getting his own life, you
know. He has an interview this afternoon."

"That's great! Why didn't he tell me when he came by
last night?"

"I guess he didn't want to get his hopes up in case he doesn't get the job, but he was really excited earlier. I dropped him off before I went to pick you up, and he said he'd get a ride back to my house."

"From who?" Taylor's protective instincts came to the fore. "He doesn't really know very many people."

"Relax! Remember Jinx? He's going to play chauffer for me."

How could he forget the guitarist with the roaming hands and the boundary issues? Like a bad penny, the guy was bound to turn up again. "There wasn't anyone else who could help Blake out?"

"Not on such short notice, no." She eyed him with a frown. "What's the problem? Jinx is a perfectly nice guy and fun to be around. He and Blake have already hit it off."

"The problem is—"

The more the guitarist was around Blake on their time off from the band, the more he'd be in Cara's presence, too. That was the crux of the matter, and he wasn't about to spew his jealousy to the woman he wanted to win over. It would just make Taylor look like a jerk.

"Nothing," he amended. "It's fine."

"O-kay." Clearly she didn't believe him, but didn't push it. "I'm going to scout around your kitchen and see what I can throw together for dinner while you take a nap."

"You don't have to do that." Though part of him loved the idea of her taking care of him. "Really, I can manage if you want to go home."

"There's nowhere else I'd rather be," she said softly.

Leaning over, she gave him a sweet kiss. Just a press of lips to his, no tongue, but it brought his body to life like nothing else could. Taking more, he returned it, enjoying this woman pushing into him, soft and warm. Her breasts grazing his chest, her hair tickling his face. His cock stirred and he shifted, trying to get more comfortable. But the only relief he'd get would be if he were buried balls deep in her.

"Go," she said on a laugh, pulling away. "Get some rest."

"And if I'm a good boy?"

"We'll see."

Damn. Sending her a pout, which made her giggle, he headed upstairs. Making his room without incident, he stretched out on the bed and had to admit to himself that he was still tired. Before long, the weight of sleep pulled him under.

Straight into the nightmare he couldn't escape.

"Think you're so smart, asshole? Thought you could come in here and be a big hero?" Connor Wright screamed in his face.

"No, I want to help." Sweat rolled down Taylor's back. "We can end this peacefully—"

"Peace? You want peace?" Wildly, he waved his gun at the three cowering people in the living room. The hostages Taylor had been sent in to help.

One of them was Jennifer Wright—Connor's estranged wife.

"Choose!" Connor bellowed, pressing the gun into the back of his head.

"Choose what?" Taylor fought to keep calm.

"You want peace? Choose one person to live."

God, no. "Connor, let's talk about—"

"Which one gets to walk out, huh? Choose, goddamn you!"

"You know I can't do that," he stated evenly. "But you and I can figure something out. Let them go and keep me instead."

"They deserve to die!"

"No! Everyone deserves to live."

"The fuck they do! They all support my conniving bitch of a wife! They all deceive me!" Connor screamed, out of control. "You had your chance!"

Before Taylor could move, the man swung the gun toward the housekeeper—

And Taylor could only watch in horror as her head exploded all over the custom drapes.

Taylor bolted upright, dragging air into his lungs, heart threatening to burst in his chest. He clutched the bedcovers, sweat trickling down the sides of his face. Sickness churned in his stomach. Self-loathing.

Yeah, Connor Wright had stolen the last of his innocence as a young cop that black day. Shown him true horror and the total destruction one human being could suffer at the hands of another. Afterward, he'd never harbored any doubt he deserved the cruel punishment of the nightmare that had lasted four hellish years.

The awful weight of his responsibility had never left him. Never would.

"Shut off the self-blame," he ordered himself. "It's over and done. Just survive today."

Taylor glanced about, listening, combing a shaking

hand through his hair. How long had he been asleep? Christ, had anyone heard him cry out? Faint voices drifted from downstairs, along with the rich aroma of something cooking. No one came to investigate.

Grateful for this small favor, he pushed to his feet with a groan. His entire body throbbed as though it had been run over by an eighteen-wheeler, and backed over for good measure. His splitting head was causing the room to swim, and he wondered whether putting food in his empty stomach was a good idea. The answering rumble demanded he try, and soon.

Glancing to the bedside table, he found the bottle of painkillers the doctor had prescribed for him. Cara must've brought them up. Curling his fingers tight around the container, he peered at the large oval capsules. Once, he would've been tempted to lose himself to the darkness. To take them all and end the pain. If Cara had any idea, she might not have left them there, though he was much stronger now.

Setting his jaw, he plunked the bottle onto the nightstand. He'd take one, but not on an empty stomach. He shed his jeans, the careful movements drowning him in waves of dizziness. Retrieving a pair of clean black briefs, jeans, and a dark button-up shirt, he shuffled stiffly into the adjoining master bathroom.

Turning on the nozzle, Taylor let the water warm for a minute while he pushed up his hair and picked off the bandage taped to the side of his head. He frowned into the mirror above the sink, examining the wound, which had been taped, since stitches wouldn't work. Not bad, except for the gouged flesh and surrounding knot, which promised to turn a dazzling display of every shade of purple known to man. But, hell, he'd survived far worse. This hardly rated.

He nudged aside the curtain and stepped into the hot spray. A long, appreciative sigh escaped his lips. "Ahhh . . . damn . . . yes."

For a time, he simply stood and let the water sluice over his body, soothing aching muscles and flagging spirits. As happened frequently of late, his thoughts drifted to the woman inhabiting his kitchen, and his cock began to rise.

Taking himself in hand, he enjoyed the sensation of squeezing the hardening flesh. He imagined it was her hand palming him, her thumb sweeping over the slippery head. Her mouth sucking his rod, taking him deep in her throat. Lips and tongue stroking, laving . . .

He couldn't last. With a groan he came, ropes of seed bathing the tile, to be instantly washed away by the spray. Sagging, he was sated for the moment—but only in the way a starving man was satisfied by wolfing a small dish of ice cream when what he really needed was a steak dinner.

When the temperature began to cool, a twinge of guilt pricked at him for using all of the hot water. Hurriedly, he shampooed, soaped himself, and rinsed.

Mindful of his head wound, he toweled off his hair, then the rest. Getting dressed again proved more of a challenge than he'd thought, given the dizziness that hung on. By the time he'd finished, perspiration dampened his brow again. For about two seconds, he considered skipping dinner, giving in to fatigue. Maybe he could sleep off the pounding behind his eyeballs that threatened to pop them out of his skull. A loud reminder from his empty belly got his ass moving instead.

As he descended the stairs, several voices reached his ears. There were obviously more people in his home than just Cara and Blake, and there was so much talking and laughing, he had trouble making out the individuals. As he reached the entryway to the kitchen, his brows rose.

Whatever was cooking smelled fantastic, and Cara moved about tossing salad and then checking on something in the oven. Standing around visiting were Shane, Daisy, their seventeen year-old ward, Drew, and Blake—

And the guitarist. Jinx.

His hackles rose and he forced his attention away from the man. His friends were imbibing a bit, Shane and the rocker with beers, the women with glasses of red wine. Blake was complaining loudly, but in a good-natured way, about being stuck with a glass of iced tea.

"Dudes, come on! I'm gonna be twenty-one in a few months. So what's the big deal?"

"The big deal is that it's against the law for you to consume alcohol before you're twenty-one," Shane said dryly.

"No, it's not! It's against the law for me to order alcohol from an establishment and be served. It's not if an adult orders it for me and gives it to me!" His expression was triumphant. But short-lived.

"Sorry. Smart as you are, no can do. You'll have to deal with tea and soda a little longer."

"Shit. You suck."

Taylor's chuckle drew the attention of the group, and

he stepped inside. "Did someone forget to issue me an invite to my own party?"

Cara smiled at him, a little flushed. "I hope you don't mind. Shane and Daisy came to check on you, and then I told Jinx to go ahead and drop Blake off here so we can make a celebration out of dinner."

"A celebration? Of me almost getting my head blown off?"

She rolled her eyes. "No, idiot. Blake, you want to share?"

The boy beamed. "So, I got the job at Guitar Center!"

Cheers erupted, and from the expressions on Shane and Daisy's faces, the news was a surprise. Taylor stepped over and pulled Blake into a hard hug. "Congratulations, man! I knew you could do it."

"Thanks."

"I already knew," Jinx put in from his spot leaning against the counter. He eyed Taylor with a smirk. "Kid was so excited he had to tell *somebody* when I picked him up from the interview."

Taylor eyed the other man as he let Blake go. *I'll be damned. The asshole is baiting me.* Instant tension stretched between them, but he was determined to be the bigger man. No way was he going to allow a petty pissing contest to ruin Blake's big evening.

"Thanks for being there for him," he said pleasantly, earning a look of surprise from Jinx. "I appreciate it."

"Sure thing." Just like that, some of the man's confrontational demeanor eased.

Taylor looked to Cara. "So, what are we eating to celebrate?"

"Lasagna, because it's Blake's favorite. And Italian cream cake for dessert."

That earned groans of appreciation, and in minutes they were all sitting around Taylor's dining table. Suddenly it struck him that he'd never had this many people at his house for something so . . . domestic.

Beer, pizza, and a ball game? Sure. Friends and co-workers at the station took turns hanging at one another's houses for the male bonding ritual, as many of their wives and girlfriends liked to tease. But this was completely different. This felt like he had a family. In his house, taking up his space, talking, eating and having a good time.

And it felt pretty awesome.

Well, except for Jinx, who kept staring at him as though he'd very much like to punch him. A childish part of Taylor wanted to mouth *bring it*, but he squashed it. Hard.

Blake kept everyone entertained with the story of his interview and how he had to audition for the job—as in playing the guitar. Made sense for a place like that to require their employees to be damned good on the instrument they were selling.

"There's more to it than just playing," Blake said with enthusiasm. "You have to know the mechanics, how they're made and where, the different brands and their tones. Sometimes players bring them in for repair, and I can do some minor stuff."

On and on he went, with Jinx chiming in now and then as a fellow guitarist, and Drew asking a ton of questions. Taylor smiled as he envisioned the boy going home and talking Shane into letting him have a guitar. Every so often the band member would return his attention to Taylor and let his gaze linger in challenge. Taylor pretty much ignored him. Even though he was getting seriously annoyed.

Taylor enjoyed watching Cara and Daisy interact, and he listened to them talk about her band and then Daisy's job at the Sugarland Police Department as a juvenile officer. Blake and Cara were interested in hearing how Daisy met Drew and worked with him after his dad died, and how he came to live with Shane, his godfather. Drew's expression was still sad, the events being only a few months old, but there was no mistaking how much the boy loved his guardians.

Blake and Drew hit it off, too, talking nonstop the rest of the evening as they cleaned the kitchen. Eventually Shane rose and ushered his brood to the car, but not before the boys made plans to hang out sometime. Jinx finally, thank God, made his move to leave as well. But he grinned, asking Cara to walk him out. She hesitated, glancing uncomfortably at Taylor, but then shrugged and followed him outside. Into the darkness. Alone.

Son of a bitch!

Taylor paced while Blake flipped on the TV. A minute passed and seemed like twenty.

"I like Drew. He's cool," Blake said in an upbeat voice.

"You know he's straight, right?"

The younger man gave him a droll stare and said nothing.

"Well, probably. And he's too young for you."

Blake shook his head. "No, he's not. And, anyway, you don't know for sure if he's straight. Not that it's any of your business."

"Jesus. I can't believe I'm having this conversation."

"You started it."

"I know. You're right, it's none of my business. Sorry."

"No problem." The boy laughed softly. "You know, you're too obvious. Why don't you just march out there and grab your lady?"

"I can't. I don't want her to think I'm some sort of Neanderthal. I have to play by the rules."

"Why? Dude, you think he's out there all *I can't touch you 'cause that's not allowed*? Bullshit."

Taylor glanced toward the front door. "Dammit."

"Go on, get your ass out there and stake your claim!"

The image of what might be happening out there goaded him into action. He knew he was about to commit an invasion of privacy, but there was no way Jinx was going to get his groove on with her. Not on Taylor's property.

Instead of storming out, however, he eased onto the porch quietly, listening and letting his eyes adjust. In the moonlight he spotted them standing beside Jinx's car. And the guitarist had her pressed against the passenger's door, kissing the shit out of her.

Taylor's stomach cramped and a cold feeling washed over him. Nausea that had nothing to do with his head wound caused bile to rise in his throat. What had Cara said? That she and Jinx had a history but that it was over long ago.

Apparently somebody hadn't received that memo.

A strange ache settled in his heart and he started to turn—just as Cara shoved Jinx hard in the chest, sending him backward a couple of steps.

"I told you no!" she shouted. "I—"

That was all he needed to hear. Taylor was off the porch like a bolt of lightning, his sole focus on the man who was going to pay for violating her boundaries.

"Hey, asshole," Taylor snarled, grabbing the man by the collar and yanking him back. Jinx spun to face him, and Taylor unloaded a punch to his jaw that sent the man sprawling on the driveway as Cara shouted in alarm.

"Fuck!" The guitarist struggled to sit up. "I just wanted to find out if she still wanted me, that's all!"

"Every time I see you, you're draped over her like a cheap coat." Reaching down, Taylor snatched his shirt and hauled him to his feet. "That ends here and now. Touch her again, and you'll be eating soup through a straw for the rest of your miserable fucking life. We clear?"

"Crystal," he spat, eyes glittering at Taylor in the darkness. When he spoke to Cara, his voice grew sincere. "I'm sorry. I was a fool to let you go, but I can see it's too late."

"Much," she said in a strained voice. "That ship sailed long before I met Taylor. Can you get past this and be professional?"

"Yeah." At her dubious look, he held up his hands in a gesture of surrender. "I swear."

"Okay. But if this happens again, you're fired."

"It won't." Now shuffling his feet, he glanced down at the pavement. "You're a special woman, Cara. I didn't mean any harm."

Her voice softened. "I know."

"Thanks for dinner. Tell Blake I'll see him at rehearsal."

"I will."

They watched him drive away, and Taylor didn't relax until the man's car had turned the corner. Cara was giving him an inscrutable look, and suddenly he was afraid.

"I'm sorry if you feel I went over the line. I was about to go back inside when I heard you shout no at him. Then I saw red."

"No, it's all right." Taking his hand, she walked with him back to the house. On the porch, she stopped and stepped in to his body. "I didn't kiss him, for the record. He kissed *me*."

"Glad to hear it." Taylor wrapped his arms around her and held her tight to him, tucking her head under his chin. She fit just right there, and he kissed the top of her head.

God, she felt so damned good pressed against him. Warm, soft, all woman. All his. Tilting her chin up, he molded his mouth to hers. Groaned as her body melted into his, accepting him, meeting his passion. They kissed for several long moments, until he was sure he'd erased any trace of the guitarist from his lady. That bastard had no right to touch the woman he—

He what? Was falling for? He pulled back, and her question seemed to echo his thoughts.

"What are we to each other?" she asked. "Are we dating? Just sleeping together?"

"I'd like the real deal," he said honestly. "I'd like for us to be exclusive and see where it goes."

She tightened her grip. "I'd like that, too."

He steeled himself. "But before you agree, I have something to tell you. It's serious, and I don't know if you'll want me anymore after this."

"There isn't anything you can't tell me."

"I'm afraid this might be the one exception."

Honestly, he didn't know anyone who'd want him after this. He certainly wouldn't want *himself*. But he had no choice but to reveal the secret he'd never told anyone except Shane.

And pray she'd stay.

10

Cara squeezed Taylor's hand in reassurance as he led her inside. As they passed through the living room, Blake saw them heading for the stairs and grinned.

"Guess this means we're staying here so you can *keep an eye* on your wounded cop."

"*I'm* staying," Cara said with a wink. Letting go of Taylor's hand, she retrieved her purse from the coffee table, fished out her key ring, and tossed it to Blake. "You're taking the car and going back to my house for the night."

Palming the keys, Blake snickered and shut off the TV. Pushing to his feet, he said, "See you guys tomorrow. Try to stay out of trouble. And thanks for dinner and the celebration."

She smiled. "You're welcome. Congrats again."

After he left, Cara locked the door behind him, but instead of resuming their path to the bedroom, Taylor lowered himself to the sofa in the spot Blake had just vacated. Walking over, she sat next to him.

"Whatever you have to tell me, I'm sure it can't be as

bad as me admitting to stalking you." She tried a smile, but his gaze dropped to his clasped hands.

"No, it's worse." He paused, seeming to find the right words. "So much worse, especially when I learned your sister was pregnant."

"That was hard for me to accept, too," she admitted. "But I realize now that there's nothing you could've done to change the outcome."

"But there is." The laugh that rumbled in his chest was harsh. Bitter. "I could have saved your sister and her baby, if only I had made the right choice."

"But you didn't *have* one."

"Yes, I did. Literally. Your brother-in-law—"

"Sorry to interrupt, but I do *not* count that crazy bastard as family anymore."

He nodded. "Understood. When the hostage situation began to escalate that day, Wright gave me a choice." His expression was pure misery. "He started to unravel, told me to choose one person to live."

Cara couldn't stop the gasp as her hand went over her mouth. "Who did you pick? But wait—he killed everyone, anyway."

"That's just it. I couldn't choose," he said in a quiet voice. "I told him that was an impossible decision and that everyone deserved to live. I tried to talk him down, to get him to let them go and keep me. But he screamed that he'd make it for me, and started shooting. I'm so sorry."

Her heart had been ripped from her chest, the pain was so bad. She stared at him, unable to comprehend how it was still beating, why she continued to breathe. "Oh, my God."

"I know I can never make this up to you. I don't know what else to say."

"Make it up to me?" she breathed. The room was closing in. She couldn't look at him, didn't begin to know how to respond. "I—I need time. To think."

She stood, grabbed her purse. Then she realized she'd loaned Blake her car.

Taylor stood. "I'll take you home."

"It's only a few minutes from here. I can walk." Blake could have, too, for that matter. But he'd known she was with Taylor and wasn't supposed to need her car.

She didn't mean to sound curt. Maybe she should stay, try to talk things out. But her brain was a chaotic mess, and in the center of the cacophony, there was Taylor, saying, *I couldn't choose*. It didn't make sense.

Her sister was dead. If he'd chosen Jenny, would she still be alive?

Taylor tried to protest. "I don't think that's a good idea. It's dark and—"

"I've been taking care of myself for years," she said curtly. "I can manage the short distance to my house."

He looked away and then nodded, expression resigned. He didn't try to apologize anymore, and she was glad, because she didn't know what to say. That it was okay? *Was* it okay?

He looked so miserable, she gave an inch. "I'll call you."

"All right," he responded sadly. "Talk to you soon."

As she'd claimed, the walk was brief. Once or twice, she could've sworn she heard a slight noise, maybe a footstep, and finally she whirled—only to see nothing but the empty sidewalk behind her. Would Taylor have followed to make sure she was safe? *Yes, he would. He'd make sure I got home all right, no matter how I tried to dissuade him.*

In minutes, she was letting herself in the house. Closing the door, she listened to him walk away. It wasn't until then she realized she was crying. Blake looked up from his spot on the sofa and his eyes widened as he leaped to his feet.

"What's wrong? I wasn't really expecting you tonight. Did something happen between you two?"

Taking a shaky breath, she wiped her cheeks and moved forward. Immediately she was wrapped in a fierce hug and she clung to him for a minute, soaking up the comfort he offered. Such a sweet boy.

"Come on, let's sit down," he told her.

Pulling back, she followed him to the sofa, where they sat close, the younger man studying her anxiously. "I'm all right. I just need time to process something Taylor told me."

"Can you share with me, or is it private?"

"He might get upset with me for saying anything, but I need somebody to talk to." She needed perspective. A calm third party to listen.

"I'm here, then." He patted her hand. "I won't tell anyone else."

"I know. Remember when I told you that Taylor was involved in the hostage standoff with my sister? There was more. He told me tonight that just before my sister's husband went off the deep end and shot them all, he'd given Taylor an ultimatum—to choose who got to live or they'd all die."

"Oh, my God! That's evil!"

"Yeah." More tears leaked from her eyes and she swiped at them. "*Evil* is the right word."

"So . . . why are you here?" He appeared genuinely baffled.

"What do you mean? I couldn't very well stay after he dropped a bomb like that on me!"

"Why not?"

"Because I needed to think! He told that lunatic he couldn't choose, Blake! And then Connor shot my beautiful sister and those other people." Her breath hitched on a sob.

Unable to hold in the grief anymore, she broke. Blake wrapped an arm around her shoulders and held her as she cried, the loss as fresh as if it had happened yesterday. For the longest time the young man didn't say a word. Eventually, however, he couldn't keep silent.

"I'm sorry you're hurting." Pulling back, he swiped her cheeks with his thumb. "But I'll bet Taylor is, too. It seems like you walked out on him after he shared the most awful moment in his life with you."

Staring at the kid, she tried to tamp down the sick feeling that rose in her stomach. "I couldn't deal with it right then. I had to go."

"I can understand why you'd feel that way, but I can also imagine how lost Taylor's feeling right now. He probably thinks you hate him."

"I don't," she whispered. "I'm just trying to wrap my head around the fact that he could've saved my sister and her unborn child."

"That's not fair. He didn't know she was pregnant.

And even if he had, if he'd made that choice, there's no guarantee the crazy bastard would have kept the bargain. Meanwhile Taylor would've been giving the others a death sentence. Can you put yourself in his place? Really visualize making that decision in front of the others, having to see their faces when you basically played God and condemned them to death?"

"I . . . hadn't thought of it that way."

"Your sister's husband may have been crazy, but he was smart enough to know the exact way to terrorize everyone in that room." Blake shook his head. "The bastard left a good cop so traumatized he gave up a job in a high-profile police department in a big city to move here and start over. Your life was ripped apart, but his was, too."

"God." She lowered her face to her hands. "I completely fucked up."

"Hey, I didn't mean that you fucked up. But if you guys are going to work past this, you have to look at things from his perspective also."

"Maybe you're right and I should go back over there. But I just need time to sleep on it." She rose, feeling exhausted. "I'm going to bed."

"Let me know if you need me."

After sending him a wan smile, she retreated to her bedroom, where she stripped and fell into bed in record time. Sleep didn't come easy, though. A man with sad green eyes chased her into her dreams.

The next day was a long rehearsal with the band. It was made even longer by the fact that she'd rather be at Taylor's house, trying to make things okay between them. It shamed her to think of how fast she'd gotten out of there after he'd opened up to her. She'd received a couple of texts from him and had only answered in short phrases, letting him know she was all right. She just had to talk to him in person. Texting wasn't ideal for communicating.

When quitting time rolled around, she was anxious and ready to get going. Which was why she was less than thrilled when Jinx stopped her, wanting to talk. Blake eyed the guitarist uncertainly, but Cara smiled at the younger man and told him to wait outside.

Once Blake was gone, Jinx shifted from foot to foot, looking uneasy. "I want to apologize again for last night. It was stupid of me—I mean, it's obvious you and the cop are together—but I guess a part of me wasn't ready to let go."

"It's fine," she assured him.

He sighed. "You ever take for granted somebody will always be there, and then all of a sudden it gets shoved in your face that they won't? That they've already moved on?"

"I have, but she didn't move on. She was taken from me."

"Your sister." His face paled. "Jesus, I'm sorry."

"No, you're right. We do tend to stick our heads in the sand and ignore that things change." She smiled at him. "I think of you as a friend and I hope you feel the same."

"I do," he said emphatically. "I don't want to lose that with you."

"Me, either." Giving him a quick hug, she stepped back. "I have to go. See you later."

Outside, Blake was leaning against the car. "Everything cool with Jinx?"

"Yeah, it's fine. He apologized again." Unlocking the vehicle, she got in and Blake followed suit.

"Poor guy. It must suck to think you're going to get your girl back, only to realize she's not yours anymore."

"Or never was. Jinx and I were an item for a while, but we sort of ended it by mutual agreement without much fanfare. That is, I *thought* it was mutual, but now I realize that in his mind, he was giving me space until we got back together."

"That won't be a problem for you and the band?"

"No, I don't think so. We're good." She glanced at him as she pulled out of the parking lot. "I'm dropping you off at Guitar Center, right?"

"First night on the job! You won't have me in your hair nearly as much from now on, and before you know it, I'll be able to afford my own place." He beamed at the prospect.

"I'm proud of you, but there's no rush as far as I'm concerned," she assured him. "Take your time, save some money, then explore your options."

"Thanks, Cara. What you and Taylor have done for me these past few months . . . it means the world."

"I'm glad to help, and I know Taylor is, too. I enjoy having you around, but I also remember when I went out on my own for the first time, away from my parents and their expectations of how I should run my life. It's liberating."

"I'll know that feeling soon enough. I've been on my own for a while, but surviving on the street isn't the same as earning an income and being able to pay for a place to live."

"True. You're on the right track now, and I know you'll be fine."

They chatted companionably until Cara dropped him off. "Call me if you need a ride home after work."

"Nah, I'll catch a ride."

"You sure?"

"Totally. I've got my house key, too, so don't worry if you're occupied someplace else." He winked, getting a laugh from her.

"All right. Have a good first shift!"

After he headed inside, she pointed the car for Taylor's house. With each minute closer, the knot in her stomach grew bigger. Maybe she should've gone back last night. He'd been so down, and she'd been too caught up in her own grief to acknowledge his.

Finally, she parked in his driveway and sat for a few moments, gathering her courage. Part of her wanted to turn and run, but her need to be with him overrode her fear of rejection. Getting out of the car, she headed to the porch. Rang his doorbell and waited. When there was no response, she rang it again. Then knocked. Nothing.

Which was odd, because there were lights on in the house. At least one in the living room, dim enough to be a table lamp. She'd spotted a light on toward the back of the house, where the kitchen was located. The idea that he was deliberately ignoring her almost sent her away. The sudden surety that Taylor was not the sort of man to do that kept her focus firmly on finding him.

Something was wrong. Some spineless bastard had nearly killed him, and was probably still after him. What if—

No. She couldn't voice that thought, even in her head. There was a perfectly good explanation for why he wasn't answering. Stepping off the porch, she decided to try another door.

Around back, then. Fortunately it wasn't full dark yet, the Technicolor of twilight still brilliant in the sky. Otherwise she'd be creeped out by walking between his house and the neighbors', jumping at shadows and imagining she saw a hit man behind every bush. She'd laugh at herself, only that scenario was a real possibility.

Rounding the corner of the house, she unlatched the gate in the privacy fence, slipped through, and shut it again. She was contemplating whether she could gain entrance through his French doors when she saw him.

Taylor was sprawled in a lounger on the back deck, three brown bottles—empty ones, she guessed—sitting close to where his hand hung over the armrest. His eyes were closed, the colors of the sunset illuminating his blond hair and playing over his muscular chest. Anger rose in her breast, hot and tight.

The stupid cop was asleep. Or passed out stone-cold, more likely. Snoring away on his deck as if he hadn't a care in the world, as if the situation was rosy and there wasn't a homicidal maniac out to smoke his ass.

Stomping up the steps, she marched over to his lounger, grabbed the backrest, and shook the whole chair hard as she yelled at him. "You dumb-ass! What the fuck are you trying to do?"

He came awake, sitting bolt upright, sputtering and reaching for a gun that wasn't there. "Shit!"

"Do you *want* a bullet between the eyes? Want to

make sure he doesn't miss this time?" Glaring down at him, she waited for an answer. "Well?"

"Jesus," he muttered, swiping a hand down his face. "A simple hello would've been fine."

"What the hell is the matter with you? One blip on our relationship radar and you have a death wish?"

"I'd say my being responsible for your sister's death, not to mention her baby's, is more than just a blip, as you put it." He looked away.

"Oh no." Crouching next to him, she gave him a fierce scowl. "You don't get to do that anymore. I'm not listening to that bullshit one more second, and I want you—no, I demand that you—wipe that self-inflicted guilt out of our lives."

"What?" He gazed up at her, renewed hope lighting his eyes.

"You heard me. Whether this relationship has a chance depends on whether you're going to hang on to the negative energy from that day and use it as a club to beat us both black and blue. If a relationship with me is still something you want to try, that is."

Taking her hand, he clutched it, rubbing her skin with his thumb. "I do, more than anything. I don't want the past to be a wedge that comes between us."

"Then you have to stop. Let it go. I realize now there was nothing you could've done differently to change what Connor did. You have to believe it, too. He went nuts, and that was it."

Searching her face for a long moment, he nodded. "I think I can do that. I know I can, if I have one important thing from you."

"Anything—whatever you need." She meant it.

"I need to know that you forgive me."

Her heart ached for him. Or course he needed that. Had for years, and thought absolution would never be his. And he trusted Cara enough to know that if she gave it to him, she would mean every word.

"Taylor, I forgive you," she said softly, with every ounce of sincerity in her body. "Whatever you believe there is to forgive you for, I give it to you freely. Please be at peace with this so we can move forward."

His expression was like the light breaking through the darkest of clouds. His eyes became moist but his handsome face was filled with a joy she hadn't witnessed in him since they'd met.

"For the first time in four years, I've finally found a reason to wake up in the morning and be happy about it. Until this second, I didn't remember what that felt like."

"I feel the same way." Leaning forward, she placed a soft kiss on his lips. Touched his face, careful of the bandage at his temple. "I was so scared when I found you out here like this. As though you were waiting for that asshole to come and finish you off."

"Part of me was," he confessed. "I couldn't picture you forgiving me after what I told you."

"I'm so sorry for leaving you feeling that way last night." She gestured to where the beer bottles sat on the other side of his lounger. "What about your pain meds? Please tell me you weren't drinking while taking them."

"No. I haven't had any today. Decided I'd rather drown my sorrows. I'm regretting that now." He grimaced.

"I'll bet. Looks like it's aspirin for you."

"I know something else that will make me feel better." Reaching around to cup the back of her head, he pulled her to him and kissed her thoroughly. His tongue delved inside and he tasted like beer, but she didn't mind. Underneath that, he tasted like her man. Clean. Heady.

Arousal sparked, and she was reminded that it had been too long. A few days was too long to be without him surrounding her. She wanted to fix that now.

"I need you," she said into his lips.

"Not nearly as much as I need you. Let's take this inside, shall we?"

"We could be naughty and do the dirty right here on the patio."

"And you fussed at me for *sleeping* out here," he teased. "I don't want to get caught by a killer with my dick out."

Smiling in spite of the seriousness of that possibility, she rose and held out a hand. "Up, then! Let's go!"

Inside, he made sure all the doors were locked, and then set the house alarm. The reason behind that simple act sobered her some, but not enough to damper her enthusiasm for making love with him.

He led her upstairs, and they tumbled onto his bed with her on top, laughing.

Taylor pressed his lips to hers, scattering her thoughts to the wind. She arched into him, deepening the kiss, seeking his closeness again, his warmth. If he'd tasted good, he smelled fantastic. A hint of his spicy cologne lingered and she wondered what scent he wore. Unable to resist, she rested her palms on the solid wall of his chest, enjoying how the strength vibrated from his taut muscles. The anticipation.

Angling his body, he leaned into her, easing her back onto the bedspread. Following her down, he lay half on top of her, their legs entwined. He buried a hand in her hair, brought a lock to his nose. Inhaled.

She relished his weight on top of her. Solid, strong. She could feel his heart thumping in his chest, hard and fast.

"I love seeing you here," he breathed. "Not just in my bed, but with me. Connected to me."

"Yes."

He kissed her again. Not gentle this time, but hot. Hungry. The kiss of a starving man, too long denied—not sex, but the connection he craved to someone who cared. Deeper, his mouth ravaging, tongue thrusting. She wrapped her arms around him, hands splayed across his back, urging him closer. Loving the play of lean muscle under her fingertips.

Taylor wasn't the only one who'd been denied, she realized. How had this man survived nearly four years of isolation and inner pain, of having no one to hold or comfort him? How had she?

She drank him hungrily, wishing away their clothing. Fantasizing about his lithe, naked body sinking into hers. No sooner had she envisioned it than he made it reality, shedding his jeans and shorts, sheathing himself, and then going to work on her clothes.

Soon she was spread naked under him, which was fast becoming her favorite place to be. She wanted to be ravaged. Taken.

He rubbed her clit and the sensitive folds guarding her entrance with his fingers. Heat unfurled between her thighs, became aching desire. She lifted her hips, seeking.

"Please. I need you inside me."

Groaning, he positioned his cock at her entrance. Slid deep and began to move with her, driving them both higher. Spirals of pleasure whirled through her belly as he swiveled his hips in pure, sexual rhythm, setting them both afire.

Elbows braced on either side of her head, he quickened the pace. Thrust as if he couldn't possibly get enough. Sank his cock deep inside her sheath again and again. Faster, harder. She clutched at his shoulders with a cry, her orgasm shattering her senses.

Through a languorous haze, she watched as he threw his head back and stiffened. Sunlit hair fell around his face. His eyes were closed, lashes feathered on his cheeks, lips parted. Lost in ecstasy. The muscles of his biceps and neck corded, and his body shuddered. On and on.

He was the most beautiful man she'd ever seen.

Smiling, she ran a finger down one lean cheek. "Wow, you sure know how to kiss."

Opening his eyes, he gazed down at her and smiled. "I do pride myself on my *kissing*. I pride myself even more on my shower skills."

"Do you, now?" she asked playfully. "Do you think Taylor Jr. could go another round this soon?"

He arched a brow. "Hey, I'm not twenty-one anymore but I know how to please my woman. Trust me on that."

"Oh, I do. No question."

"So, what do you say? Are you game for letting me

put my money where my mouth is? Or my mouth where my cock is, I should say."

She pretended shock. "You are a dirty boy. I don't know if I can take you home to Mama or not."

"You probably shouldn't. But maybe I'm worth the risk."

With that, he gently pulled out of her and then slid off the bed to dispose of the condom. When he returned, he grabbed her hand and hauled her up and out of the bed.

"Shower time. I'll make it the very best one you've ever had." His predatory look made her shiver in anticipation. But when he grabbed his pair of handcuffs from the top of his dresser, her pulse began to pound.

The water was running when he pulled her into the large master bathroom, which was already getting hot. Opening the glass door, he stepped in and pulled her after him, shut it, and yanked her to his front so that their naked, slick bodies were pressed together.

He felt so good. So right. Like he was made to fit perfectly to her like this. To be hers. Thinking that way didn't seem such an impossible fantasy like it did before.

"Turn around and face the wall," he said, voice husky. "Spread your legs."

She did, and felt his palms slide down her sides slowly. Then he gently took each wrist and brought it to the towel rod mounted on the tiled wall. With a snap of each cuff, she was fastened to the rod, helpless and spread for him. Her arousal flared at the knowledge, heightening as he cupped her buttocks. His work-roughened hands made her skin tingle, and she wanted more.

Again, she did as he said. She'd never been one to

take orders from a man when it came to sex, but with Taylor it wasn't threatening or debasing at all. What he did, he did for her pleasure and his. There was nothing wrong about it. Giving in to him was giving them both a ride on nothing but sensation. She trusted him.

His fingers sought her slit, rubbed the tender lips swollen and sensitive from his loving. With the water streaming over them both, it was fantastic. Warmth began to spread through her sex again as he stroked back and forth. Then forward to tease the taut nub of her clit. Back again, then slipping inside her channel. Finger fucking her until she was mindless.

Then he knelt on the shower floor and spread her ass cheeks, completely exposing her to his gaze. No man had ever done this, not quite in this position, leaving her feeling so vulnerable. But instead of scaring her, it turned her on. In a huge way.

She loved being exposed to Taylor. It must be something she enjoyed only with this man, because she'd never felt so free in her life. So sexual. He lapped at the pouty flesh of her folds, slurping, drinking as though she and the water were one and the same and he was receiving life-giving sustenance.

His tongue slipped into her sheath as far as possible, fucking her. No part of her was spared his attentions. He ate her with languid strokes and licks, and she arched into his face, babbling incoherently. She hoped he got the message not to stop. Never had anything made every part of her boil before. She was heat and desire.

She was nothing but flesh. Seeking his mouth, needing

to be devoured. He gave that to her, everything she asked for, until she came undone.

"Oh! God, yes! Fuck!"

Her orgasm shattered every thought except letting that wonderful mouth own her. He lapped her up, riding through the last of the shudders ripping from her head to her toes. She didn't want the ecstasy to end, but it had to. When she was limp, he stood and she heard sounds of him rinsing off. Then he unfastened her wrists, set the cuffs outside the shower, and turned her again, holding her close.

"Thank you," he whispered.

"You're kidding, right? Thank *you*. That was amazing."

"I mean for trusting me. I've never found anyone I was totally compatible with when it came to sex. I mean, outside the act of just getting off. Anyone can do that."

"I do trust you, and I feel the same way. We are compatible, in a lot of ways."

Smiling, he soaped her, then himself. They had fun washing each other, lathering all of those interesting nooks and crannies. Learning each other's bodies intimately. It was fun. And fun with a lover was a definite first.

After rinsing off, they got out and Taylor lavished her with attention, toweling her off and then insisting in carrying her to bed and tucking her in. She was a little sheepish about being babied, but at the same time she loved it. Another new experience—having somebody think of her first.

Even Jenny had never put Cara first. As disloyal as it might be to think that, it was true. She'd never been blind to the fact that Jenny's world existed about three feet around her body, her own wants pretty much all that mattered. But Cara had loved her unconditionally, and Jenny loved her for that, in her own way. Grief made it easy to forget the less pleasant facts about someone.

Settling in beside her, Taylor gathered her close and settled her head on his chest. He enjoyed having her sprawl half on top of him, and she was glad to oblige. He made a nice, warm pillow.

Sated, she drifted into a cozy sleep, and into sweet dreams.

Dreams that were abruptly shattered by the sound of breaking glass and the shriek of the house alarm.

11

Taylor bolted upright, every nerve electrified.

An outright home invasion, despite the alarm that would alert the neighborhood—and his fellow cops. This he should've counted on, but it was something he really hadn't thought the killer would attempt.

Yanking on his jeans, he grabbed his gun from the bedside table. Cara was sitting up, eyes huge in her pale face. Grabbing his discarded ankle holster, he pulled out the smaller handgun and gave it to Cara, who took it and stared at it as though it were venomous.

"Point and shoot," he ordered her. "Stay here, and if anyone comes through that door except me, uniformed cops, or Shane, aim for the center of the body and pull the trigger until there aren't any bullets left."

"Okay! Be careful!"

There was a control panel for the alarm on the wall in his bedroom. He could've shut off the racket, but the more people roused by the noise, the better. Maybe the killer would take off. If not, the noise would mask his progress through the house, and he knew his way around better than anyone.

Even now, backup was coming. He knew that and it reassured him. Moving slowly, he gripped his gun and eased down the stairs. Nothing moved in the moonlit shadows of his living room that he could see, except a curtain billowing in a slight breeze. The broken window. He paused, not moving toward it, knowing the window could just be a way to draw him out. Cautiously, he edged farther into the room, looked to his left.

He saw the huge silhouette a split second before a cough punched the wall next to his head. A silencer. He dove to one side, firing a round, and was gratified by a harsh grunt from his enemy that he heard in spite of the wailing alarm.

The other man stumbled into an end table, knocking a lamp to the floor with a crash. Being wounded sent him into retreat, and he ran as Taylor fired another round. He dove through the broken window and Taylor gave chase.

For a big bastard, he moved fast. Taylor cleared the window in time to see the killer reach the edge of the trees. As he did, Shane roared up in his car and, having already spotted the assailant, threw open his door and gave chase. Shane was closer to the man and vanished into the trees, hot on his heels.

Taylor heard crashing sounds ahead of him and followed. Here the neighborhood gave way to a park used by everyone and enjoyed during the day. At night, the acreage was a fun-house maze of hiding places and obstacles, minus the fun. It was hard to see shit out here, even on a bright night like this one.

At least he had the noise of their pursuit to guide him—until it stopped. He halted too, taking in the shapes of the different types of playground equipment ahead of him. The creek was beyond that, just over the rise. Had the killer taken refuge there, in the brush along the bank? It seemed likely.

Scanning around him, he kept to the trees and tried to make his steps as light as possible. He wanted to call out to Shane, but alerting the killer to his whereabouts would be stupid in the extreme. So he kept going silently until he had the creek in view.

Beside the creek, there was a shape on the ground. At first, he felt a surge of triumph because he'd obviously wounded the suspect badly enough to catch him and get some answers. But the closer he got, a ball of dread began to form in his gut.

The form on the ground wasn't nearly big enough to be his assassin. As he jogged over, the sight that greeted him in the moonlight damned near stopped his heart. Shane was lying half-in, half-out of the creek. Facedown in the water.

"Fuck! Shane!"

Grabbing his partner by the shoulders, he rolled him onto his back and dragged him from the shallows. Safely on the bank, he checked to see if Shane was breathing. He wasn't. But there was a steady pulse in his throat, which was good.

Quickly, he administered CPR, alternating breaths with pushing the water from Shane's lungs. The second his partner began to cough and sputter was the greatest sound ever.

"Thank God." Taylor hung his head in relief.

"Fucker . . ." He had another coughing fit. "Tried to . . . drown me."

"Almost did."

"Thanks for the save." He tried to sit up, so Taylor helped him. "He get away?"

"Yeah. But he's hurt, so maybe he'll turn up in an ER."

"Doubt it. Too big a risk."

"Kind of like busting into my house in the first place." He shook his head in disbelief.

"Why didn't he just shoot me?" Shane wondered aloud.

"Simple—he's not getting paid to kill you. One cop is enough. So he slowed you down, knowing I'd come along and tend to you instead of chasing him. He's able to get away."

"Makes sense."

"You need the paramedics?"

"No, man. I don't want to scare the crap out of Daisy and Drew if I can help it. They've had more than enough scares when it comes to me."

As they picked their way back to Taylor's house, Shane coughed some more, but basically seemed all right. By the time they trudged onto the front lawn, his place was swarming with their brethren and curious neighbors. Among them stood Cara, looking lost until she spotted him and Shane heading her way.

Breaking into a run, she flew into his arms and held him tight. "I was so scared! Where'd you go?"

"Chased him to the park, but he got the drop on Shane. I had to give up pursuit."

Looking to his partner, she eyed his wet clothes and hair. "Are you all right?"

"Never better." He punctuated the claim with another cough.

Taylor snorted. "You'll probably end up with some sort of weird flesh-eating bacteria from breathing in that nasty creek water."

Shane sent him a glare. "Thanks for that image."

"I'm always here to help."

One of the uniforms, Cunningham, ambled up to their small group and hitched a thumb toward the house. "Think he'll come back tonight?"

"No. Honestly, I think he'll try a different tactic next time."

"We'll keep extra patrols on the street tonight and the next few days, just in case."

"I appreciate it." The killer would just wait until they were gone to strike again and they all knew it. But it was peace of mind for now.

"No prob. A couple of guys found some plywood in your garage, and they're boarding up the hole from the broken window. That'll do until you get somebody out to fix it."

"Thanks, big guy."

The redheaded cop waved off his thanks and went to join the others. Shane told him good night, claiming he needed to get home and change, then swill his mouth out with bleach to kill the microbes that were no doubt partying in his system this very minute.

After they went back inside, Taylor looked at Cara.

"I'll understand if you want to go home. Or somewhere far away from me, at least until this is over."

"No."

"You could go back to California, stay with your mother—"

"I'd rather boil my eyeballs and eat them for breakfast."

In spite of the situation, he laughed. "Well, in that case. Want to try and get some sleep?"

"Or something."

It was a long while before they got any sleep, restful or otherwise.

In light of the previous night's events, Rainey gave him the day off.

Taylor wanted to get the hell out of Dodge, and was happy when Cara felt the same way. She took off from her bartending job that evening so they'd have the entire day and night to themselves before reality intruded again.

A day of much-needed fun started with breakfast and extended to some shopping in Nashville, a movie, and a drink at a bar on Second Avenue. That didn't mean Taylor was less vigilant. He watched every move from anyone nearby, especially since he now knew the assailant by his sheer size. He couldn't understand why this asshole kept coming for him, but he'd have answers soon.

"You up for a drive down by the dam?"

"Sounds nice."

The evening shadows were getting long when they pulled in to the state park down on the Cumberland. He found an isolated spot to park and grabbed a blanket from the back of his car. Then they headed for an even more secluded place close to the river, one where they couldn't be seen by anyone for miles around.

His kind of place.

Taylor spread the blanket and they stretched out, with him simply holding her and enjoying the closeness. Soon, her hand began to roam and his cock took immediate notice.

He smiled. "Christ, what are you doing to me?"

Her hand slid up his thigh, brushed the telltale bulge pushing at the zipper of his jeans. "Isn't it obvious? Take them off."

"Out here?"

"Nobody has followed us all day." She grinned wickedly. "Nobody can see, either. Let's play."

Taylor stared at Cara, his body humming with pent-up sexual tension. His cock was now hard as an iron spike. Every nerve ending on sensual overload. Hell, he'd never been a saint. And knowing a special woman like Cara, a lady who was privy to all his painful secrets, who wanted him in spite of his past, proved to be more than he could battle. Not that he ever tried very hard where she was concerned.

She sat with her full lips turned up in a gentle smile, waiting for him to make the next move. His call. God help them both, he had to touch her. Had to possess this goddess with her purple-streaked hair framing her pretty face. Her breasts were small but perfect, her slightly darker nipples erect little pebbles. Begging for his fingers. His tongue.

With effort, he dragged his gaze back to her lovely face. His hands shook as he cupped her cheeks, brushed his thumbs over her lips. He had to be sure she understood the score with him.

"Our past was one obstacle to overcome, and we're doing it. But in my line of work, what happened to Shane tonight can happen to any of us anytime. You've got to know what you're signing up for with me."

She lifted a brow. "You keep people safe, but to do that you're sometimes at risk. I understand that and I won't be held hostage by fear. I trust in the future now like I never have before."

"You humble me, baby. What did I do to deserve you?"

"Oh, Taylor. Make love to me," she whispered. *"Now."*

Admiring her, he skimmed his palms down the graceful curve of her neck to her slim shoulders. Brushed his fingers across the swell of her breasts, her puckered little nipples. Marveled as always at the sensation, the pleasure of touching her.

My woman.

Reverently, he helped her undress; then he rolled the taut peaks between his fingers, pinching them lightly. Bracing her weight with her hands flat on the ground, she leaned back, spreading those long, toned legs. Offering herself to him.

Drinking in her natural beauty, he groaned, his heart pounding at the base of his throat. She was all silvery skin, curves of breasts, and lean hips, a dark nest of curls at the V of welcoming thighs.

He stood next to her, unzipping his jeans, pushing

them past his hips. His erection sprang free, hot and hard. Throbbing to the point of real pain. Already a drop of cum beaded at the head of his penis. Eager to be buried deep, shoot inside her heat.

Smiling, she sat up on her knees and tugged his jeans to his ankles, pulling them as he stepped free. She laid them aside and wrapped her fingers around his erection, stroked, swirled the pearly drop around the head of his penis. He gasped at the wonderful, wicked bolt of desire sweeping him.

"Cara, I'm not going to last," he croaked. "I can't—"

"Shh, it's okay. Don't hold back."

Her tongue laved the tip, licking away the sticky wetness as she continued to pump his shaft. He shuddered, balls tightening, the heat rising in his loins, on the verge of losing control too soon. Her other hand found his sac, kneaded gently, and his breathing hitched.

Unable to help himself, he let his gaze drift down to watch. The sight nearly undid him. Beautiful Cara, kneeling between his spread legs. Working his cock with her silky touch, her warm, wet little mouth. Taking obvious enjoyment in reducing him to a mindless puddle. Demanding all of him.

Oh yeah. She can have me. Whenever, however she wants. From now on.

She took his length deep, sheathing his cock to the very base. He buried his hands in her wild hair, closing his eyes in ecstasy. Hers now. All hers.

"Cara. Oh, God!"

He pumped his hips slowly, in tandem to the pull of her sweet mouth. She sucked eagerly, teeth scraping, tongue sweeping the ridge of his dick. So damned good. He wanted more. Harder, deeper. How could she take all of him? He didn't want to hurt her.

Then he wasn't capable of thinking anymore. She grabbed his hips, urging his thrusts. There was nothing but the rising throb of heat threatening to burst him into a million shards. Blow him apart.

He gave himself over. To Cara. Gave her what they both wanted. Fucked her hard and fast. "Just like that. Fuck, yeah—so good."

With a hoarse cry, he stiffened. Shot into her, pumping on and on. Riding the waves crashing through him until he stood trembling on legs that barely held him upright.

When the last of the aftershocks had faded, she released him and wiped her mouth with the edge of her discarded shirt. His rubbery knees folded and he sank down in front of her. She looked at him with a saucy grin, and his heart turned over.

Unbidden, a surge of raw emotion took him by surprise. Happiness swelled in his chest, real and powerful. And a fierce protectiveness. He was falling for her, and he wanted a future for them. Given the chance, he'd send the son of a bitch trying to take that away from them straight to hell.

"Mmm," she purred, slanting him a sexy look. "I loved doing you. I think you've corrupted me."

"I like the sound of that."

"And I don't know if you're ready to hear this, but it's more than sex to me between us. You're special to me and I . . ." Trailing off, she bit her lip.

He knew what she'd been about to say. She might not

be ready to say it, but joy spread through him, rain on a barren, parched desert. No one had ever told him he was special. Except his parents long ago.

The long, lonely years, it seemed, were coming to an end. She'd brought him happiness, and he wanted to give in return. Something to express the wonder of having his eyes opened, a blind man able to see at last. She was a miracle.

He retrieved his shirt, spread it on the ground behind her with great care. Taking her chin, he kissed her. Reveled in the dark flavor of himself on her lips. Him and no one else, if he had his way. Ever. The knowledge aroused him all over again, his softened cock waking anew.

He laid Cara back gently on his shirt, following her down. Cradling her, he pressed butterfly kisses to her lips, nose, chin, forehead. She rested a hand on top of his head, running his hair through her fingers, and he loved the sensation.

Dipping lower, he turned his attention to her breasts. Capturing one tight pebble in his teeth, he groaned, sucking it. Feasting like the starving man he was. She arched into him, gripping his head, gasping encouragement. He swirled one peak, then the other, as one hand skimmed down her flat belly.

His fingers found the springy nest of curls and lower still, to her wet sex. Her thighs parted for him, hips urging his touch. He stroked the hot, sensitive nub, the pouting lips, slick and ready for him. Suckled her breasts, teased her clit until she writhed, unable to take any more.

"Taylor, please," she moaned, yanking his hair.

He lifted his head, regret spearing his gut. "I have protection, but it's at the house."

"I'm on the pill and I'm healthy."

Her words sent a thrill through him. "I'm healthy, too. Cara, baby, are you sure?"

"Yes! Now, please . . ."

He needed no further encouragement. Positioning his body over hers, he guided the tip of his cock to her moist opening. Worked it in slow, making certain he wouldn't hurt her.

And in one long, delicious stroke, pushed deep. Her tight sheath gripped his cock with silken heat. She clutched his shoulders as he began to pump. In as far as possible, his balls rubbing against her bottom. Relishing the feeling of being buried inside her. Then out, inch by wicked inch. Skin deep, inside her again. Wanting to crawl in and never come out. Fusing their souls.

Never, ever anything like this. The power of their connection shook him. Humbled him. She was a gift, a treasure. He held her close, making sweet love to her under the waning light. That's what she deserved, and he gave all he had to give.

Her nails dug into his back. "Oh yes. Yes. Faster!"

The feral male animal in him came undone. *Mine.* Clutching her tight, thrusting hard, their bodies slapping together. Hot, blazing, burning him up. Higher and higher. *Gonna explode—*

"Come with me, baby," he demanded.

Hips bucking, she cried out. Her release shattered him. Seated deep, he let her carry him over the edge into oblivion. Her orgasm milked his cock as he spurted into her, harder than before. More than he'd thought possible.

Raising his head, he looked into her face and swept a damp tendril of hair from her eyes. She gazed at him, smiling dreamily, a woman well satisfied. A new emotion clogged his throat. One he wasn't brave enough to name. Yet.

She kissed his shoulder. "Wow. You're an awesome lover, handsome. I saw stars."

Damned if he wasn't smiling back. Hell, he'd have to be dead not to feel a bit of smug male satisfaction. Crazy how a guy's fortunes could turn on a dime.

"Naw. I was inspired by a gorgeous lady—that's all."

"Sweet talker." She reached up, played with his hair.

In spite of himself, he laughed. "Jesus, I don't deserve you."

"Kayne?"

"Hmm?"

"Shut up."

"Yes, ma'am."

He sank willingly into her arms once more, set about making up for all those lost, lonely years. As he made love to her again, a realization warmed him.

A man didn't have to die to touch heaven, after all.

The weekend was bright and clear.

Cara had been on alert for the rest of the week after the terrifying break-in at Taylor's house. More and more, they didn't want to be apart. They also didn't want their nemesis to be able to pinpoint a set schedule. So they alternated between staying at his house or hers, in no set pattern. They were at her house a bit more, only because Blake grumbled about the precautions and the fact that they didn't want him staying alone.

However, the complaints had lessened when Taylor explained how Blake could be used as leverage with Taylor or Cara. He could be kidnapped or worse. That truthful information went a long way toward changing his sour disposition.

Another thing that made Blake happy was that when Taylor went over to Chris's house to tinker with the old Chevelle, Taylor invited him to tag along. Blake was thrilled. He'd been buzzing like a fly around Taylor, Shane, Drew, and Chris all morning, asking a zillion questions about every single feature of Chevelles, and extolling the various virtues of every muscle car ever produced.

Rolling their eyes, Cara and Daisy had unanimously declared it must be a guy thing, and retreated to the house. The two of them were there now, sipping iced tea and getting to know each other better.

Cara learned that Daisy, Taylor, Chris, and Shane had been instrumental in solving the mysterious death of Drew's famous father, a veteran NFL player. Drew, being a scared sixteen-year-old, had been keeping some heart-wrenching and dangerous secrets in that regard, and the fallout had nearly destroyed their family before it had a chance to form. The boy was recovering now, and though he loved his dad, he'd really bonded with Daisy.

"I'm so happy for you guys," Cara said with a smile.

"It goes to show that family truly means the people who love and support you."

"You sound like you know a bit about that."

"My family sucked, to be honest. My mother is still alive, but she's an addict. A rich one who wears all the right clothes and has cool friends, but is still an addict."

"I'm sorry to hear that." The other woman frowned.

"Don't be. It is what it is."

"You seem to be forming a family yourself," Daisy observed. "You're rather fond of Blake and Taylor."

"I am," she admitted. "I'm more than *fond* of Taylor."

"Falling?"

"Yeah."

"He's an easy man to love, or so I'd think if I didn't have Shane."

"He is. He's awesome, and I feel like a teenager every time I think about him."

"I'm glad. Taylor needed someone to love, and I'm happy it's you."

"That's so nice of you to say." The kind words had her tearing up some. "If you knew our history, you might not feel I was right for him."

"I already know," the other woman admitted. "I hope you don't mind that Shane filled me in."

"A few weeks ago, I might have minded. Now, not so much. He and I have made our peace with each other as far as my sister's death."

"That's good. Holding on to pain will only make you more unhappy." Daisy smiled. "Want to see what the guys are up to out there?"

"Sure."

Strolling outside, they joined the men and observed one of the strange male-bonding rituals involving messing with cars. Cara thought cars were neat, but couldn't quite get as excited as the guys.

"So, what are you gonna do with her now that we've just about got her running again?" Chris asked, patting the hood.

"I don't know. I've had this one for a long time and she's special to me, but I don't need two cars. Especially since I've got the Challenger. It's newer."

"But the Chevelle is a classic," Blake insisted. "You can sell it!'

"I never said anything about selling it, but that's an idea. The upkeep on two muscle cars, the insurance, the registrations, inspections, all that shit. Too much."

"Then sell the Challenger. It's new, not a classic."

"I like driving it, though. I don't want to sell it. I sure wish there was another solution." At that, the three adult men exchanged knowing looks. They'd obviously planned something, but Cara didn't know what. A glance at Daisy, who shrugged, confirmed she didn't, either.

"I guess there's only one thing to do," Taylor said, pulling the key ring from his pocket. "I'll have to let someone use it so it doesn't get rusty sitting in my driveway."

"What?" Blake looked horrified. "You're going to let someone else use it? You can't just hand over the keys to a classic car to some— some stranger!"

"Who said it would be a stranger?"

Taylor was grinning at the kid. And he still wasn't getting it. "Dude, take the keys."

"Huh? Why?" The boy appeared totally confused.

"Because you're the one I want to drive my car."

Blake was dumbfounded. "But—but—"

"Holy shit!" Drew exclaimed.

"You've got two jobs now, and you need transportation. I've got an old car that's been rebuilt and is not going to do well if it's allowed to gather dust. It's a win-win situation for everybody."

"I . . . I don't know what to say." The boy's eyes filled with tears.

"Just say you'll car-sit for me. And when you're on your feet, if you want to keep the car, we'll work out something."

"You mean it?"

"Yes, I mean every word."

Blake closed the distance and hugged Taylor hard. "Thank you. I'll never forget this."

"I'm glad I was able to do it. I almost sold the thing for scrap when it took a dunk in the river. Now I'm glad I didn't."

"Me, too!" Taylor glanced at Drew, practically vibrating. "Want to go for ride? If it's okay with everyone else?"

"Fine with me. The car should be good to go. I guess we'll test the theory."

The boys climbed in and Blake fired up the car, which emitted a throaty purr. After getting a stern warning from all three men to drive safely, he waved and pulled out onto the street.

"That was a damned decent thing you just did, partner," Shane said. "Who knew you had it in you?"

Taylor knew he was teasing but punched him, anyway, and everyone laughed. It was just about as perfect a day as they'd had.

It was to be the last one for a long while.

Taylor received a text from Chris shortly after he arrived at the station on Monday. *Got info 4 u. C me.*

Curious, he wandered to Chris's desk and found the man pouring over lines and lines of print with names and numbers. "Are those what I think?"

Chris looked up, blinking at Taylor for a few seconds as though he couldn't see very well. Then it passed and the man shrugged. "If you mean Max Griffin's phone records, then yes."

"And are any of them ringing more bells than the other?"

"You could say that." He looked up at Taylor. "Most of the calls, including the day he died, were between Griffin and a man named Dmitri Constantine."

Taylor's heart jolted and he stared at Chris. "I know that name. Constantine was . . ." he broke off. How much to tell Chris? As it turned out, not much.

"Constantine was the name of the man who was with you in that house in Los Angeles. He was there the day Connor Wright went crazy and he was killed." He gave Shane and apologetic look. "I do my homework."

"How could Griffin talk to a dead man?"

"He can't. Damon Constantine was the man in the house with you. He was Dmitri's brother."

"Meaning, if this whole thing with the hit man ties back to that day, then—"

"Then you could have a revenge plot in motion," Shane put in, joining them.

"But why wait four years to make me·pay for getting his brother killed?"

Shane tapped another paper and held it up. "He recently got out of prison. He went in right after the slaughter because of some money-laundering shit against him. White-collar stuff."

"All right. Why do I get the feeling there's more?"

"Because there is. Three guesses who worked for Dmitri as his PA."

Taylor stared at them, his blood beginning to pump. This could be the missing link. The tie they needed to wrap this up in a neat bow. "Jennifer Wright."

"Exactly," Chris said. "Now, it could be nothing. It could be that the Constantines and Griffin knew each other through Jennifer Wright, and nothing more than that. Maybe Max and Dmitri kept in touch, nothing more sinister than that."

"And donkeys fly," Taylor said. "If they're such good acquaintances and all, how come Dmitri wasn't down here in our faces, demanding we find Max's killer?"

"Good point."

"So, the question is, when do I leave for a little side trip to L.A.?"

"As fast as you can book it—two seats, because I'm going with you," Shane said.

"I can handle this."

"But you're not going to alone, period. Not with some psycho Terminator asshole after you. Forget it."

Taylor took off early to pack, and Cara was there

when he got home. All the way to his house, he'd been in a dilemma. He couldn't leave her and Blake unprotected.

"What's going on?" she asked, following him into the bedroom and watching as he got out a small gym bag.

"Your sister worked for Dmitri Constantine. Did you know this?"

"Of course I did. I could've told you who she worked for, but it never came up."

"This is important. Jenny worked for Dmitri. Max knew all of you. Phone calls between Dmitri and Max continued up until Max's death."

"That doesn't mean anything by itself. But on the whole, it's pretty curious. I can't imagine what they'd have to discuss."

"Was Max acting as Dmitri's attorney?"

"Not that I'm aware of." She paused. "Do you think he had control of Max?"

"It's a possibility. And if he lost that control, say, if Max was running here to warn you about something, then he might be forced to act."

Cara looked sick. "My God."

"Yeah." He sighed. "Shane and I need to interview this Dmitri guy. Where can you and Blake go while I'm gone? I'll fly out this afternoon and stay overnight. Come home tomorrow."

"Where I'll stay won't be a problem. I'm going with you."

"Cara, no. It's not safe."

"And it's safe here? I'll take my chances with you, where I'll be a lot safer."

He couldn't argue that. "What about Blake?"

"Why don't we see if Daisy minds if he stays with her and Drew, since Shane will be gone, too?"

"Good idea."

In an hour, the details were settled and Blake knew where to stay after work. Taylor and Cara headed to the airport, where they met Shane.

Time to finally get some answers.

But he had a feeling he wasn't going to get the ones he needed.

12

The flight was turbulent, and Taylor hoped that wasn't a portent of things to come.

That and the ever-present smog, one fact of life in Los Angeles that he'd hated with every fiber of his being. He much preferred the clear blue skies of Tennessee to this crap any day.

Next to him, Cara's head was resting on his shoulder. Across the aisle, Shane played a game on his computer tablet. Or he could be planning World War III. Who knew?

At last they came in for a landing, the smoothest part of the flight. Cara stirred and gave him a tired smile, and he gave her a kiss. After collecting their luggage, they hailed a cab and found a cheap motel room not far from the airport, in case they had to make a run for it. They didn't plan on staying longer than necessary.

At the motel, they checked in, Shane in his own room. They'd stay tonight and rest, see Dmitri tomorrow. Or, rather, he and Shane would make the visit while Cara remained out of sight. Once they had their impressions of Constantine, maybe dropped some bait, they'd leave for home.

Taylor stretched out with Cara, pulling her into his body. "You hungry?"

"Not for dinner."

"You're insatiable."

"Only when you're on the menu."

He grinned, liking that. A lot.

"How's your head?" she asked, touching the smaller bandage he'd switched to.

"Better. The flight gave me a bit of a headache, but I'm fine."

"Why don't we rest for a while? I'm tired."

She was probably just worried about him, and the thought lightened his heart. He fell asleep with the soft sound of her breathing filling his head.

Reaching over, Cara brushed her fingers over Taylor's whiskered cheek. She didn't want to wake him, but she couldn't help herself. Drinking in the sight of him, she touched his beloved face. Traced his brow, his sensual mouth. Thick blond hair fell around his face. Nuzzling her hand, he didn't speak, just opened his eyes and gazed at her. Such longing and tenderness radiating from them, it took her breath away.

"Taylor . . . I love you." There. For better or worse, she'd taken the plunge. From his sharp intake of breath, whether she'd done the right thing remained to be seen. God knows she hadn't been able to hold it in any longer, especially now.

Pulling her into his arms, he crushed her against his

chest, buried his face in her neck. "Oh, God, Cara. I love you, too. So damned much."

Wrapping her arms around him, she hugged him close. Reveled in his solid warmth, his spicy male scent. Listened to his heartbeat thumping a tempo under her ear, steady and strong. The idea of that strength and vitality suddenly being stilled forever was unthinkable. Horrendous.

Drawing back slightly, she lifted her chin. "Make love to me."

Tonight, neither of them questioned whether *making love* was what they were doing. The promise in his gaze was more meaningful than any pretty words he could've whispered.

Taylor pulled his T-shirt over his head, lean muscles rippling with the movement. He dropped it to the floor, then unzipped his jeans, sliding them over his hips and legs. Kicking them aside, he grabbed the edge of her white tee, tugged it up and off.

"You're so beautiful," he said gruffly. "Let me taste."

Bending, he captured a nipple in his mouth, flicking it to a peak with his tongue. His teeth grazed the hard little nub, and she gasped at the tiny needles of pleasure. He repeated his attentions on the other nipple, then sank to his knees in front of her.

Tilting his head up, he kept his eyes locked with hers as he hooked his fingers in the waistband of her jeans and underwear. Slowly, he eased them down her thighs. She wiggled out and he pushed them away with a low, sensual command.

"Spread your legs for me, sweetheart."

She complied and—*Oh, shit.* The decadent sight of

her gorgeous, naked man kneeling at her feet sent her pulse racing. His mouth was so close to her sex, his warm breath tickled a bit. But his gaze remained on her face as his strong hands spanned her waist.

"This is what you deserve, my girl. To be cherished, worshipped. Held and loved for the rest of your life, by a man who can give you his soul." He paused, his voice hoarse as he went on.

"I can give you those things for as long as I have breath left in my body. Baby, I hope that's enough, because in the end, I'm a humble cop. My heart is all I have to give."

If she hadn't been a total goner before, that clinched the deal. This man who kept both sorrow and joy buried inside had stripped his soul bare for her, offered his heart on a silver platter. If possible, the bond between them deepened, her love for him intensified to the point of physical pain.

She touched his cheek, tears pricking her eyes. "Oh, honey. You're all I need, never doubt that. I'll grow old loving you."

A myriad of raw emotions flashed in the depths of his eyes, and his jaw tightened. His bittersweet thoughts telegraphed as clearly as if he'd spoken aloud.

"Love me," she whispered.

Leaning into her, he pressed gentle kisses to her tummy. Her flesh quivered in anticipation as he worked lower, nuzzling the downy thatch between her thighs. One finger found her moist slit, rubbing along the nether lips, stroking. He spread the wetness, gliding deliciously around the sensitive clit.

"Ohh, Taylor . . ."

"More?"

"Yes, *yes*."

He spread her folds, fastened his mouth to her throbbing sex. His talented tongue laved every inch, dipping, exploring. Suckling like a man enjoying a piece of caramel, he ate her. Unhurried, skillfully. Panting, she clung to his shoulders to keep from falling over with sheer pleasure. His hot, wet mouth sucked and pulled, driving her close to the edge, so close.

She yanked at his hair. "Stop! Fuck me, *please*."

Without moving, he looked up at her. His gaze glittered with pure male lust, and no small amount of satisfaction. "You sure?" More flicking with that devil tongue.

"Oh! Yes, now!"

Chuckling, he stood and scooped her into his arms. He deposited her on the bed, then crawled between her splayed legs. Lord, he was a pagan god. A very hungry pagan god, lean muscles bunching as he guided the tip of his jutting cock to her opening.

He was beautiful. All hers.

Pushing inside, he seated himself to the hilt, covering her body with his. Filling her. Cradling her in his arms, he began to move, sliding out, the head of his penis nudging her entrance, then in again. Inch by glorious inch.

She held him tight, fingers digging into his back as he made slow, sweet love to her. Entwined, they moved together, lost in the miracle of two people fusing their souls. Creating a bond even death could never break.

Angling, he stroked her clit, increasing the tempo. The fire became a blazing inferno and she matched his thrusts, hips rising to meet him. Burying her face in his neck, she urged him on.

"Oh, Taylor, yes, yes! Faster, harder!"

"God, baby."

Pressing her close to his heart, he loved her with abandon. They flew higher, the rhythm of their bodies as perfectly attuned as a symphony. *This is the way it should be. So wonderful, so right.*

"Cara, oh, Jesus . . ."

One thrust, two, then he buried himself deep, throwing his head back with a hoarse cry. Stiffening, he came deep inside her, the hard, hot rush of his release triggering her own. The explosion of heat and electricity rocked her and she clung to him, throbbing against his cock.

"I love you," he whispered raggedly. "God, how I love you."

Gradually, the storm abated to gentle waves and she floated back into her body. Smiling, she reached up and raked his hair out of his face. He was gazing at her with so much love and something like reverence.

She swiped a tear with her thumb, throat constricting. "Love you more."

Laughing, he rolled to his back, scooping her into his arms. She settled happily against his chest, hugging him close.

"Damn," he sighed with contentment.

"You tired?"

"Yeah," he admitted.

"How are you feeling?"

"No worse than when I woke up earlier."

"Which means?"

A pause. He kissed the top of her head. "I still feel a little off. Like the world isn't totally on its axis."

"Dizzy?"

"Some. Listen, don't worry about me, baby. By tomorrow, I'm sure I'll be fine."

He seemed positive, but that didn't erase her worry by a long shot. "Sleep," she said, caressing his face.

But from the even rise and fall of his chest, the directive wasn't necessary.

He was already gone.

Cara had one item of closure she needed to attend to the next morning before Taylor went with Shane to shake down Constantine.

"I need to see my mother," she told him. "And I'd like for you to go with me."

He considered her for a moment, before nodding. "If it's important to you, I'll be glad to."

"I think I mentioned this before, but my mother isn't the most pleasant person to deal with. She's an addict and might be confused or hateful. Or she could seem normal and greet us with open arms. Either way, I won't be coming back here often, and I'd like for her to meet you."

"You want her to know your life turned out fine without her money, addictions, and neuroses?" he guessed.

She smiled. "You already know me so well. Yeah, I guess you could say I want her to know I'm fine. That I chose not to turn out like her."

"I can understand that."

"Can you? I'll bet your parents are awesome."

"They were awesome, but they passed away years ago."

"I'm so sorry."

"It's all right. I may not know firsthand how bad parents can be, but I've dealt with plenty of people who are how you describe your mother. I can handle her."

"Thanks for doing this," she said with feeling.

Shane drove them to a secluded estate in the hills outside L.A. and whistled as they pulled up to the gate with the code box. "Jeez. I could get used to this."

"Maybe, if you didn't have to live with my mother."

"Point taken." She told Shane the code and he pulled up the long, curving driveway, parking in front. "I'll wait out here."

Even though he was joking, he didn't have to tell her not to take too long. No way would she stay longer than necessary. At the front door, she simply used her key and let them in. The first person she saw was Lettie, the woman who took care of the house and her mother. She was paid well to do a big job, and she was happy to see Cara.

"Oh! Welcome home! It's been too long!" She eyed Taylor with appreciation. "And who is this handsome man?"

Hands off, Lettie. "This is my boyfriend, Taylor Kayne."

"Nice to meet you, sir." Giving a little bow, she faced Cara again. "I'll get your mother."

When the woman disappeared, Cara led Taylor into the formal living room, where they remained standing. He sensed her need not to get too comfortable.

"Boyfriend?" he asked with a grin.

"Was I overstepping?"

"Are you kidding? I love you and you love me. I like the sound of being yours and you being mine."

"Me, too."

Taylor remained collected but she couldn't help fidgeting while they waited. She was glad at least one of them was calm. Especially when her mother walked in, impeccably dressed in beige linen pants and a silk blouse, her hair fixed and sprayed so that not a strand could move if a tornado swept through.

"Cara, darling." Moving forward, she embraced Cara in a hug that was like greeting a marble statue. Stepping back, she eyed her daughter's ripped jeans and glittery T-shirt with distaste. "You always come home looking like a refugee from Woodstock."

"Wrong era, Mom." *At least I don't take fifteen kinds of drugs like they did then—and, oh, like you do.* But she didn't say that. "How have you been?"

Her mother scrutinized the two of them. "Doing fine." She eyed Taylor like he was a bug. Or a juicy steak. With her, one could never tell. "And who are you?"

"Detective Taylor Kayne," he said, extending his hand. After a moment, she took it briefly in one of those limp grasps. If Taylor was disgusted, he said nothing.

"I'm Melinda Evans. I'm sure my sweet girl has told you all about me."

"Nothing but good things," Taylor said, lying through his teeth. He rewarded her mother with a broad smile that made him look like a movie star.

Melinda blinked at him, then smiled shyly, clearly taken with him. "Well, thank you. Though I must say that's a surprise."

"I just came by to introduce you to Taylor. He works for the Sugarland Police, and since his home is there, that's where I'm staying."

"You're not moving home?" Melinda actually seemed a bit sad about that.

"No. I have my own life there, but I'll visit. And you can come there, hear my band play sometime."

"I don't know—"

"And you can stay with me, meet some hot, eligible bachelor cops," she couldn't resist adding.

That perked her mom right up. "Oh? Well, maybe sometime I'll have to make a trip. When I'm feeling better." She shot an uncertain glance at Taylor before looking at her daughter again. "And I am feeling better. Much."

Code for "being sober again."

"Good for you." She gave her mom a genuine smile, and was surprised to have it returned. "Have you been careful, not left the house like I told you?"

"Of course, but I don't understand what this is all about," she complained.

"I'll tell you about it soon, okay? I just can't get into it right now."

"All right. Stay for lunch?"

"I'm sorry, but we can't." For the first time in ages, she actually regretted that. Her mother didn't act human very often, and she was going to miss out. "Next time?"

"Of course." Her smile looked sad. Lonely. "Taylor, it was nice to meet you. Perhaps I'll get out your way in a few weeks."

"It would be my pleasure to have you come for a visit. Let's set something up soon."

Now her mom looked outright pleased—a minor miracle. "I'd love that. We'll discuss it."

Melinda walked them to the front door, and before Cara left, she got a hug that was much different from the one she'd received when she arrived. "Be happy," her mother said.

"I will," she whispered. "I love him."

"And he loves you, I can tell. Treat him better than I treated your father, all right?"

"No worries there."

One last hug and she headed to the SUV. As Shane pulled out, she kept glancing backward until she couldn't see the house anymore.

"Your mom doesn't seem like such an ogre."

"She's not too bad when she's sober, but she's usually full of cutting remarks. Finds fault with everything. She must've liked you a lot, because that's the warmest I've seen her in ages."

"Hey, I have that effect on all the women," he teased.

"Ha! Just don't practice too much."

"Only on you, baby."

"God, you two are making me gag," Shane complained. But a laugh ruined his attempt at grumpiness. "Can we focus on the mission here?"

That sobered them up. Time for the boys to coax Dmitri into coming out to play.

Shane walked beside Taylor into the fancy office building. "So, we mess with him a little. See if he seems to be hiding something, and bait the hook."

"Sounds about right."

"The problem with baiting hooks is sometimes you catch a shark."

"It's what we do."

They walked into the building, secure in the knowledge that Cara was inside the rented SUV, waiting for them. The lobby was busy, and a harried receptionist missed their arrival when she turned her head to address someone. They slipped past and rode the elevator to the tenth floor, then got out and walked straight down the carpeted hallway leading to Dmitri's office.

Nobody stopped them, probably because they looked like they belonged, wearing their suits and charming smiles leveled to disarm anyone who thought to get in their way. No one did. Until a young secretary outside Constantine's office looked up to see them headed for his door.

"Do you have an appointment? You can't go in there!"

Shane winked. "This won't take long, honey."

They strolled inside to find Dmitri on the phone. His dark eyes widened when he saw them—and something unpleasant passed over his features when his attention settled on Taylor.

"Gentlemen? May I help you?" His tone suggested he'd rather have them escorted out.

"Maybe," Taylor said. Time to mix the truth with a lie or two, see if they bore fruit. "I'm Detective Taylor Kayne of the Sugarland, Tennessee, Police Department, and this is my partner, Detective Shane Ford. We're here about a murder case we're working back home, and it's come to our attention that you know the victim. We're hoping you can shed some light on that for us."

"Me? What would I know about a murder? Who's this victim?"

"His name is Max Griffin."

"Max? He's dead?" His surprise sounded fake. Nor did he show much remorse.

"I'm afraid so. He was shot in the forehead, point-blank range, in one of our motels. We don't like that sort of thing happening in our town, and we want to catch who did this."

"Yes, of course. But I don't know how I can help."

Reaching into his jacket, Taylor removed a folded sheaf of papers. "You can start by telling us what you and Griffin talked about on your frequent phone calls. Especially the one he made to you right before he was murdered."

Again, the predatory look. More than dislike, it was akin to hatred. "I don't recall. We were golf buddies and occasionally had dinner together. Raised funds for charities with our wives—things like that."

"Your wife? Are you married?"

"Yes." His face grew pinched. "Does that matter?"

"You tell me. Does it?"

"I think not."

"Okay." Purposely, he switched gears fast. "You used to have a personal assistant named Jennifer Wright, didn't you?"

The man actually paled, though he did his best to maintain a calm outward appearance. "Yes, I did. She died when her crazy husband killed her and my brother in a stand-off—as you well know, since you were there, Detective."

Ooh, careful there. Your shark's teeth are showing.

"How would you recall that I was the officer inside the house that day? It's been four years." He tried to sound baffled.

"I remember everything about that horrible time. I read the papers, and the news wouldn't stop talking about it."

"I see. How did you feel about Jenny, Mr. Constantine? Was she more than just a PA to you?"

"I don't see how that's any of your concern," he said in a cold voice. "But the answer is no."

"Murder is always our concern," he replied in friendly tone. "Especially when a new one has something in common with an old one."

There could be no missing the subtle threat in Taylor's voice. He was serving notice to Dmitri, letting him know they'd made the connection back to him.

Taylor went on while the man in front of them seethed. "We don't like loose ends, and we'll tie them sooner rather than later. You know what I think?" He leaned forward, one hand on Constantine's desk. "I believe Jenny was more than a PA to you, and that you can't risk that ever getting out to your wife, to the people you work with. Prison was enough of a black mark. But this?"

"Shut up about Jennifer," he snapped. "You don't know anything."

"I know I can subpoena her medical records to determine whose baby she was actually carrying. What do you think the tests would show? How far did you go to make sure Max would cover up your mistakes? How far did you go when he refused to play your games anymore?"

Bingo. Cold rage was etched on the man's face. Here

in his own offices, he could do nothing to really shut them up. Taylor gave him a smirk and walked out, Shane right at his side.

When they were safely downstairs, Shane murmured, "I hope you know what you're doing. You leaned on him pretty hard. I thought he was going to pull a gun and shoot us both."

"Not there. But he'll come for me, which is what I want."

In the SUV, Cara was waiting anxiously. "Well? How'd it go?"

Shane put the vehicle in gear and started straight for the airport.

"Dmitri is guilty as hell, in all of this up to his eyeballs." Taylor sighed. "I know you said your sister was unhappy in her marriage. Did she ever confide in you about being more than Dmitri's PA?"

Cara blanched. "No. But that doesn't mean she wasn't. I've often wondered why Damon was there helping her pack that day, even if she claimed he was a friend. He was Dmitri's brother, and I never liked Dmitri much. It seems like something he would do, sending his own brother to do his dirty work, moving his mistress out of her husband's home."

"And it would explain why Connor completely lost it that day. What if he found out the baby wasn't his, but Dmitri's? A man couldn't murder his own baby, but another man's? If he's crazy enough, he could."

"And Connor was crazy."

Cara looked miserable. "Now what?"

"We go home. I'm going to get our guys together and

make a plan. He's going to come after me, and when he does, we're going to trap him."

"We can fix you with a wire," Shane suggested. "When you goad him again, we get a confession on digital."

"Assuming he'll come after me in person now, as I think he will, that'll work."

"We'll be nearby, move in and grab him before he can blink."

Operations like those were iffy at best. But in dealing with people like Constantine, who were full of hatred and the need for revenge, wringing a confession was a preferable way to go. The only other way was to catch his hit man or other employee, and get a confession from them, and then they were going on hearsay, which was inadmissible. They'd need records of transfer of funds, and it was hard to prove murder for hire when excuses could be made for the use of the money.

They made it to the airport and onto the plane without incident, and Taylor was able to breathe a temporary sigh of relief. He knew the reprieve wouldn't last long.

He just had to hold on a bit longer. He'd baited his shark.

Almost time to reel him in.

Cara watched as Chris, Shane, and a couple of technical guys from the station outfitted her man with the latest in electronic-listening wear.

The "wire" actually didn't include a wire at all, unlike on old TV shows, where the bad guy finds the cords running under the cop's jacket and rips them out. This device was a high-tech mock shirt button, and it made her feel better to know that he was sporting something virtually undetectable. Chris fussed with the placement, finally getting it the way he wanted.

"There," he said, straightening. "Shane and I will be in the van first, monitoring. Then a new shift will take our place after twelve hours, and we'll rotate like that until we get this bastard."

Taylor's phone rang and he answered. After a short, terse exchange, he hung up. "Constantine has left L.A., but there's no proof he's on his way here. Our people have lost him."

"Dammit," Shane swore. "He could be anywhere. Even left the country."

"Maybe, but I don't think so. Is that it?" Taylor studied his button microphone in the hallway mirror.

"For now. Go on about your business, but stay away from Cara after this." Shane waved a hand between them. "Say your goodbyes for the time being. It's safer for her that way."

The rest of the troops left, and she stepped into Taylor's arms, sinking into his comforting heat. "I'm glad Blake is staying with Shane and Daisy until this is finished."

"Me, too." He frowned. "I don't want to say good-bye, even for a few days. I hate that this bastard is taking over our lives. He's as crazy as Connor was."

"To kill to keep your indiscretions secret? Yes."

"People have killed for less. To feel powerful, for money. Passion. Seems like Dmitri fit all of these."

"I'm sorry my sister got caught in Connor's wrath, too."

"So am I. I would have liked to have met her."

"She wasn't perfect, but none of us are. She would've liked you."

Talking about that, the truth of it, made her sad. She clung to her man and didn't let go for a long time. When she finally pulled back, he took her upstairs and made love to her for the better part of the afternoon—with the microphone stuffed in the closet.

Later, when he dressed again, he snickered into the device. "Sorry, guys. For our ears only."

She pictured them rolling their eyes, and laughed. "Hungry?"

"I could eat. Let's go find something, and afterward I'll take you home, where one of the officers is going to stay with you."

She didn't like it, but had no choice.

As they entered the kitchen, a whisper of sound made her turn to her right—and she shrieked to see Dmitri standing in Taylor's kitchen with two other men, his gun trained on them, smiling as though he'd been invited for dinner.

Taylor had no chance to reach for his weapon.

"Take your gun out nice and slow," Dmitri said. "Drop it to the floor."

Jaw ticking in rage, he did. Every muscle was tense with the need to fight, but they were outnumbered. "Is this how you did away with Max? Got the drop on him in that motel room and put the bullet in the middle of his forehead?"

The reminder made tears sting her eyes. But she knew he had to get a confession.

"That was my associate, Snyder," he said, pointing to the huge man in question. This must've been the one Taylor chased the other night and shot. The man had a bandage around one biceps. "Snyder took care of Griffin for me, since the man was no longer inclined to cooperate in keeping my secrets. And Web is here as extra insurance that *this* job gets done right."

The other man was younger, smaller and wiry, but appeared no less vicious. He raked Cara with a lascivious look, and she felt ill. She'd die before she let this creep touch her that way.

"Is that why you're here? To make sure the job gets done, since Snyder wasn't capable on his own?"

The barb struck home and Snyder unloaded a punch to Taylor's midsection that doubled him over. She cried out, grabbing his arm to steady him. Gradually he straightened, expression stony. She hoped he didn't goad them much more, but that hope was futile.

"Takes a real pussy to kill old men and con married women into sleeping with him."

Dmitri's eyes narrowed. "There was no con. She was lonely, and I wanted her. I always get what I want."

"Since she's dead, I'm inclined to disagree."

That earned him another hard punch. He coughed and stood up again, this time with more difficulty.

"What did you do? Blackmail Jenny into being with you?"

"There was no need, since she was in love with me. And when she turned up pregnant with my child, even better. She wanted to be with me, and she didn't want darling hubby to find out before she was out the door."

"But he did find out," Taylor pressed. "How? Did you tell him after all?"

"No. I don't know how he learned about the baby, and I guess I never will. Could be that she told him herself, out of desperation when he caught her packing, but we'll never know. What I do know is that you're going to pay for getting Jennifer and my brother killed."

"Connor killed them," Taylor said firmly. In that moment, Cara knew he really had forgiven himself. "I did the best I could in a bad situation. I believe he would've killed them all no matter what."

The gun waved as Dmitri fought his anger. "It no longer matters what you believe. You murdered my brother, my lover, and my child. Now you're going to die."

Cara caught Taylor's gaze for a second and knew he was thinking the same thing.

Where are Chris and Shane?

Chris was guiding the van into a parking place when the sound feed on the microphone crackled. Taylor and Cara had been on their way downstairs to eat something; then Taylor was taking her home. Now Chris was getting some annoying interference.

"Are those other voices?" Chris said quietly.

"Shh."

They listened intently, catching pieces of phrases. With the feed acting up, it was hard to tell who was speaking.

"Should we go back?"

Shane listened harder, fiddled with some of the buttons on the sound recording system. The unit crackled again and the feed cleared up.

"Takes a real pussy to kill old men and con married women into sleeping with him."

"There was no con. She was lonely, and I wanted her. I always get what I want."

"Since she's dead, I'm inclined to disagree."

The sound of a hard punch could be heard. Coughing.

"What did you do? Blackmail Jenny into being with you?"

"There was no need, since she was in love with me. And when she turned up pregnant with my child, even better. She wanted to be with me, and she didn't want darling hubby to find out before she was out the door."

"But he did find out. How? Did you tell him after all?" Taylor pressed.

"No. I don't know how he learned about the baby, and I guess I never will. Could be that she told him herself, out of desperation when he caught her packing, but we'll never know. What I do know is that you're going to pay for getting Jennifer and my brother killed."

"Connor killed them," Taylor said. *"I did the best I could in a bad situation. I believe he would've killed them all no matter what."*

"It no longer matters what you believe. You murdered my brother, my lover, and my child. Now you're going to die."

Chris laid rubber, wheeling the van from the lot.

13

In the van two miles away, Shane shouted to Chris, panic blinding him.

"Go, goddammit, go, go!"

Dmitri Constantine had waited years to make Taylor pay for the death of his brother and unborn child. Now he planned to have his vengeance.

His companion floored the accelerator while Shane prayed.

If Dmitri Constantine touched one hair on his friends' heads, he was one dead son of a bitch.

"I can almost forgive Max's sudden attack of conscience that led him to disobey me. This is going to give me great pleasure."

Dmitri shoved Taylor into the room, hard, and Taylor stumbled and fell to her knees. *Shane!* She knew Taylor had to make sure his partner heard enough to put this creep away for good.

If Dmitri realized the button was a wire, they were screwed.

Taylor sat up and looked into Cara's eyes, his face etched with regret as he spoke for the benefit of the van's recordings. "Dmitri here was having an affair with Jenny. The baby Jenny was carrying was his, not Connor's. She wanted to leave her husband for this cocksucker, though God knows why—"

That earned him a swift reprimand. Dmitri lunged, swinging the butt of his gun to deliver a blow to the side of Taylor's head. Cara cried out as he slumped to the floor. Immediately, he pushed to his hands and knees, head hanging.

His shaggy blond hair enveloped his face, blood dripping to the polished floor. Just as he tried to stand, Constantine kicked him forcefully in the ribs, sending him crashing sideways into the coffee table.

"I loved Jennifer. You killed her and my child! You should have chosen *her* life when you had the chance!" Lips pulled back into a feral snarl, Constantine advanced, kicking him again and again in the ribs, the head. Moaning, Taylor curled into the fetal position, but it offered no protection against the vicious onslaught.

"Stop!" Cara screamed, dropping to his side. "You're killing him!"

Her plea penetrated Constantine's rage, but not for the reason she'd obviously hoped. While she gathered Taylor into her arms, the man stood back, face flushed from exertion.

"You're right." He gave a cold smile. "I can't have him dying on me too quickly, after all. That would be rather anticlimactic. Boys, let's take these two to a place where

I can introduce them to the full meaning of a slow, painful death."

From somewhere outside, the squeal of tires could be heard rounding a corner down the street.

Constantine gestured with his gun. "Take them out the back and hurry the fuck up. Put them in your truck; make them keep their heads down. You know where to go. I'll follow in my car."

They won't get away. Shane is coming, she consoled herself. But not fast enough to stop them. Yet. *Thank God Blake is at work!*

Snyder reached down and jerked Taylor from her arms, half-dragging him toward the kitchen. "Try anything, and your sweetheart gets a bullet in the head." Web went along, the muzzle of his gun against Taylor's temple.

Pushing up, she started after them, her knees like water. Constantine walked behind her, his gun digging into the small of her back. All the way through the kitchen and out the back door, she numbly tried to grasp how things had gone bad so quickly. How this could be happening in broad daylight.

These men were planning to kill them. And Dmitri would make sure Taylor suffered first.

They were taken to a double-cab pickup parked next to the back fence. Taylor was shoved headfirst into the backseat of the truck, his forehead smacking the doorframe. He dragged himself in and collapsed across the seat, unmoving.

"You can kneel on the floor beside him. Move it!" Snyder growled.

She got in as the truck peeled out, and wedged herself between the seats, facing Taylor. His beautiful green eyes were half-open, and his bruised cheek lay against the leather upholstery in a smear of blood.

"Cara." He coughed, grimacing in pain. "I'm so sorry."

"Don't talk, baby," she whispered, taking his hand. "We'll be fine."

God, don't let that be a lie. Constantine, that monster, had beaten him badly. A widening patch of dark hair glistened, sticky with blood. A crimson droplet trickled from his temple down his exposed cheek, like a tear. Grabbing the edge of her shirt, she leaned over him, wiping it away. When she dabbed the side of his head, he winced, sucking in a sharp breath.

No use. Pressing on the wound didn't staunch the flow, and only hurt him more. She settled back again, squeezing his hand.

"I love you," he said, closing his eyes.

"I love you, too, so much." No response. "Taylor?"

He'd passed out, a mercy for him. But she felt so alone and scared, she wanted to cry.

No time for the luxury of tears. Constantine's thugs were silent as the truck left the paved road and began to bounce wildly over rough terrain. She couldn't tell whether Shane had caught up and given pursuit or not.

You have to stay calm. Think of a way to help.

But nothing came to mind just yet. There was no thought of anything except survival.

Bending to Taylor, she kissed him on the cheek and whispered her love to him, again and again.

14

Shane hung on as the van tore around the corner. The driveway of Taylor's house came into view.

"Around back—cut them off," he yelled to Chris.

Constantine had hurt his partner. He could tell by the sickening thuds of a body being struck repeatedly, Cara's frantic scream. Yeah, the asshole was fucking dead.

Oh, God, this nightmare was his fault. He should've moved faster. Everything had exploded in their faces with such dizzying speed, he was reeling with gut-wrenching fear.

The department's new surveillance van was state-of-the-art, jacked up with all sorts of spy equipment, definitely not built for high-speed pursuit. Chris did his best, barreling down the driveway and taking out the mailbox on its post, which splintered with a sharp crack and went flying. He swerved, barely missing a tree as the van careened around the side of the house and across the lawn.

"Jesus, they're heading through the woods," Chris hissed, fighting the wheel. "We're not catching them in this fucking tank."

Dammit, he was right. The big truck and Constantine's car were almost out of sight. They needed backup *now*.

Ahead of them, the car swung to the left, allowing the front passenger of the truck a clear target. One of the thugs stuck his arm out the window, and Shane found himself staring down the sights of the man's pistol.

"Shit!" He dove behind the dash as bullets pinged off the grille, smacked the windshield.

Cursing, Chris jerked the van to the left, hunching down behind the wheel. Keeping cover, Shane pressed the button to lower his window. The hail of bullets abruptly ceased, and he bolted upright, levering his torso against the door and sticking his pistol out the window.

"Swing it to the right," he yelled to Chris.

His cousin did, lining him up with the truck again. From inside the cab, Snyder's jerky movements told him the guy was probably slamming in a new round.

Shane couldn't risk firing at the men inside the cab, for fear of hitting Taylor or Cara, and the sorry bastards knew it. He squeezed off several shots at the right back tire, but the bouncing of the van ruined his aim and they ricocheted harmlessly off the tailgate and bumper.

Reloaded, his nemesis returned fire. Shane ducked inside as more bullets pelted the windshield. This time, glass shattered, spraying shards. Chris let out a soft grunt, and the van swerved left. Shane glanced over to see his cousin slumped, face bloodied.

"Oh, God."

Loose, out of control, the vehicle veered off the worn path, bucking like a wild horse across the uneven ground.

Shane lunged for the wheel as the two vehicles ahead disappeared into the woods, making their escape.

With his partner, whom Constantine planned to murder.

He'd failed Taylor.

That was his last, agonizing thought as he scrambled to reach the brake. He stomped down hard, sending the cumbersome van into a sideways skid. He fought, but couldn't correct the motion or stop in time.

He hit the copse of trees at forty miles an hour.

The impact tossed him like a rag doll. His head smashed into something, snuffing the light, hurling him into darkness.

From far away came the screeching, tearing of metal.

More glass shattering.

A final, jarring collision.

Silence.

Gradually, Taylor became aware of the truck slowing. Of Cara stroking his hair. And the band of pain tightening around his ribs like a fist. His head throbbed in tempo to his pulse.

He tried to move. A mistake. Nausea cramped his belly, and he groaned.

"Taylor?"

Opening his eyes, he looked into Cara's sweet face. "Hey, baby. Not much of a courtship so far, huh?" He tried a smile, but it came out lopsided. "Next time I'll just bring flowers."

Her pretty green eyes filled with tears. "Oh, honey. Don't talk. Save your strength."

"I'm okay," he lied. Looking past her, he noted that their captors didn't seem in a particular hurry now. Snyder sat calmly in the passenger's seat, facing ahead. Heart sinking, he turned his attention back to Cara. "Shane didn't catch up."

She combed a lock of hair from his eyes, her expression sad. "No, sweetie. There was lots of gunfire and . . . I think they wrecked."

God, no.

"Shut up back there," the other man barked, making Cara jump.

Anger swelled, hot and choking. He owed those two sons of bitches—and Constantine—big payback. How to dole out retribution in his condition, one injured man against three, posed a slight problem.

Somehow, before they killed him, he'd find a way to take the fuckers with him.

Sweet Jesus, what will they do to Cara once I'm dead?

No, don't think about that. If he did, he'd lose his mind and any opportunity to get out of this mess. *Watch, plan.* Try with everything in him to keep them away from her until he drew his last breath; that's all he could hope for. Buy some time until Shane located them, if he was able.

The truck stopped, idling, while the rumble of a mechanism came from outside. Then they were moving again, the sunlight disappearing. He struggled to sit up, Cara grabbing his arm to steady him, and saw they'd driven into a cavernous parking garage. If anyone had worked here, the place was deserted now.

"Where are we?" he asked their captors. "Is this a warehouse?"

"Shut up." Web opened his door.

Web was out of the truck and yanking open Taylor's door in two seconds. The wiry younger man proved stronger than he looked. He grabbed Taylor's shirt, dragged him out of the vehicle, and threw him to the concrete with a forceful shove. Dammit, he hated for Cara to see him this beaten. The punk never would've bested him in a fair fight.

Before Taylor could stand, he found himself staring down the barrel of Web's pistol. Grinning, the man pressed the muzzle between his eyes. Strange calm stole through him. No, he wasn't going to die like this. Dmitri had something much more sinister planned, and he wouldn't let his minion kill him this easily.

He was right.

"Web!" Dmitri shouted, emerging from his car. "Quit pissing around and get those two inside now!"

Web glanced from him to Dmitri and back, the smirk vanishing. Obviously he was displeased. *This one actually loves the kill. Snyder, for all his efforts as an assassin, is the brainless muscle.*

Taylor stood, shoulders knotted with tension as Snyder waved Cara out of the truck with his gun. Web got behind him, giving him a push toward her. He limped over to her, gait unsteady, his body aching. Dizziness threatened to topple him, but she hooked her arm through his, acting like a human crutch. No one stopped her, and he was careful not to lean on her small frame too heavily as they followed Constantine.

He led them to a security door with a square panel to the left of the frame. Making no move to block the box from view, he punched in a six-digit code. Taylor memorized the combination, praying he got a chance to say it for Shane.

A buzzer whined and the lock popped. Inside, they were confronted by three white, sterile-looking corridors branching off left, straight ahead, and right. Constantine turned down the one to the right. A cold finger trailed down Taylor's spine and he thought, *This is the end. I won't leave here alive.* Beside him, Cara was tight-lipped, her face white.

God, why had he let her stay with him after he'd been injured? Constantine obviously had planned to kidnap him when the other attempts on his life had failed, and she'd gotten in the way. If only he could wish her away from this evil place. He'd never wanted to experience this horrible helplessness again, and the rage made him want to tear these monsters limb from limb.

Near the end of the corridor, Constantine pulled a set of keys from his pocket and unlocked a door on the left. At the same time, he jerked his head to indicate another set of doors across the hall. "Web, make sure everything is ready."

"Sure thing." The man left, ducking into the room.

Constantine turned to Snyder. "By tomorrow we'll be in Europe, setting up our new lives. Is Mr. Kayne's grave prepared?"

Shit. Cara clung to him, shaking.

"Yes, sir. Dug it earlier in the hills west of town, where you told us. What about her, though?" He shot an uneasy glance at Cara.

Constantine waved a hand in dismissal. "We'll take

care of her later, after I've had my fun. I'll find out if she's as sweet as her sister."

Taylor lunged at him. "Don't touch her, you bas—"

Snyder countered with a swift kick in his sore ribs that sent him sprawling through the door Constantine had unlocked. Gasping, he pushed up. Cara stumbled inside and immediately wrapped him in her arms.

They sat, holding on to each other, giving what little comfort they were able. Over the top of her head, he glared his hatred at Dmitri.

"So touching. Brings a tear to the eye," the monster said. "Enjoy these next few minutes, because that's all you have. Don't bother trying to escape. This is a solid ten-by-ten storage closet with no vents and a lock you can't pick. I'll return soon; don't worry."

The door slammed shut, engulfing them in darkness. Letting go of him, Cara reached over and tried the knob anyway, to no avail. She settled into his arms again, snuggling her face into his neck, and they clung together. He breathed her scent, could still smell the flowery shampoo she'd used in her hair.

"I love you, Cara, more than my own life. Whatever happens, never forget that," he whispered. Fingering her silky purple-streaked hair, he searched his heart for the right words.

"I could bitch about how unfair it is that my time might be cut short just when I finally know what it means to have someone to love. But at least I found what so many others spend their whole lives looking for and never find. And in the end, nothing else matters."

He had so much more to say, but his throat locked up.

"Oh, Taylor. I'll always love you, never doubt that."

She tilted her head up, and he bent to her. His lips grazed hers, gently at first. Then deeper, kissing her with every ounce of passion in his soul. Kissed her as though for the last time. The last breath. Suspended in this moment, no more words necessary between them. He tasted the salt of their tears, bittersweet.

Finally, he pulled back and spoke to the button on his lapel. "Hey, partner. Are you out there? We're in a warehouse of some kind, and make it quick, if you don't mind," he quipped, letting his sarcasm come through. God, this sucked. "Through the parking garage, code on the security door is five-five-one-zero-zero-two. Take the right corridor. We're in a storage closet at the end of the hall on the left, but not for long. There's another room across the way, and that's where Constantine's taking us next. *Hurry*."

He paused, closing his eyes in the dark, even though he couldn't see. "Shane, if I don't get to tell you in person ... I don't think I ever thanked you for what you did, pulling for me to get the position at the department after the nightmare in Los Angeles and dragging me out of hell. So, I'm doing it now. You're a fantastic partner despite all the shit I give you, and I love you like a brother."

His voice broke and he couldn't say more. Just held on to Cara and prayed for one more miracle.

I don't care what happens to me. Please keep Cara safe. Swear to God, I'll never ask for anything else.

Sitting in the rear of the mangled van where he'd been thrown, Shane clamped a hand over the nasty gash in his arm. Blood dripped between his fingers and onto his chest from the cut on his face. Tangled wires hung from black consoles like globs of spaghetti, and something sharp poked him in the spine.

By the grace of God, the receiver putting out the transmissions from Taylor's microphone survived the wreck. But if help didn't arrive soon, the blessing would become a curse. He'd be forced to listen to his partner's murder as Constantine carved him into pieces.

"Chris?" A groan was his answer, and relief swamped him. His cousin was alive.

Fishing around, he located his cell phone under the driver's seat. The captain was on his way, and several of the other detectives were scrambling to locate the warehouse Taylor described. But not fast enough. Not by a long shot.

Seething, he heard Constantine spouting his vile poison. Ordering his partner's imminent burial somewhere west of town. If that happened, even with search dogs they'd never find Taylor in time.

Listening to Taylor and Cara essentially telling each other good-bye yet desperately clinging to their love, unraveled him. Slowly, painfully. As if that weren't heartbreaking enough, the asshole had to go and spill his guts to Shane.

"You're a fantastic partner despite all the shit I give you, and I love you like a brother."

"Oh, Jesus Christ . . ." He panted through the agony of vicious claws raking across his heart. No, the shit wasn't going down like this. He would not accept that. No way in hell.

He was spared from contemplating more horrifying images of Taylor's death by the grinding of an approaching vehicle, maybe two or three, judging by the noise.

One motor shut off, then another. Three doors slammed in succession, the crunch of footsteps rapidly jogging for the van through the weeds.

"Shane?" Austin called, anxious. "God, look at this mess."

Buddy, it gets worse. "I'm in the back. Chris is in the front and he needs medical attention."

More rustling. The van's double rear doors jerked, refusing to budge.

"Damned frame must be bent," muttered another.

After several hard yanks, the doors gave, swinging outward with a loud squeal. Austin and Tonio Salvatore filled the open space, a barrel-bellied lieutenant named Henry Palmer hovering behind them. Grim-faced, Austin and Tonio reached for him, taking him by his upper arms, easing him to sit on the edge of the van.

The captain bent close and peered at the cut on his forehead. "This one's making a mess, but it doesn't look deep."

"Good."

"Let's see the arm."

Reluctantly, he moved his hand. Tonio whistled through his teeth and Austin winced. Even his own stomach did a flip at the sight of the two-inch gash, not long but deep, the ragged flesh laid open. "I must've hit the corner of the listening console."

"That needs stitches," Tonio said.

He shook his head. "No time. Constantine has Taylor

and Cara. We have to move before he kills them and skips town."

"Constantine." Austin's mouth tightened in rage. To the lieutenant, he called, "Palmer, I need you to wait here, take care of Chris and wait for the paramedics."

"Yes, Cap. They need to hurry."

Shane was torn between desperation to get to his partner and worry for Chris. But he knew Chris would order him to get moving. He looked at Rainey. "We need to go. We're running out of time."

Austin grabbed his good arm, steadying him. "You hurt anywhere else?"

"I'm good." Except for the ache in his lower back and pains in about ten other places. Rainey eyed him with skepticism.

"Right. A trip to the ER will make sure of that."

That wasn't happening. Not with his partner out there in danger. His cell phone chirped, and he knew that wasn't happening yet. Tensing, he answered with a sharp, "What have you got?" He listened, holding the phone in a white-knuckle grip. Anxiety warred with a small dose of relief. Back at the station, the rest of the team had come through in spades.

"Good work. We're headed there, so send us some backup, right fucking now."

He hung up, heart racing, and glanced at Tonio. "Help me find my gun and something to wrap my arm," he said. The other man did as he asked, and Shane jogged for the captain's SUV, half-limping as he spoke over his shoulder to his companions.

"The guys got a probable location. It's an abandoned warehouse a few minutes from here."

"All right," Austin nodded, big hand resting instinctively on the handle of the gun at his hip. "Let's do it."

After Tonio returned with Shane's gun and a small hand towel, the deputy helped to wrap the cloth tight around his arm. Austin and Tonio climbed into the front, the captain taking the wheel and roaring off, tires spinning.

Awash in fear and regret, Shane closed his eyes. *Hang on, partner.*

But second chances were almost nonexistent, and few men got one without paying a heavy price. Nothing was for free. His partner knew that better than anyone, and he had the scars to prove it.

Taylor had done penance for his mistakes a hundred times over. Had paid with his soul. He wasn't going to pay with his life.

No, that privilege belonged to Dmitri Constantine.

Because Shane was going to kill him.

15

Cara burrowed into the warm comfort of Taylor's arms. Let his solid strength surround her, giving the momentary illusion that everything would turn out fine.

"We're not going to just roll over and die," he whispered against her neck.

"You've got a plan?"

"Other than to fight like hell? Not exactly."

She tightened her grip on him. "Fighting works for me."

His soft laugh chased the gloom. "That's my kick-ass rock-and-roll girl."

"That's me. What can I say?"

"When we get out of here, we're going to take a vacation. Just you and me, somewhere tropical. Lots of fruity drinks with umbrellas, and plenty of beach sex."

"Sounds yummy." They were facing death, yet she'd never heard him sound so calm and sure. This was a man she'd love forever.

If they both saw tomorrow.

"What about Blake?" she asked.

"Oh, I have a feeling he'll be fine." The smugness in his voice had her studying him.

"Why do I get the feeling you're up to something?"

"Well, I may have meddled a little bit."

Her mouth fell open. "You found his brother, Jon, didn't you?"

"Even better—I called him and we had a chat. Let's just say I opened his eyes to a few facts he didn't know."

"What did he say?"

"What I expected. Jon said he had no idea, that his parents had told him Blake stole money from them constantly and had gotten into drugs. They poisoned Jon against him, warning him that Blake would be calling Jon next and not to let him get away with conning him, too."

"And he believed that?" She wanted to smack the man for his stupidity.

"Yeah, and so he hung up on Blake when he called. Blake was left thinking Jon had rejected him for being gay and didn't contact him again. By the time Jon thought it through and realized his parents had played him, Jon couldn't find Blake anywhere."

"But if we don't get out of here, Blake might never know the truth!"

Taylor reassured her. "I gave Jon his brother's phone number and new address. Those two will be all right eventually. Jon has been sick with worry."

A rattle at the door sent her heart into her throat. They scrambled to their feet, Taylor grunting in pain as he pushed her behind him. Light from the hall flooded the tiny closet, and she blinked against the glare as her vision adjusted. Constantine held a large pistol, the barrel strangely oversized, sort of like a flare gun, pointed at the center of Taylor's chest. His face twisted into an ugly sneer.

"Showtime." His dark eyes gleamed with malice. "Let's go."

He stepped aside to let them pass, and Cara pressed as close to Taylor as possible. She'd always prided herself on being capable of handling just about any situation, but that didn't include sadistic murderers. She'd better learn fast, because their window of opportunity would be unmercifully short.

"Nice toy," Taylor remarked coolly, gesturing to the odd gun. "Voodoo darts?"

A dart gun! Cara's stomach rolled.

Constantine smiled, cold. Evil. "Nah, just good, old-fashioned poison. You'd actually have a chance at surviving a gunshot wound and it wouldn't cause nearly enough pain. Get a load of this—you die slow, writhing in agony."

Taylor returned the chilling smile. "Maybe we should test it on you."

Web shoved him forward. "Get moving!"

Snyder wasn't there. She'd been so focused on Constantine, she hadn't noticed. A minuscule flicker of hope took root and grew. Without Snyder's bulk to contend with, the odds were looking better. Constantine appeared to be Taylor's equal in size and strength, but Web didn't have much going for him except attitude. Once disarmed, Taylor would crush the punk like a gnat.

First, they had to somehow get both of their captors' weapons out of the picture.

Taylor took her hand, squeezing her fingers in reassurance as they stepped into the room across the hall. The sight hit her like a fist to the stomach, and she stood on shaking knees, staring.

The setup was actually very plain and simple, functional, for its monstrous purpose. A long, dirty wooden table sat next to a cart loaded with all sorts of sharp tools. A syringe half-filled with clear liquid and a small amber bottle rested there as well. Implements of torture they planned to use.

"Kayne, on your knees," Constantine barked from behind them. Addressing Web, he ordered, "Keep your gun to his head. If he so much as flinches, blow his brains out."

Taylor's eyes met hers steadily. Arching a brow, he gave a barely perceptible nod, telegraphing the message, *Be ready.* Then he knelt, clenched fists the only sign of his anger. Web pressed the muzzle of the pistol against Taylor's temple, smirking. A typical runt eaten with Little Man Syndrome who'd be nothing without a weapon, one who sure wouldn't smile if Taylor got that gun away from him.

Constantine swaggered past Taylor and positioned himself beside the cart at one end of the table. Shooting Cara a wolfish smile, he waved her to stand next to him. "Over here, sweetheart. And since you won't be needing them anymore, take your clothes off."

"What?" she sputtered.

"Torture is much more satisfying if the subject is vulnerable." He chuckled as though he'd made some great joke.

As he kneeled on the tile floor, Taylor's face was tight with rage, every muscle in his body a coiled spring. It was then she noticed the circular metal drain between them, close to her boots. For the blood. Her eyes widened in horror.

"No," she heard herself say. "I won't do it."

His expression turned smug. "You don't have a choice."

"Yes, I do. You can peel them off my dead body, loser." Taylor made a strangled noise, but she didn't dare look at him. Constantine's eyes narrowed dangerously. As she'd suspected, she wasn't showing nearly enough fear for his taste.

"Big talk for such a puny little girl."

And that was where people who didn't know better were forever underestimating her. This egocentric lunatic was no different. Her mind stilled, clarified. Though she had to concentrate to keep her knees from knocking, she managed to gaze at him with contempt.

"Then it shouldn't be too hard for a macho guy like you to force me to do what you want. Bring it, asshole."

"You're forgetting that Web has a gun to your lover's head. One word from me—"

"And he'll die quick and painless rather than slow, like you wanted. Gee, I wonder which he'd prefer." Constantine's face darkened. Before he could reply, she angled her head toward a rectangular crate resting by the door they'd entered. A coffin-sized box, she noted, squashing a wave of panic.

"Is that for me?"

The smile returned, a crazed light in his dark eyes, and her flesh crawled.

"Not for you, my dear. I said I have a special place to bury your lover, but did I say he would already be dead?"

Caught off guard, she stared at him in horror. After Constantine forced Taylor to watch her die, the sick bastard planned to bury him alive.

Oh, God, no.

Constantine laughed. "I think my Jennifer would be pleased with her murderer's execution."

Taylor's voice, low and cold, echoed throughout the stark space. "You're the reason she's dead. If you hadn't drawn her into your sick little world, she'd still be alive."

Constantine whirled, leveling the dart gun at his chest. "Shut your lying mouth the fuck up."

"I have to wonder if she really loved you as much as you think. Maybe she was leaving you *and* Connor that day," he taunted.

"I said shut up!" The gun wavered.

Cara's breath caught.

Taylor's eyes were feral with hatred. "You were responsible for getting Damon killed, too. It was terrible how your brother cried when Connor stuck the gun to his head. Begged. And I couldn't keep his brains from splattering all over the living room."

Everything exploded at once.

With a bellow of rage, Constantine stiffened his arm, taking aim as Taylor lurched upward and slammed the back of his head into Web's face. The younger man's howl of pain reverberated off the empty walls, blood spurting from his nose. Before Constantine could pull the trigger, Cara launched herself at him with all the strength she possessed.

Her momentum knocked him sideways, propelled him into the unstable cart, which immediately shot across the slick tile. Unable to regain his balance, he stumbled and fell into it, cart and man hitting the floor with a resounding crash. Tools slid and rolled in every direction. The dart gun lay several feet from his outstretched hand. With a violent curse, he began to push to his hand and knees. She reacted quickly, out of pure instinct.

She kicked him in the jaw with the hard toe of her boot, using enough force to send a shockwave of pain through her foot and shin. His head snapped to the side and he collapsed with a groan, unmoving.

No time to celebrate. A shot went wild, whizzing past her to slam into the wall. Taylor and Web were rolling around on the floor, locked in deadly combat. The gun was sandwiched between them, each man struggling to turn it on the other. Web had Taylor on his back now, the position and Taylor's earlier beating working to the younger man's advantage in spite of his smaller size.

Using his upper-body weight as leverage, the grinning creep began to angle the muzzle toward Taylor's chest. Gritting his teeth, Taylor bucked to try to throw him off, but the kid stuck like a burr.

No! Cara's heart slammed against her ribs as she scanned the debris for a weapon. Anything.

She spotted the syringe lying next to a pair of scissors, and dove for it. Panting in fear, she grabbed the thing and pushed up, running for the battling pair.

Web shoved the muzzle at Taylor's heart. "Gotcha."

"Noo!"

Her earsplitting scream caused Web to start. He hesitated a split second too long.

Screeching in fury, she drove the long needle into his back, injecting him with the vile contents. He stiffened, gasping. His eyes widened, fingers slack, releasing his hold on the gun. Taylor relieved him of the weapon and pushed him off, standing with a grimace and favoring his injured side. Odd gurgling noises escaped Web's throat as his face contorted in agony. She'd never seen anything so horrifying in her life.

"Sweetheart, don't watch," Taylor murmured, folding her into his arms.

"My God," she whispered, stricken. She burrowed into his body, a warm, safe haven from the madness. "I did that to him. Taylor, he's practically a boy."

"A boy who was ready to kill us both. His choice."

"Is he dead?" She shuddered.

"I—I don't know." He let her go for a moment to crouch beside Web. "I can't find a pulse."

"Oh, Taylor, how horrible!"

Taylor returned to her, gathering her into his embrace again. "Yes, it's awful. But it's justice."

A shuffling from the floor a few feet away had Taylor whirling, putting her behind him once more. Constantine sat up, moaning, cupping his jaw in one hand. Cara hoped she'd broken it.

"Don't move," Taylor warned, training the gun on their nemesis.

Constantine thought about it, she could tell. His dark gaze slid to where the dart gun rested just out of reach, then back to Taylor. If hatred alone could kill, her man would be dead. Constantine wasn't ready to give up, and the danger wouldn't end until help arrived. *Please let Shane and Chris be all right, and be bringing reinforcements.*

"You and your little bitch are going to die for this," he hissed.

"Big talk for such an insignificant worm," Taylor mocked.

"Ah, but I have something you don't."

"And that is?"

Cara felt something round and unyielding press into the back of her skull, and her knees went weak.

"My promise to splatter her brains all over you," Snyder rumbled from behind her. "Drop the gun and get inside the crate. Unless you'd rather have your precious lover take your place."

The awful moment stretched taut, the three men frozen in anticipation of the deadly outcome. Whether Taylor gave in to the order or not, they probably weren't going to make it out of this alive. *Probably.* A slim hope was all they had.

"Don't listen to him, Taylor. Take his pistol away from him and shove it up his fat ass," she encouraged.

Snyder jerked her backward, against his chest, wrapping a beefy forearm around her neck. The muzzle dug into the side of her head. "Stupid move, Kayne. You can't take us both and keep her alive. Won't work. Get in the crate."

He didn't answer, just turned very slowly, glancing between Constantine and Snyder. Assessing. Face stony, shrewd gaze calculating. Here was the cop who'd survived years on the force, learning from his mistakes, and he wasn't going to give in. She'd never loved him more.

He looked straight at her and whispered two words. "Fall down."

Instantly, she went limp in Snyder's arms, knocking him off balance as Taylor rushed him. He couldn't hold her and block the attack, so he dropped her.

Took aim, and fired.

"Nooo!" The scream ripped from the depths of her soul, mingling with the echo of the gunshot.

Taylor grunted as the bullet punched his chest, stumbled, and launched himself at Snyder. Another gunshot and the two collided, toppling to the floor. The gun skittered away, knocked loose. Straddling the big man, Taylor hauled back his arm and slammed the heel of his hand into the other man's nose in an upward thrust, with all the force he could muster.

A sickening crunch, and the man went limp as a bloated whale, staring sightlessly at the ceiling. Cara clapped a hand over her mouth, willing down the bile. Taylor had killed a man nearly twice his size with a single blow, by shoving the bridge of his nose into his brain.

A movement caught their attention, sparing her from dwelling on it further. In those few seconds, Constantine had crawled for the dart gun. His fingers closed around the butt and he jerked it upward, kneeling, the triumphant gleam in his eyes mixed with madness.

"You can't win, Kayne," he chuckled.

"Neither can you." Taylor stood, weaving on his feet, and stepped away from Snyder's body. Blood soaked the left side of his shirt, across his chest. Breathing hard, wheezing, he placed himself between the deadly weapon and Cara.

Shaking with fear, Cara went to his side, tried to edge in front of him. "Taylor, no!"

"Get behind me *now*," he hissed, blocking her once more.

"Constantine!" Shane's voice boomed from the doorway. "Police, drop your weapon!"

Cara sagged, almost falling over. *Oh, thank God.*

"We've got this place surrounded. You've got nowhere to go, so drop the gun."

Cara saw the men using the door for cover, arms extended, pistols trained on Constantine. They had a clear shot.

"Face facts. It's over," Taylor said coolly.

Constantine's face contorted with hatred. "Yes, I guess it is. In that case, join Jennifer and my brother in hell."

He pulled the trigger just as Shane and the captain opened fire on Constantine.

Cara cried out as Taylor's legs folded. He sank to his knees and she went with him, gathering him into her arms as he collapsed. The lethal dart had missed and was embedded in the wall behind him. But the gunshot wound to his chest was bleeding profusely, pumping with every beat of his heart.

Lovingly, she smoothed the silky blond hair out of his pale face. She adored everything about him. His smile, the way he cared for kids like Blake. How he tried so hard to keep others safe, as he'd tried to do for Jenny. His quirky sense of humor. The tender way he made love. If only he wouldn't leave her, so she could spend the rest of her life showing him the joys of having someone special to love. *Please stay.*

Shane crouched on the other side of his partner, and she glanced up at him. Looking at Taylor, he shook his head, eyes filled with tears. Like her own.

"Come on, buddy. Help is on the way. Hang in there—you hear me?"

Taylor swallowed, struggling to breathe. His green eyes were glazed and unfocused. He reached for Cara, and she took his hand, squeezing it. "Thank you for loving me. Sweetheart, I wish . . ."

Talking was too much, and he fell silent. Battling to stay alive for her.

"I know, baby," she reassured him, choking on tears. Her throat burned, and her chest ached as though her heart had been ripped out. "Just don't go, okay? Stay with me. *Please,* Taylor."

He tried to smile up at her. "Bossy."

His body went limp in her arms, his dusky lashes sweeping down. She shook him, terror punching her in the gut.

"Taylor, honey?" Nothing. Placing her fingertips on his neck, she found his pulse slowing. "No."

Shane's cell phone bleated. He snapped a terse greeting, and listened. "We're on the way." He flipped it shut, and hefted Taylor into his arms. "The medics are here. Let's go."

Tonio stepped forward, gesturing toward a wide section of board lying on the floor. "You're injured. Use that—it'll be faster."

Austin nodded, face grim. "We'll say a prayer for Taylor."

"Thanks," Shane said hoarsely. Tonio took Taylor's feet, Shane hooked his arms under his partner's shoulders, and they carried him to the wooden board, laying him on it gently. Wasting no more precious seconds, Shane took off, making his way as fast he could through the maze of corridors. Racing against time to save Taylor.

On the way out, Cara didn't spare a glance or so much as a prayer for Dmitri Constantine, sprawled dead on the floor. *May he rot in hell.*

No, she saved all her prayers for the man she loved. The man who'd fought so bravely and saved her life. The man who, when all seemed lost, refused to give up.

God, I'm begging you. Don't let me lose him.

16

God, he was so cold.

Was this death?

Not yet. Being dead wouldn't hurt so damned much.

His veins, his blood, were on fire. Boiling. Even his eyeballs. He couldn't see, but heard people shouting over some awful racket. Noise and movement, the sensation of lifting, going airborne.

A delicate hand stroked his brow. "Taylor, come on, sweetie. Fight for me, for us."

I am, he tried to say. But his lips were frozen. The noises around him took on the weird quality of a dream. Began to fade.

Baby, don't leave me!

He didn't want to. Just a taste of happiness, stripped away too soon. Not nearly enough, but it had to be.

Because he couldn't hold on. Cara sobbed brokenly, clutching his hand.

He doesn't have more time! Do something, goddammit! Shane, ordering the world to jump at his command, as usual. He almost smiled.

Tired. *Can't breathe.*

Too late, Taylor thought, saddened. *Cara, I love you.*

The weight eased from his chest, the pain vanished. Warm light soothed his battered body, and he found himself cradled in strong, loving arms and white robes. A good place to be.

Except Cara wasn't here.

Heartbroken cries followed him into the darkness.

Dejected, Cara hunched in the chair beside Taylor's hospital bed. Her churning insides felt chewed up and spit out, her face swollen from crying until everyone worried she'd become ill. She couldn't possibly eat, and she'd nearly thrown up a mere few sips of coffee.

Now she sat staring at his waxen face in a sort of numb stupor. Thick lashes rested against his paper-white cheeks, his tangled hair spread over his pillow. His full, sensual lips held a faint blue tinge. Except for the barely perceptible rise and fall of his chest, he looked like a beautiful corpse.

The nightmare ride to Sterling would remain forever burned into her memory. Taylor had stopped breathing for so long, they were certain he was gone. Then the surgical team had brought him back, giving him a fighting chance, but with no guarantees. Blood loss and the beating he'd received had left him clinging to life, where he hovered forty-eight hours later.

Compelled by the need to touch him for the thousandth time, she scooted her chair close and propped an elbow on the pillow by his head, combing her fingers through his hair.

"Wake up, handsome prince," she whispered in his ear. "I'm not going to stop bugging you until you do."

He stirred, tilting his head toward the sound of her voice. She gasped, heart hammering with hope, and stroked his cheek. "That's right, big guy. Come back to me."

Taking a deep breath, he shifted a little, groaning.

"Taylor?"

"Cara . . ."

Thank you. Her throat tightened with emotion, but she had no tears left. Overcome by joy, she kissed his forehead. "I'm here, honey. Let's see those gorgeous peepers."

"Don't shout." He moaned. "Headache . . ."

Smiling down at him, she said, "I'm whispering. The doctors said you weren't going to feel too great when you woke up. You're a disaster, buddy."

His lashes swept up, pale green eyes staring at her, unfocused and befuddled. "Huh?"

"Never mind. Just relax and take your time waking up. The worst is behind us, and I'm not going anywhere."

Closing his eyes on a sigh, he reached for her hand. Hanging on to her as though she were his lifeline, he drifted into sleep once more. Settling in and laying her head on the pillow beside him, she gave in to the flood of exhaustion that sheer terror had held at bay for hours on end.

When she awoke, the afternoon sun slanted through the curtains, lengthening to evening. Her arm was wrapped around Taylor's middle. The twinge stabbing her neck said she'd been like this for a while, and she wondered why the nurses hadn't shooed her off.

Someone was toying with her hair. Sitting up, she found Taylor smiling at her. She smiled back, touching his dear face. His color wasn't so pasty anymore, but he had dark smudges under his eyes.

"Hey, you. How do you feel?"

"Lucky to be alive." He started to reach for her, but frowned at the IV in his right hand and assortment of wires running from his chest, attached to monitors looming around the bed. Reaching into the top of his gown with his left hand, he plucked at one of the patches. "Damn, I'm wired to blow. Can't even hold you."

"No, you don't," she scolded, pulling his wrist toward her and taking his warm hand in hers. "Leave those alone. They're showing the doctors how much better you are."

"Yes, ma'am." He poked out his bottom lip, imitating a pouty little boy.

A giggle escaped, her love for him multiplying a thousandfold. Did he have any clue how wonderful he looked sitting there, the sad shadows of the past banished from his sparkling eyes?

"Taylor, I love you."

"I love you more, sweetheart." His gaze dropped to his lap. He studied their clasped hands for a minute, then lifted his head to study her from under spiky lashes. "I want to make us permanent, Cara. I want to marry you, to see our kids running wild all over town, giving us gray hair. What do *you* want?"

All right, she just *thought* her tears had dried up, dammit. His face blurred, her voice shook. "I'd say that's the best idea I've ever heard."

Careful of the IV and the bandages covering his gun-shot wound, she climbed onto the bed next to him and snuggled into his waiting arms. Listened to his heartbeat, steady and strong. Reveled in the heat of hard male, all hers, and pushed aside the horror of nearly losing him forever. He held her tight, kissing the top of her head.

The door opened and Shane walked in, amazed delight spreading across his handsome face as he approached the bed. "God, you *are* awake! I leave for a few hours to shower and change, and look what happens. It's about damned time, too."

"It's good to see you, too. For a while, I didn't think that was gonna happen."

Claiming the vacated chair, Shane sat and laid a big palm on his partner's shoulder. "One of the nurses said she peeked in a short while ago and thought you'd probably wake up soon. You have no idea how terrified we were. A bunch of the guys from the station have been here, some of the firefighters from Station Five, and Blake, too. That kid's been going out of his mind." Overcome, Shane propped his elbows on his knees, buried his face in his hands.

"Hey, man," Taylor said with gruff affection and humor. "This *must* be the part where we hug, right?"

Shane laughed at what must've been an inside joke between them, raised his head, and wiped at his eyes. "Yeah, I think maybe it is. First, though, you two are grinning like a couple of naughty kids in a candy store. What gives?"

"I asked Cara to marry me and she said yes," he said happily.

"Hey, congrats!" Shane shook his head, giving them both a smile. "When are you doing the deed?"

"We've already done *the deed*, many times! Now we just need to make it official."

Cara rose quickly to see Taylor waggling his brows suggestively at his partner. Her face heated and she swatted him on the shoulder. "Taylor Kayne!"

Both men laughed. The happiness and contentment rumbling from Taylor's chest deflated her embarrassment like a leaky balloon. Never had she seen him like this, so completely at ease.

Taylor was finally free of his demons.

"If I had my way, we'd be married today. But I guess Daisy will want to help Cara fuss over whatever girly stuff goes with the ceremony. Say, a week?"

"A week!" She shot Taylor a look of mock dismay. "I couldn't possibly plan it for a week from now. Make it two."

"You're on, baby." He gave her a soft kiss on the lips, then pulled back, love shining in his pale green eyes.

"And I don't want girly stuff, either," she informed him. "I'd like the wedding and reception held at your place, in the backyard. What better place to begin our lives together than at our place, surrounded by the people we love?"

He kissed her again, on the nose. "*Our* place. Sweetheart, you've got it. Anything your heart desires."

"Sounds perfect," Shane said, beaming. "We'll have ourselves a wedding bash Sugarland won't soon forget."

"How's Chris?" Cara asked Shane.

"Better." His expression clouded some. "He's not

well, though. He's got some health issues going on that he finally leveled with me about. Thing is, the doctors don't really know what's wrong."

Taylor looked worried. "I'll be honest—Chris told me recently that he hasn't been well. I'm glad he finally let you in on the secret. I told him that he'd better, or I'd have to do it for him."

"Thanks, partner. I sure hope he'll be all right."

They lapsed into silence, lost in their own thoughts. Cara was concerned about Chris, too. But she couldn't help but bask in the sheer bliss of starting her life with Taylor.

Shane stood, smiling. "I need to get home to Daisy, but I'll be back. Get well, because we've got some major celebrating to do, my friend."

"Shane." Taylor swallowed, suddenly hoarse. "Thanks for everything. If it wasn't for you bringing in the cavalry—"

"Gotcha, loud and clear. And you're welcome. Now get well so I can have my partner back, and get busy making that pretty lady of yours happy so I can stop rescuing your ass."

Taylor found himself swept into a bone-crunching hug. He laughed and returned it, thumping Shane on the back. They parted and Shane straightened, lips curved upward, eyes dancing. With a cocky wink, he was gone.

"Your partner's quite a man," she observed.

"Ahem." Taylor arched a brow.

"But not nearly as much a man as you. So big . . ."

His expression grew smug. "Keep talking."

"So sexy, smart, and strong. Will that satisfy your ego for now?"

He made a huffing sound. "Only until I get sprung from this joint. Unless you want to play Dirty Nurse Does Taylor?"

The man looked so hopeful, she couldn't help but feel sorry for him. "Poor baby. Don't worry. We'll play when you've regained your pep. After the wedding, of course."

"What? That's two weeks away!"

She giggled at his horrified expression. "Kidding. Goodness, you're easy to provoke."

"Go ahead, have fun at my expense while I'm at your mercy. Because the second we're alone, I'm going to turn you over my knee for some serious punishment."

"Ooh, promise?"

He pulled her into his arms, cradling her against his chest. "It's a date, sweetheart."

Safe in his arms, Cara drifted. Home at last.

Neither of them budged for a very long time.

Taylor pulled the Challenger up outside the Nashville apartment and squeezed Cara's hand. She bit her lip in worry, but he had a good feeling about this. Turning to look at Blake in the backseat, he smiled.

"You ready?"

Blake's eyes were huge in his face. Hand shaking, he shoved a spiky shock of brown hair from his face. "You sure about this? What if he doesn't really want to see me?"

"He does. Trust me. And you know what? Even if the worst was to happen and he tossed you out, that would be his loss. You've got us now, and we won't let you down," he encouraged.

Fortifying himself, Blake sucked in a deep breath. "Okay. Will you guys come with me?"

"Tell you what. We'll get out, but we'll hang back out of the way. You need us, we'll be right behind you."

Giving them a tremulous smile, Blake got out of the car and started up the sidewalk. Taylor got out as well, meeting Cara on her side of the car.

"I'm scared for him," she admitted in a whisper. "What if this goes badly?"

"Like I told Blake, we'll be there for him. He's going to be fine, but this is something he has to do. If he doesn't, he'll always regret not reaching out."

"You're right. I'm just nervous."

He was too, but somebody had to *not* be losing their mind. Unfortunately that was himself.

Staying a few yards behind, they watched as Blake knocked on the apartment door. A few seconds later, it opened and a tall man in his midtwenties stepped outside. He was a large version of his younger brother, with the same brown hair and big eyes. Older and more muscular. Tough-looking.

But there was nothing tough about the regret etched on his face. The love.

"Oh, Christ, little bro," Jon choked. "I thought I'd never see you again. I fucked up so bad. Can you ever forgive me?"

A few heartbeats passed, agonizing seconds as Blake stared at Jon. Weighing his sincerity. Then, a small smile curved his lips. "I'll let you make it up to me, asshole."

With a sob, Jon yanked his brother into his arms and didn't let go for a long while.

Cara turned and Taylor folded her against his chest, his happiness truly complete. The people he loved were happy and fulfilled.

"Hey, let's all go inside," Jon called out to them, draping an arm over his beaming brother. "Pizza and beer?"

"That sounds fine." Taylor smiled.

Extremely fine.

Blake's life—*all* of their lives—were on the right path. At last.

The day of the wedding dawned clear and beautiful. Not nearly as lovely as his wife, Taylor noted with pride, but damned close.

He watched her bounce among the guests, sunlight catching the deep purple streaks in her black hair. Being Cara, she had already changed out of her finery into comfortable, holey jeans. His fiery, sexy little rocker. His. At times, he still wondered whether he'd died after all.

Three days after he'd awakened, the doctors declared him well on the road to recovery and allowed him to go home, provided he rested plenty. Right. He hadn't lasted two hours after they arrived before making passionate love to her. Forget two *weeks*.

". . . and it took us almost an hour to get him into his pen again. That's the craziest bull— Hey, earth to Kayne."

Taylor blinked at Chris. He'd forgotten the man was standing on his left, talking to him. Blake stood on his right, eyes sparkling with humor. "I'm sorry. What?"

"Oh, man," Blake chortled, slapping him on the back. "You've got it bad, dude."

"Nope. I've got it *good*."

Chris nodded. "That you do, and it's about time."

Yes, it was. Happiness like this still felt weird, but in a wonderful way. Making love to Cara, working in a job he liked. Mentoring Blake. His life was great.

With Cara at his side, he could accomplish anything at all.

"Gentlemen, will you excuse me?"

He ignored the knowing looks of his friends as he made a beeline through the revelers toward Cara. The men, he noted, had broken out the longnecks iced down in the washtub on the back porch, and someone had turned up the stereo, blasting a rowdy, unrepentant Toby Keith. He smiled, shaking his head. Let them have their fun and their beer. For his part, Cara provided all the buzz he needed.

As he neared where she'd gone to stand under a large oak tree by the back fence, he saw she was speaking to Austin. At his approach, the two of them turned. The expression on Austin's angular face reflected warmth and friendship. Something new from his usually gruff boss. The captain extended a hand in greeting.

"Kayne, terrific ceremony," Austin said sincerely. "Great party, too."

"Whatever makes my wife happy," he replied, gripping the other man's hand briefly. Cara slid an arm around his waist, tilting her face up for a kiss. Bending, he complied with pleasure, wondering how soon to grab his lady and ditch the celebration without appearing rude.

"Wow," she breathed when he straightened. "Did you miss me for the whopping ten minutes we were apart?"

He grinned. "Fifteen, and it sucked."

Austin cleared his throat. "I'm gonna leave you love-birds alone. Catch you later. And congratulations. I'm happy for both of you."

After the captain moved out of earshot, Taylor turned Cara to face him, resting his palms on the dip of her waist. "You look so damned hot."

To prove his point, he lowered his head for another kiss. Their mouths locked, and she went liquid in his arms. His tongue swept inside, searching. Pressing into him, she urged him deeper. Several guests laughed and a couple of men let out wolf whistles, but damned if he cared. If not for their rapt audience, he'd have her flat on her delicious backside in the grass, pounding between those lovely thighs.

At last he broke the kiss, panting. Wrapping Cara in his arms, he crushed her against his chest, burying his face in her curls. A powerful wave of emotion clogged his throat. "God, I love you," he rasped. "A few months ago, if anybody had told me I'd soon have everything I ever dreamed of, I'd have said they were crazy."

"Taylor?"

"Hmm?"

"Let's take this celebration somewhere private, shall we?"

"Can we play Dirty Nurse again?" Waggling his brows, he leered at her like a hungry wolf, making her giggle.

"Only if you're a really good patient," she whispered.

With that, he bent and scooped Cara into his arms, striding for the house. Her happy screech mingled with more wolf whistles and a few catcalls, and he laughed aloud as she squirmed without making any real effort to get loose.

His forever. This incredible woman.

The miracle he'd cherish for the rest of his days.

About the Author

Bestselling author **Jo Davis** is the author of the popular Firefighters of Station Five series, written as Jo Davis, and the dark, sexy paranormal series Alpha Pack, written as J. D. Tyler. *Primal Law*, the first book in her Alpha Pack series, is the winner of the National Reader's Choice Award in Paranormal. She has also been a multiple finalist in the Colorado Romance Writers Award of Excellence and a finalist for the Bookseller's Best Award, has captured the HOLT Medallion Award of Merit, and has been a two-time nominee for the Australian Romance Readers Award in romantic suspense. She's had one book optioned for a major motion picture.

Connect Online

www.jodavis.net

Turn the page for an exciting preview
of the first in the Torn Between Two Lovers
e-book trilogy by Jo Davis,

Coming in October 2013 from InterMix.

Anna Claire sipped her dirty martini and observed the restaurant from her soothing darkened corner. From back here, nobody could see her slip off her Pradas under the table and stretch her aching feet.

This place was her domain, her baby. Every stick of furniture, every glass, every fork, knife, and spoon belonged to her. The staff moved as efficiently as a well-oiled machine under her ownership and also the direction of her brilliant head chef, Ethan Collingsworth. They respected her and were quite terrified of Ethan's wrath, an arrangement that suited her just fine.

She didn't need to be bosom buddies with her employees to be a success. Quite the opposite had proven true in her previous business experience. She merely needed intelligence, persistence, and lots of money.

Anna had plenty of all three.

Which didn't explain why she was sitting alone in a corner booth of her own high-end New York establishment, feeling sort of down, when by all rights she should be basking in the glow of two years of hard work come to fruition, from conception to success.

Soft laughter and a tinkling of glasses drew her attention toward a table on the far side of the main dining room. A group of four was having some sort of celebratory gathering, and they looked happy as they toasted with champagne. At ease and on top of the world. A promotion, perhaps, or the landing of a big account. An engagement or a pregnancy. Whatever the occasion, Anna couldn't help but feel proud that they'd chosen her restaurant for their celebration. On the way to her own table, Anna had welcomed them and told them so.

But as she watched, a sense of melancholy stole over her. Nobody had ever really celebrated *Anna's* accomplishments. Even her own mother didn't get her, didn't understand what drove Anna to succeed, especially in the restaurant business. Margaret Claire was set in her ways and her thinking and never minced words. Like many parents, she had the power to make Anna bleed from hundreds of tiny invisible cuts, even if she didn't realize it.

Her mother stared at her incredulously. "Let me get this straight—you worked hard to make that little café of yours a success, and now you're going to just throw it away ... spend a ton of money to open a fancy restaurant in New York City." The older woman sighed. "Honey, you were doing well as a manager, and then you went out on a limb with the café and did all right. But this? I don't understand why you need to take a risk this big."

Anna's heart froze. Was she kidding? "This restaurant has been my goal for as long as I can remember! You haven't listened to a word I've said!"

So unbending, her mother. Such a product of her own upbringing as the daughter of a steelworker and a teacher. The Claires were good, salt-of-the-earth people who worked hard and loved harder. But the fact remained that they were also narrow-minded in their view of what equaled success—and that typically involved punching a clock nine to five and earning a retirement after forty years or so of working for someone else.

She tried again. "Mom, did it ever occur to you that *employees have to work for somebody? Someone intelligent who knows their business? And that the boss might as well be me?*"

Margaret Claire just stared at her daughter as though she'd spoken in tongues and sacrificed a chicken in the front yard.

"Miss Claire?"

Anna snapped to the present and blinked at the man standing in front of her table. She'd expected to see one of her waiters but instead was greeted by a tall man dressed in kitchen whites. In the dim lighting, it took her a moment to focus on his features.

He was a big man, fit and broad shouldered, and she could only guess at the muscles hiding under the drab required uniform. His short, golden brown hair was mussed in that sexy, just-rolled-out-of-bed look that turned her on when a man knew how to pull it off—and this one did. His full lips quirked upward, and she found herself wondering, not for the first time, how he would taste. Brows that were a bit darker than his hair arched over expressive blue eyes, which conveyed a very male interest he couldn't quite hide, or hadn't bothered to, from day one.

The last idea intrigued her in spite of herself. What kind of man would hit on his boss? One who was either very stupid or very confident.

Anna had always found confident men to be extremely sexy.

"Mr. James? What can I do for you?" She made it a point to know the name of every single employee, so his came effortlessly—and the question emerged more flirty than she'd intended.

Grayson James, the new prep chef, was one rung on the ladder above the janitor of this building. At age thirty-three, he was a bit long in the tooth if he hoped to make head chef one day, but he'd come highly recommended from Le Cordon Bleu, one of the most prestigious cooking schools around. That, and his letters of recommendation from the senior partners at his former law firm, had been enough for Anna. She'd hired him on the spot, despite a few reservations Ethan had voiced.

Who was she to hold back someone determined to follow his dream?

"Chef sent me to see if you wanted anything special for your dinner," he said in a smooth, deep voice.

A radio voice, her mother would say if she were here. Anna toyed with her martini glass, trying to ignore the warmth that pooled in her middle at the sound and traveled south. The man was an employee and she had no business drooling over him, much less playing this flirtatious cat-and-mouse game with him for the past few weeks. But she supposed what he didn't know wouldn't hurt anyone.

She cocked her head, lips curving upward. "I highly doubt Ethan did any such thing."

He made a face. "Busted. But how else was I supposed to get away to talk to the most beautiful woman in the whole place?"

Pleasure curled through her insides. "You've got a big, steely pair, Mr. James. I like that."

Something hungry, predatory, flared in his eyes, and he leaned over slightly. His voice was husky as he parried her thrust. "Do you? That's good, because I happen to like a woman who knows what she wants and isn't afraid to grab it."

"I'm afraid of very little," she said, eyeing him in appreciation and not bothering to hide it.

"And yet I sense you holding back with me."

"I'm careful in every aspect of my life. A little common sense is a good thing."

"Not when it interferes with the fun of living, I think. I guess I'll have to make it my mission to loosen you up, boss lady." Her brows shot up, but he didn't wait for a response. "Would you like to order something?"

You. Naked on a platter with an apple in your mouth. "What's Ethan's special tonight?"

"The duck over a bed of sautéed greens, with a mushroom wine sauce drizzled on top."

"Sounds fantastic. I'll have that."

"Wise choice." The man actually winked at her and grinned. "Ethan does get testy when the patrons don't follow his recommendations."

Damn the man for having the most alluring dimple on the left side of his mouth.

"Everything he creates is beyond compare. Our diners can't go wrong, no matter what they order."

"True. I'll let him know your choice." He waved a hand at her glass. "Another?"

She debated, then nodded. "I think I will."

He laughed. "So long as you're able to walk at the end of the evening, that's fine."

She barely managed to keep her mouth from falling open at his forwardness. If any other employee had made that remark, she would've reprimanded him. When it came to Gray, however, she couldn't be upset when his playfulness was edged with genuine concern. "Thanks, but I'll be fine. I won't be behind the wheel, and I only live five blocks away."

"But you could stagger in front of a tour bus," he said innocently. "Then who would sign my paychecks?"

As she opened her mouth to retort that he wouldn't have to worry about that if he was no longer working here, she was shocked when he turned his back and simply walked away. The arrogant bastard just left her sitting there, his carriage and attitude screaming that he wasn't the least bit intimidated by her position as owner. Any of the others, save Ethan, would bow, scrape, and stammer in her presence. But not this man.

That damned confidence she couldn't resist. Somehow, in the space of a couple of weeks, the prep chef had homed in on her weakness and filleted it like a sea bass in Ethan's kitchen.

The second drink and her duck were delivered with a flourish, but with no further sign of Mr. James. It surprised her to realize she was disappointed. That small exchange had left her feeling more charged than she had in a while. Almost like she'd been awakened from a deep sleep.

Her meal had never tasted better, and she wondered whether a certain sexy prep chef had anything to do with that. Thoughts of him replayed in her head as she ate, and by the time she was ready to leave, she found her eyes straying toward the doors to the kitchen. Was she really so eager to get another glimpse of the man? *You're the boss. Just go in there and check on things. You don't need an excuse.*

When she was finished, she did just that. But only because she needed to close her office and retrieve her purse, she told herself. Mr. James was hard at work chopping vegetables when she walked through, and he barely acknowledged her with a nod. There was no cocky grin this time, no heat in his gaze. No familiarity. But then she caught Ethan observing him and not bothering to hide it, so that made sense. The chef was his boss as well and was much more stern and scary than Anna. No way would anyone in his right mind invite a tongue-lashing from Ethan.

Grayson James, on the other hand, could give me a tongue-lashing of a different sort. A very welcome one.

Good God! Annoyed with herself, she went through some paperwork and studied some orders for fresh meat and vegetables. Then she left twenty minutes later, locking her office and passing through the kitchen without letting her attention stray to the object of her fantasies, and took the elevator down to the lobby.

Fatigue dragged at her as she pushed through the revolving door, and she suddenly wished she'd called a cab.

But that was ridiculous for a mere five-block walk, even this late at night. At least the city never really slept, and there were cops on almost every corner this close to Times Square.

That's what she told herself, anyway, as the bright lights of her restaurant's block gave way to the lengthening shadows of a residential area with fewer people about. Though she was tired, her senses were on alert for any movement. Any person who didn't belong.

So she was jolted with terror when a hand grabbed her arm and yanked her into an alley between two apartment buildings. "Hey!" she yelled. "Stop!"

Another shriek was abruptly cut off by a palm clapped over her mouth as she was pulled backward, farther into the darkness. The hand was covered by a ragged glove with the fingers cut out, because they were digging into her cheek.

Every horror story she'd ever heard about women being abducted and assaulted flashed through her mind, and she exploded in movement, fighting him like a wildcat. Twisting and bucking, she managed to make him lose his grip for a moment—just long enough to sink her teeth into the side of his hand as hard as she could through the glove's material.

"Ahhh! Fuck!" Jerking his hand away, he shoved her back into the side of the nearest building, then spun her around and pushed her face-first into the bricks before she could glimpse his features or clothing. "Scream or bite me again and I'll snap your pretty neck! Got it?"

She nodded, heart slamming against her rib cage. "Wh-what do you want? Money? It's in my purse."

"And where's your purse?"

She jerked her head as much as she could in the direction they'd come. "Over there. I dropped it."

"Hmm. Maybe I'll go back for that," he said in a low voice. "But I'm thinking the real prize is right here in my hands. Begging for a piece of this." As emphasis, he ground his groin into her ass.

"Y-you don't want to do this," she said, breathless with fear. "Someone will come and you'll be caught. Just take the money and go."

"Nobody's coming. Why can't I have both?"

"People live here. You don't want to risk jail."

"As if guys like me care about getting sent to Club Fed. Three squares a day, exercise, reading, and TV. Hell, I could even study for a trade, which is more than I get on the street."

"Please," she begged as his hand began to creep under the hem of her blouse. "Don't — "

Just then, the man's weight vanished from her back. Before she could register why, she heard a vicious curse and the sounds of flesh hitting flesh. Spinning around, she spotted two men bouncing off the wall and into some garbage cans, sending the receptacles flying and causing a loud clatter. In the dim light, she could barely make out a large man punching a slightly smaller man. The more slightly built one was dressed in a hoodie, the bigger one in jeans and a T-shirt.

She had to do something. Get help before her rescuer got hurt.

Just as she was about to turn and run, the attacker shoved the bigger man away from him and fled. He was fast, booking it down the alley and skidding around the corner. Gone, just like that. The bigger man stood under a sliver of moonlight, chest heaving, his tense stance suggesting that he was tempted to give chase. Instead, he faced her and took a couple of tentative steps.

"Ma'am? Are you all right?"

His voice was so familiar, but she was badly shaken. She could hardly think straight as she replied, "I feel sick."

"Here, let me help you." Taking her gently by the hand, he led her out of the alley, stooping to grab her purse on the way and hand it to her.

"Thank you," she said.

"You're welcome."

Tears pricked her eyes, a testament to how frightened she'd been. She hadn't cried in years, since she'd finally learned to swallow being a disappointment to her mother.

Her rescuer urged her back onto the sidewalk, under a streetlamp. Then he turned to speak but stopped, mouth hanging open. "Anna! I mean, Miss Claire," he corrected himself. "My God, I can't believe it's you. Are you sure you're okay?"

"I— Mr. James," she stammered in surprise. "Yes, I think so."

As if to reassure himself, he stepped close and took her hands in his, rubbing them as though to ward off a chill. Then he turned her a bit and inspected her from every angle.

She gave a watery laugh. "Really, I'm fine." Except for the nausea, which threatened to upset her dinner.

"You don't look fine," he replied, eyeing her with a

concerned frown. "Just to be sure, I'm going to walk you the rest of the way home."

"Oh, that's not necessary."

He shook his head. "I insist. Which way?"

"No, I mean it's really not necessary because I live there." She pointed to the building on the corner.

"You're kidding! That's where I live, too." He smiled. "Then it's definitely no trouble at all to see you safely to your door."

"I don't—"

"Please? For my peace of mind?"

He looked so handsome, so worried, that she had to smile back. "Fine. That would be nice. Thanks."

"First, though, we should file a report. I should've thought right away of calling the police."

She considered that, then blew out a breath. "I think that'll be a waste of time. I'm not hurt, and he didn't take anything. I didn't even get a look at him, so my input isn't going to help much."

"Are you sure? They can at least have it on record."

"No. Really, I just want to get home."

He hesitated, then relented. "I can understand that. Come on."

Tucking her hand in his arm, he escorted her the rest of the way to their building and inside. As they crossed the spacious lobby, she briefly wondered how a lowly prep chef could afford to live in a neighborhood like this, where the apartments were so expensive. Then she remembered that he'd been a hotshot attorney of some kind, so that made sense. He'd probably socked away plenty before changing careers.

As they stepped into the elevator, his finger hovered over the number panel. "Which floor?"

"Six."

He smiled again, a blinding slash of white that made her knees a little weak. "What do you know?"

"You, too?" She blinked at him.

"Yep. I'm curious, though. How is it that the boss lady missed the fact that I live in her building, on the same floor?"

She shrugged. "I make it a point to memorize names and faces because I like my employees to feel as if they matter to me—and they do. But my manager, Jeff Wilson, does all of the hiring paperwork and tax forms, and he collects the employee information sheets we keep on file. If I need to know specific information about one of you, I can look it up."

"I met Mr. Wilson, but I don't see him around much," he mused. "He doesn't take a very active role on the floor."

"Because that's not what I hired him to do. He does most of the paperwork, ads, and marketing."

"So you can be among the people, which is what you enjoy most."

"Yes."

"And yet . . ." The elevator arrived at their floor, and they got off.

She stopped and faced him. "What?"

"I don't know if I should say." His gaze settled on hers, assessing.

"You can speak freely. You *did* just save my life." She grinned in encouragement.

He relaxed some. "It's just that you seem very reserved most of the time. Aloof. It's interesting to hear you say that you enjoy being around your staff and guests when you don't really show it."

She stared at him in surprise. "I don't? But . . . I speak to people all day. I ask them how they're doing, if their meals are excellent, what they're celebrating. Things like that."

"What about the staff?"

"What about them?" She started to feel defensive. "I ask them if they need anything, what I can do to help them. I inquire about any incidents that may have occurred, how the kitchen has been running, check on the special reservations to make sure the staff is prepared."

"Yes, you do. You're a good boss," he allowed.

"Why, thank you," she said dryly, giving him a droll look. "I'm so glad you approve."

He ignored her sarcasm. "But when was the last time you actually *talked* to any of them?"

"What the hell do you mean? I just told you I talk all day!"

"When's the last time you asked one of them anything personal?"

"Personal?" She was at a complete loss. "Like what?"

"Jesus." He pinched the bridge of his nose, then dropped his hand and regarded her in part amusement, part exasperation. "You know Brandon the waiter?"

"Brandon Gates. Of course I do."

"Right. But did you know his pet iguana died yesterday?"

Obviously one of them had been dropped on their head. And it wasn't *her*.

"So? As long as Ethan didn't serve it in the soup, what does that have to do with me?"

The bastard actually laughed. An honest-to-God laugh that made his eyes crinkle and her toes curl. Made her insides warm in the most pleasant way.

"Christ, you're so uptight, you squeak when you walk."

"What?" She gaped at him. "Listen, Mr. James—"

"I saved your life, as you pointed out," he murmured, moving closer. Reaching out, he gently touched her face with the rough pads of his fingers. "I believe we've moved on to first names, Anna."

Her breath caught in her chest, her nerves dancing at his touch. The hunger in his eyes, his nearness, torched all of her arguments to dust. At five-eight she wasn't a short woman, but the top of her head barely reached his chin. That was a secret thrill of hers—a big, tall man surrounding her. Pressing her down, covering her lips with his.

He was so close, their mouths almost met. Then he stepped back, and it took her a moment to adjust. To realize he wasn't going to kiss her after all. Flushing, she attempted to cover her embarrassment by fishing in her purse for the keys to her apartment. Finding them, she gave him a smile she didn't feel.

"Well, Gray, I should get home."

She turned and started down the hallway and he kept pace beside her, apparently not ready to relinquish his role as her protector. Suddenly her ordered world had been unbalanced, not just by the attack but by Gray's nearness, and she wondered if that's what he intended.

At her door, she unlocked it and faced him. "Thank you for saving me. I can't imagine what might've happened if you hadn't been walking home right behind me."

The idea made her feel sick again.

"I'm glad I was there." A shadow passed over his face and was gone. "Let me come in? You've had a shock, and I want to see you settled before I leave."

Settled. That would be the very last thing she would feel if she allowed him inside; of that, there was no doubt. Some force that obliterated reason and good sense had her opening the door anyway, stepping aside to welcome him to her home.

"Nice place," he commented.

"I imagine it's the same as yours."

"Just the floor plan." Looking around, he appeared impressed. "I definitely don't have your sense of style."

"I can't claim much credit, except for the colors. I picked those and then hired a decorator."

"I like the browns with the deep red accents. It fits you."

Curious, she studied him as she set her purse on the bar. "How so?"

"The browns are subtle, understated, and strong. Alone, they might be boring to the eye, and then bam! The red is exciting. Just like those flashes of your true personality when you let them out, as you did in the hallway a few minutes ago."

"Seriously?" A laugh escaped before she could help it. "You are so full of shit."

"And like now," he said, looking smug. "*Miss Claire* would never have said that, but *Anna* sure did. I obviously know what I'm talking about."

"I don't know whether to be flattered or frightened by the armchair psychoanalysis."

"Flattered—what else?" Gesturing toward the couch, he ordered, "Sit down. What do you want to drink? Wine? Something stronger?"

Bemused, she did as he said—for the moment. "Isn't that my line? This *is* my apartment."

"You can offer one to me some other time." He disappeared into the kitchen and began to rummage around as his voice drifted to her. "You know, sometime when you haven't been attacked by a mugger."

The image caused her to shiver, and she unwillingly began to relive the encounter. "I'll just have some water. Get whatever you want for yourself."

In moments he was back, the sofa dipping as he sat beside her and twisted the tops off two bottles, handing her one. "I don't often drink this late at night. Gives me insomnia."

"Hmm." There was something odd about that man in the alley.

"Are you sure you're all right?" he asked in concern.

"He talked too much."

"What?"

"The mugger." Anna lifted her gaze to see Gray studying her, brows furrowed. "He was all talk. He never did much except push me around and scare me. Isn't that weird?"

Gray leaned forward. "What else?"

"He smelled nice, like he had on his best cologne. And . . ."

"And?"

She gasped. "The man wasn't armed! He didn't have anything in his hands."

"Are you sure? Could be that it happened so fast, you missed a small knife or something in his grasp."

"No, I'm positive. The mugger wasn't armed, he spoke articulately, and he smelled nice. Something is off about the whole thing."

"That is strange," he said thoughtfully. "You should be more careful from now on. In fact, I'll be walking you home for a while. Just in case."

In case the man returned. Fear overrode the inner whispering that it was smart to keep a distance from this sexy man, no matter how much she wanted him. "All right."

Their eyes met and a strange flutter of butterfly wings took off in her stomach. Gray was looking at her as though she was the answer to every question he had, and it was wonderful. Confusing. Arousing.

"You're so beautiful," he said with reverence, touching her face with the pads of his fingers.

"I don't remember the last time anyone told me that."

"You deserve to hear that every single day, because it's true."

"Thank you." Drawn to him, she reached up and traced his lips with one finger. "You're a very handsome man yourself."

"I wasn't fishing."

"I didn't think you were." She paused. "Why me?"

His face registered surprise. "Why am I interested in you?"

"Yes."

"Besides your beauty, you're smart, successful. Kind. I think you need to unwind a lot, and I want to help you do that."

God, he smelled good. Woodsy and manly, and it made her body ache to be touched. Completed. "Then help me, Gray."

For a few moments he didn't speak. His hand covered hers and he waited, giving her time to voice an objection. When it didn't come, he leaned over and closed the distance between them. Brought their lips together, parted hers with his tongue.

His kiss was liquid fire. Slowly, he licked her mouth, his sensual exploration sparking an electrical storm throughout her body. All thoughts of why it was a bad idea to see an employee blew to dust. Pushing into him, she sought more. Needed more from this man. It had been far too long since she'd come alive this way.

All too soon, the kiss was over and Gray moved back. Confused, she tried to pull herself together.

"Will you be okay tonight?"

Only if you stay. But of course she wouldn't say the words.

"Yes, I'll be fine." She forced a smile. "Go on, get some rest. You're on the late shift again tomorrow."

Rising, he looked down at her. He didn't seem eager to go—more like resigned that it was for the best. And it was.

"Give me your cell phone."

"Why?"

"So I can program my number in for you."

"Oh. Okay." Fishing around in her purse, she found the device and handed it over.

He punched a long series of buttons; then he handed it back. "Here you go. Call me if you need anything at all, Anna."

Her name on his lips, the intensity of his gaze made her feel like a wounded antelope in the sights of a lion. The thing was, she didn't want to escape.

"I will."

With that promise extracted, he gave her a wicked half smile and walked out the door, shutting it softly behind him. Following him, she looked up and then stood gazing at the colors in her living room, trying to see them—and herself—through his eyes.

Brown for steadiness and strength, red for excitement. Being alive.

Somehow, it seemed he'd taken all of the red with him when he left.

Grayson closed the door behind him and stood in the middle of his sparsely furnished apartment, frustration and guilt riding him hard.

As he'd started getting to know Anna Claire over the past few weeks, he'd slowly come to realize she was nothing like he'd first assumed. He'd thought she was too straitlaced and wondered why she hadn't snapped like a brittle twig. Maybe a little stuck-up, too. But she wasn't.

She was driven, determined, smart, and sexy. Kind to her employees and patrons, yet aloof to the former, perhaps because she was their boss. The woman was complicated, and yet he felt he was coming to understand what made her tick. She needed to have some fun, enjoy life a little.

He intended to help her along in that area.

A knock at the door interrupted his musings. "You took a hell of a risk," he growled as he opened the door. "Don't you ever use your brain?"

Simon King strolled inside and faced him, wearing a grin. "I changed clothes, and nobody saw me come here. It's not like she got a good look at me, anyhow."

Gray rolled his eyes. "She knows something is off, you idiot. Once she calmed down and had time to pull herself together, she said you were too articulate and you smelled good. And it didn't escape her notice that you weren't armed."

The cocky grin slid off his face. Good.

"Shit. I didn't expect her to be so aware of those kinds of details. Most women wouldn't be when they're so scared."

"Anna's not most women, Simon." Gray sighed.

"Yeah? Well, at least we accomplished our goal," his partner pointed out. "You got invited into the lioness's den. The question is, did you get a free pass to go back?"

"Most likely. She's a tough one, but I think this was the edge I needed."

Simon considered that. Thankfully, he didn't mention just how far Gray might still have to go to capture their prey. "Did you get the trace put on her cell phone?" he asked instead.

"Yeah. I'll get the rest in place next time I go over there."

"Which will be when?"

"Hopefully tomorrow."

"It would be quicker if you just broke in and did the job."

"And more risky, too, in a building like this, with all the apartment doors facing the hallway and no access from the outside. No, being invited in is a much better scenario."

"All right. It's your call." Simon paused. "Who do you like for this, partner? Honestly?"

Gray rubbed the back of his neck. "That's the million-dollar question."

And that's why he and his partner were on this case, and why Gray had infiltrated the staff of Floor Fifty-Five. Several of Anna's employees were running drugs, using the restaurant as a cover and base of operations. His job was to learn the names of everyone involved, how and where they were hiding the drugs—and whether Anna was in on the scheme.

Lowering himself into an easy chair, he answered. "I'm the low man there, so working my way into confidences is proving harder than I expected."

"Whoever's behind this is mob connected, my friend. They're going to be suspicious of anyone new and it will take too long to earn their trust, so forget making buddies. Just find the evidence and get out."

"I have to tell you, my gut says Anna's not involved."

"You sure that's not your dick doing the talking?"

Despite the seriousness of the situation, Gray laughed. "Not at all."

"That's what I figured." His partner shook his head. "Be careful, okay?"

"I wouldn't be anything less."

But after Simon left, he couldn't help but think *careful* wasn't going to be a word that applied at all where Anna was concerned.

LOVE
ROMANCE
NOVELS?

For news on all your favorite romance authors,
sneak peeks into the newest releases, book
giveaways, and much more—

"Like" Love Always on Facebook!
🅕 LoveAlwaysBooks